YOUNG WRITERS

**Word Up!**

YOUNG WRITERS' CREATIVE WRITING COMPETITION 2002 FOR SECONDARY SCHOOLS

# *EASTERN COUNTIES*

Edited by Lynsey Hawkins

First published in Great Britain in 2002 by
*YOUNG WRITERS*
Remus House,
Coltsfoot Drive,
Peterborough, PE2 9JX
Telephone (01733) 890066

HB ISBN 0 75434 110 0
SB ISBN 0 75434 111 9

# FOREWORD

This year, Young Writers proudly presents a showcase of the best short stories and creative writing from today's up-and-coming writers.

We set the challenge of writing for one of our four themes - 'Myths & Legends', 'Hold The Front Page', 'A Day In The Life Of . . .' and 'Short Stories/Fiction'. The effort and imagination expressed by each individual writer was more than impressive and made selecting entries an enjoyable, yet demanding, task.

*Word Up! Eastern Counties* is a collection that we feel you are sure to enjoy - featuring the very best young authors of the future. Their hard work and enthusiasm clearly shines within these pages, highlighting the achievement each piece represents.

We hope you are as pleased with the final selection as we are and that you will continue to enjoy this special collection for many years to come.

# CONTENTS

Emma Witney-Smith 1

Ashfa Rani 2

Imogen Bexfield 6

Coleridge Community College, Cambridgeshire

Cathleen Crawford 9

Ruby Davies 10

Ixworth Middle School, Suffolk

David Firth 11

Martin Borley 12

Katherine Thwaites 13

Anastasia Porteous 14

Frances Busson 15

Linton Village College, Cambridgeshire

Benn Oliver 16

Jack Glossop 17

Daniel De'Ath 18

Tom Davies 19

Hannah Warner 20

Rachel Davies 21

James Farenden 22

Tom Sargeant 23

Ed Bonsey 24

Will Woodgate 25

Luke Little 26

Anna Tumber 27

Euan Corrin 28

Jasdeep Rai 29

Edward Dickinson 30

Callum Mayfield 31

Emily Durley 32

Laura Dickens 33

Lewis Cracknell 34

Chris Negus 35

Catherine Orgee                                36
Helen Jedrzejewski                             37
Tom Miller                                     38
Daniel Fletcher                                39
Simon Blackman                                 40
Kayleigh Orloff                                41
Jessica Plumb                                  42
Laura McCann                                   43
Katherine Wright                               44
Bob Read                                       45
Niels Meissner                                 46
Natasha Withers                                47
Ines Collings                                  48
Samantha Green                                 49
Hannah Norman                                  50
Sarah Smith                                    51
Jo Malins                                      52
Rachel Kiddie                                  53
Stephen Orriss                                 54
Annabel Palmer                                 55
Ella Prior                                     56
Amy Dockerill                                  57
Nathan Lumby                                   58
Jake Weston                                    59
Chris Cornwell                                 60
Francesca Elliott                              61
Sam Penfold                                    62
Rachael Newton                                 63
Emma Laidlaw                                   64
Hannah Burns                                   65

Margaret Beaufort Middle School, Bedfordshire
Annabel Walker                                 66
Sean Houghton                                  68

Northgate High School, Norfolk
Martha Hodgson                                 69
Amy Young                                      70

| | |
|---|---|
| Holly Buckingham | 72 |
| Shannon Fuller | 73 |
| Lee Tomlin | 74 |
| Elizabeth-Rose Matthews | 76 |
| Hannah Creed | 77 |
| Andrew Stevenson | 78 |
| Rachel Rayns | 79 |
| Harriet Brandwood | 80 |
| Emma Hall | 81 |
| Samuel Braysher | 82 |
| Chris Dewing | 83 |
| Stephanie Kemp | 84 |
| Matthew Barley | 85 |
| Rachael Herman | 86 |
| Jessica Kipper | 87 |

**St Mark's School, Harlow, Essex**

| | |
|---|---|
| David Okusi | 88 |
| Lauren Grundy | 89 |
| Lelldorin Gaskell | 90 |
| Christopher Lloyd | 92 |
| Elaina Crehan | 94 |
| Matthew Bowden-Scott | 95 |
| Lindsey Colley | 96 |
| Kayleigh Henderson | 97 |
| Jordan Weir | 98 |
| Holly Bailey | 99 |
| Natasha Christmas | 100 |
| Daniel Hockley | 101 |
| Jaye Hacker | 102 |
| Ross Ashcroft | 103 |
| Sam McFarlane | 104 |
| Sarah Cholerton | 105 |
| Amy Pemberton | 106 |
| Catherine Fisher | 107 |
| Elizabeth Woodland | 108 |
| Donna Murphy | 109 |
| Joseph Calvino | 110 |

| | |
|---|---|
| Tom Mortimer | 112 |
| Kayleigh Hart | 113 |
| Emma Lingard | 114 |
| Rick Coghlan | 115 |
| Katherine Saville | 116 |
| Alice Holdstock | 117 |
| Keiron McGlone | 118 |
| Erin Walters | 119 |
| Thomas Jewell | 120 |
| Michelle Tomlin | 122 |
| Daniel Spiller | 123 |
| Jade Rencontre | 124 |
| Laura Fleming | 125 |
| Joe Earll | 126 |
| Lee McDonnell | 127 |
| Brooke Fryer | 128 |
| Tara Arnold | 129 |
| James Kennard | 130 |
| Danielle Warwick | 131 |
| Alex Keene | 132 |
| Emma Bell | 133 |
| Vincent Cuming | 134 |
| Luke Bowering | 135 |
| Dan Stack | 136 |
| Jazmine Marsh | 137 |
| Kenneth Kwok | 138 |
| Lauren Cunningham | 140 |
| Fu-Wah Kwong | 141 |
| James Cox | 142 |
| Natalie Walsh | 143 |
| Natalie Strong | 144 |
| Jack Dench | 146 |
| Patrick O'Sullivan | 148 |
| Sam Cunningham | 149 |
| Matthew Mouncey | 150 |
| Callum Healy | 151 |
| Jack Wieland | 152 |
| James Hammond | 154 |

Matthew Wood                          155
Kane Read                            156
Catherine Donovan                    157
Christina Gargan                     158
Amy Hartgrove                        159
Nicole Kelly                         160
Kristle Kilburn                      162
Andrew Swanton                       163
Aimee Bloomfield                     164
Elisabeth Charge                     165
Jack Pavitt                          166
Danielle Lamb                        167
Dominic Steingold                    168
Stevie Hamill                        169
Graziella Castronovo                 170
Jodie Davey                          171
Sarah Packer                         172
Amber Selway                         173
Kwasi Debrah-Nkasah                  174
Joanna Bergh                         175
Lisa Adnitt                          176
Mun Loi                              178
Stacey Barbet                        179
Gemma Buck                           180
Stephanie Difrancesco                181
Prashant Thakrar                     182
Lewis Quinlin                        183
Yasmin Uddin                         184
Laurence Ashoori                     185
Jamie Reilly                         186
Isobelle Ancient                     187
Rees Foxwell                         188
Kylie Airey                          189
Louise Spicer                        190
Amy Tovell                           191
Toni Beard                           192
Harry Doyle                          193
Qasim Ali                            194

St Paul's Catholic School, Milton Keynes, Buckinghamshire
    Holly Grady    195
    Luke Atkins    196

St Peter's School, Huntingdon, Cambridgeshire
    Chloe Brown    197

The Cedars Upper School, Bedfordshire
    Tanya Rowland    198
    Sarah Barrett    199

The Highfield School, Hertfordshire
    Glyn Spencer    200
    Kirstie Robson    202
    Rebecca Barnes    204

The John Bramston School, Essex
    Steven Smith    207
    Charlotte Deighton    208
    Dominic Burton    210
    Justin Hook    212
    Emily Brown    213
    Hayley McGarry    214
    Suzanne Curl & Emma Brett    215
    Jazmin Harrington    216
    Jamie Long    217
    Danielle Elton    218
    Emma Sands    219
    Alex Rudd    220
    Mark Brown    221
    Angela Baker    222
    Naomi Williams    223
    Leah Batcock    224
    Chris Doe    225
    Edgar Legaspi    226
    Kristina Fleuty    228
    Gemma Davies    230
    Victoria Matthews    232

Kirsten Frost 234
Leigh Clements 236

The Prittlewell School, Essex
Joshua Forman 238
Helena Bray 240
Sasha James 241
Andrew Moore 242
Amy Such 244
Anja Forman 245
Matthew Fowler 246
Jade Gilbert 247
Simon Burman 248
Michael Dowley 249
Alex Monteith 250
Louise Champion 251
Jason Walden 252
Chelsea Skinner 253
James Wagstaff 254
Joe Freeman 255
Sarah Jones 256
Larni Munns 257
Amber Fletcher 258
Jenny Searle 259
Scott Eagling 260
Jenny Harrold 261
Hannah Parkin 262
Carl Harrold 263
Amy Louise Heathcote 264
Jade Easterford 266

William Edwards School, Essex
Charlotte Humphrey 267
Luke Stanton 268
Elizabeth Dale 269
Jenna Yeomans 270
Andrew Baker 271
Katherine Furner 272

Luke Walsh                    274
Sarah Henderson               275
Katie West                    276
Elizabeth Cooledge            277
Rebecca Gray                  278
Ben Kelly                     279
Daniel Gray                   280

Wymondham High School, Norfolk
Julia Alderson                281
Thomas Phillips               282
Daniel Lee                    283
Kayleigh Miles                284
Carly Buckenham               285
Hannah Burroughs              286
Stephanie Garnett             287
Molly Harrison                288
Kate Cooper                   289
Laura Gedge                   290
Hayley Goodrum                291
Madeleine Piggot              292
Kirsty Bell                   294

# The Stories

# DRAGONSONG

Night faded slowly into day, taking with it the last glimmering of twinkling stars. The weary sun peeped up over the horizon, stretching its dazzling rays over land and sea alike, casting waves in fiery hues of red and orange. And the sky waited, empty, for the dawn chorus.

Aboard the Dragonstar, Nayru watched the sky avidly. Her ship had sailed eastwards for months, far past the last known archipelago and, as far as civilisation was concerned, over The Edge. And finally, after months of endless, fruitless searching, weeks of frustrating solitude and uncooperative weather, she had reached The Edge.

The Edge, it was rumoured, was where the world ended and dragon country began. It was where the waters of the world poured in a never-ending torrent off into eternal oblivion. It was where legend became fact and fact became legend, where dreams and nightmares alike could come true. It was the home of magic, of colours, of life itself. It was a place of mystery, of chaos, of order, of danger and of immense, breathtaking beauty.

And as Nayru watched with bated breath, the sun finally rose past the horizon and they finally came, wheeling and tumbling in the air in sheer ecstasy. Scarlet, sapphire, violet, gold, they all heralded the rising sun as one. And as one, they began to sing, filling the misty morning air with soft bell-like chimes, with brazen trumpet-like shrieks, with glissandos, arpeggios, ornaments. It was beautiful. It was heart-rending. It was Dragonsong.

*Emma Witney-Smith (15)*

# THE BLOODY HAND!

The stars were twinkling brightly; the moon was shimmering in the dark and gloomy night. Blackbirds, whistling, curling and looping in the air, silhouetted against the darkening sky.

It was a year since Peter's world had been rocked upside down with the sudden disappearance of his grandpa. Life had not been the same for Peter and his grandma.

Peter lived in Shropshire with his grandma; though he loved his grandma very much, it was not the same without the presence of his grandpa. It had been a very tough year for both Peter and his grandma but they managed to pull through. Peter was adamant to find out what really had happened to his grandpa. He asked several questions to his grandma but was told to carry on with his own life.

In Shropshire, no one told Peter anything, which made Peter even more determined to find out the truth. All Peter knew about was the stranded car of his grandpa's.

All the villagers kept themselves separate and away from other people so they were not much use to Peter. If Peter did question them, they would just tell him to keep out of things that did not concern 13-year-olds. That kind of answer made Peter anxious about what had happened to his grandpa.

However, tonight Peter was very confident that he would find out the truth and get some of his questions answered; like why was his grandpa's car found stranded on top of Shropshire Hill?

Peter's heart was pounding fast as he was now halfway up the great hill. He could hear robins singing and owls howling. Within a few minutes Peter had reached his destination, the top of the great hill! Peter waited for a second until he got his breath back and then he turned around, it was just then, as he looked forward, he got the biggest shock of his life, it was a forest! However, not just any old forest, this was a forest with a face!

Peter knew that there had never been a forest on the top of Shropshire Hill, also he had never seen a forest with a face. Peter could not take anymore so he turned away. He was feeling cold, numb, and scared. Peter felt he had to look again and in doing so, he got a further shock! The face was his grandpa's! It was like it had been squashed into the trees! Peter was absolutely horrified; he noticed that the face was very prominent. 'Grandpa? Is that you?' Peter asked the face of his grandpa. There was no reply, only howls from inside the forest. 'I don't believe this, I'm talking to a forest! A face on a forest! What has happened to me? I must pull myself together.' Peter whispered this all to himself, as he was too frightened to speak loudly; in case, something lurked out of the forest and attacked him.

What should I do next, Peter thought. After a few minutes he had decided to go on ahead and enter this dark and spooky forest. He took three steps forward and found himself inside the gloomy, spooky forest. Peter's mind was racing with thoughts; what would he find? Would it be nice or horrible? Peter soon got his answers to those questions.

The leaves rustled and crunched as Peter walked slowly on them. he heard a chilling scream; he looked up only to find himself on the floor after tripping over something. He got up and looked down, but wished he hadn't as he saw a rather gruesome, alive, blood-leaking hand! The red, thick, slimy blood was leaking out of the hand, the fingers were moving!

Peter let out a scream! he was terrified. Peter looked at the bloody hand, for him just looking at it, made him freak out! He had to run! 'I mmmmuuussst run!' he shouted, quite loudly. He ran, which was a big mistake as he found himself being chased by the blood-leaking hand. He didn't know where he was going, but ran with all the power he had in his legs! 'Hhhhheeelllppp! Help! Anyone!' screamed Peter.

As the bloody hand chased Peter, the dropping of the blood made splashing noises which were very gruesome! Panting and breathing hard, Peter's legs were very tired, unlike the bloody hand, which hadn't stopped. Peter stopped and turned around once with a devastating consequence!

He felt it! That gruesome bloody hand had gripped the back of Peter's neck. Peter felt the blood gripping on his back, he screamed for help! Suddenly he heard a rather ghastly and ghostly voice. 'Peeeettteeerrr! Run as fast as you can, get away from it!' It was the deep voice of his grandpa.

'How? What shall I do? Please help me! Grandpa!' cried Peter!

'Peter, I can't do anything, only you can, lick the blood, the hand will stop,' replied his grandpa.

The bloody hand's grip got firmer and deeper into Peter's neck; he was desperate to get away from it and so licked the blood! The bloody hand loosened the grip that it had on Peter's neck.

'More Peter, lick more!' shouted his grandpa.

Peter did so and the bloody hand let go of Peter's neck.

'Run away Peter!'

'Grandpa, what about you?' asked Peter.

'Forget me, you go!' replied his grandpa.

Peter ran and ran but again the bloody hand was on the trail of Peter. The bloody hand was getting faster and faster after Peter. Peter was getting slower and slower, the forest was spooking Peter, but he got even more spooked when he saw all these heads, arms and legs all after him!

Just when he thought he had escaped from the spook forest, Peter was grabbed by three bloody hands, which had their gruesome fingers on Peter's neck and back. Peter was sweating, covered in blood and his heart was thumping hard. Peter struggled to get the bloody hands off him. He was so desperate to get away; he bit one of the bloody hands! Peter now was drenched with blood. He remembered what his grandpa had said, and so licked, licked, and licked all the blood he could see.

Suddenly all three bloody hands were off Peter, he took a huge breath and with all strength he had, he grabbed a long log! Without thinking twice, he smashed the log on every bloody hand, arm, head, or leg he could see!

What Peter had done was very clever, as it had worked; all the blood had been squashed out of the hands and without the blood, they could not survive!

Peter ran out of the bloody forest and as it was 1 o'clock in the morning, everyone was in bed so he decided to jump into his cosy bed. Peter knew the truth and decided to keep his terrifying adventure to himself; after all, who would believe a 13-year-old?

*Ashfa Rani  (14)*

# DESERT DISASTER

Excitement flooded through me as we sped along the runway. Just me and my two friends on a private jet to Egypt - how cool!

I had not a care in the world as we soared up into the sky, leaving cold, wet, dreary England behind.

Adrenaline rushed through me as we flew into a world of fantasy where real cars looked like miniatures and the whole world had become a toyland.

Several hours later, just as I had managed to dose off, a huge bang came from the back of the aircraft. As I turned round, to my horror, I saw a man dressed entirely in black emerge from the toilet. His face obscured by a balaclava and a revolver in his hand.

He spoke in a cool, clear and collected voice, 'If you do as I say, no one will get hurt.' I broke into a cold sweat. My clammy hands clasped together as beads of perspiration trickled down my forehead. My dreams of a perfect holiday shattered into a thousand pieces. Now all I was worried about was my life!

We nodded our heads vigorously and promised to do as he said. The man in black headed triumphantly towards the pilot's cabin and pushed the pilot to the floor. The plane dipped suddenly and headed straight for the ground. I closed my eyes. My life flashed before me. Everything seemed to go silent and peaceful before we hit the ground with an almighty thud.

Shards of glass shattered everywhere and the man in black was flung forward and cartwheeled through the front window. My breath caught in my lungs. He was sure to be dead. I picked my way through the rubble to the man in black. My friends and a very startled, but uninjured pilot, did the same.

The man in black lay motionless with a humungous gash in his leg. What should I do? Should I help him when only a few minutes earlier he had threatened all of our lives? I decided that no matter what he had done I could not simply stand by and watch him die. The fight for survival was now on.

I got to my knees and began mouth-to-mouth resuscitation. My friend, Mark, made a tourniquet out of his shirt to deal with the injured leg.

Eventually he revived and grew strong enough to walk on some makeshift crutches made from pieces of the mangled wreckage.

As I looked around me I saw nothing but barren wasteland. A vast open desert that stretched as far as the eye could see, broken only by the occasional clump of cacti and the contorted lump of metal that glinted and glared at us in the hot sun. ' Now,' I said to everyone, 'we all have to forget our differences and work together if we are to have any hope of survival. It looks as though we have crashed in Death Valley. Our first task must be to find a way of collecting water.'

It was Madgie, our man in black, who knew just what to do. He used the tiny sink from the aeroplane kitchen and wedged it deep into the sand. Then he covered it with a plastic bag that had survived largely intact underneath one of the seats. By making a small hole in the middle we now had a means of collecting the desert dew. It was precious little but enough to keep us alive.

Then Richard, our pilot, showed us how to use a shard of glass to prise the spines and skin from a large flat cactus leaf. My mouth was burning and my gums felt on fire, when to my relief he showed us how cooling it was to suck on the bare flesh of the cactus plant.

We all perked up and I began to believe that somehow we might make it. If only we could get help. The aeroplane radio was dead. The heat was raging down on us. We needed an SOS that could be seen from the air in case they were out there searching for us. I had to believe that they were.

It was my turn for a flash of inspiration. I gathered together all the clothes that were intended for happy careless days frolicking on very different expanses of sand. I carefully arranged them in the biggest 'SOS' I could manage and doused them in fuel from the plane.

Now all we could do was sit and wait. We each dug ourselves deep pits in the sand which were our only protection against the searing sun.

I awoke to the sound of beating wings, humming in the distance. I summoned all my strength to drag myself out of my pit and set light to our silent message in the sand. My trembling fingers were barely capable of striking the match. Then all at once there were flames everywhere and with them all of our hopes.

The sound of helicopter wings grew in the silence like a goddess sent from Heaven. What seemed like a lifetime now flashed by in the blink of an eye. We were safe.

I learnt a lot from my adventure in Death Valley. I learnt that we all have to work together to achieve.

*Imogen Bexfield  (11)*

# LEAVING

Goodbyes have never been a strong point of mine and I hated saying goodbye to them that day. It felt like I was leaving a piece of me behind. Like I had forgotten or lost something. Except I couldn't forget this - or lose it.

I wrapped my arms around my children and they had never held on to me so tight. Their shaking bodies trembled over my soul and scarred me forever. I could hear them sobbing, whispering, 'Please don't go Daddy, don't go.' Those words went through me like a dagger, I held on so tight, feeling them one last time, knowing the next time might never come. I gave them one final kiss and told them I would love them always. Still I could hear their crying words, 'Don't go Daddy, please don't go.'

I looked up, my beautiful, beautiful wife, standing tall, holding back the tears, for fear of never stopping. As I looked at her, I realised how much I loved her, how I knew now I could never live without her, yet here I was about to leave her.

I looked into her sorrowful eyes, and saw her pain, I put my arms around her, held her with all my love and softly touched her warm lips, whispered, 'I love you,' and heard the words returned.

I turned around and walked away from my family, my loving family. Oh how I love them.

*Cathleen Crawford (14)*
*Coleridge Community College, Cambridgeshire*

# THE EDGE OF THE KNIFE

I always balance on the knife's edge, reminding myself not to drop either side. My parents worry all the time, staring if I walk in late, trying to see through my excuses, panicking if I'm seen with anyone who's not trusted.

Now is a dangerous time, they say, warning me, making me stand straight and on guard. I can't smile because someone might misread it. I can't talk to strangers or be home later than five. In winter, I have to chase the dark home else Mum will worry. In summer, my strappy tops show too much 'unwanted flesh'.

I'm fifteen, but they can't trust me because of Helen. She went out three years ago and never came home. We suppose she's alive somewhere, evading the police or the questions the world will ask her. She was always the sly one, the one who could stare at Dad and lie, just to get a date or a lift home or a higher allowance. In her room, she'd tip the stolen bracelets and necklaces into a purse and slip it behind the wardrobe. When she left, I took them and threw them, sparkly and shimmering, into the lake. I guess they're still there.

My parents talk again and again about the invisible knife's edge. One false step, they warn me, will tip me into the groaning underworld of drugs and evil. Do everything right and I can have paradise as they see it; a secure home and fancy Sunday roasts.

*Ruby Davies  (14)*
*Coleridge Community College, Cambridgeshire*

# THE DOVER SOLE

Keith gets up early, 5am. He goes to the fish market at the docks to see if he can buy a Dover sole. Keith chains his bike to a metal pillar and then he runs to the 'D' section of the market. He looks and looks for a Dover sole but he can't find one. Tired and disappointed Keith rides to the supermarket to continue his search. 'Oh no,' says Keith, spotting his dad looking for a bargain fish. Keith tries to hide in the supermarket until his dad has gone. He then asks at the fish counter, but no luck.

Keith decides to ride his bike into town to see if he can come up with ideas to find a Dover sole. He goes to the fishing shop to see how much a fishing rod would cost. He thinks he can catch a fish from the pier.

Suddenly his Dover sole problem is solved; he sees a fish on the wall. He notices the words Dover sole underneath. He asks how much it costs. The man says, 'Fifteen pounds and when you press it sings!' Keith goes home to see if he has enough pocket money. Yes he does have enough pocket money to cheer up his parents.

*David Firth*
*Ixworth Middle School, Suffolk*

## ONE COLD WINTER'S EVENING

One cold winter's evening, when I was walking to the gushing stream my feet were crunching against the gritty snow. The street lamps were dim. A policeman said, 'Evening,' as he was walking by, with his hands behind his back, whistling gently. Also I saw wreathes on semi-detached houses and light patches where the cars had been. Children were playing on the frosted up puddles near the new estate.

*Ding*, 1, 2, 3, the church chimed on its iron bells. I saw muffled snowflakes leaning against the window ledge, behind the glass there were timeless patterns on the thick cosy curtains, with a gap where an old lady was knitting.

A few twinkling stars were coming out. Past a signpost a slow Mini was coming down the road, with its scratchy windscreen wipers and a sudden cough of black smoke spurted out.

Nearly there; out of town, a farmhouse with the farmer wrapped up, driving his cattle in for the night, walking up a country lane with the town's lights flickering behind me, I'm at the river, what a lovely sight!

*Martin Borley*
*Ixworth Middle School, Suffolk*

# CAN THEY KEEP A SECRET?

One day Lady Hannah was eating her toast, when suddenly her son, Master George ran in and shouted, 'Can we go to the zoo today Mum, please, please?'
'I might have to think about that George.' So she thought for five minutes.
'Well, what's the answer? Come on tell me.'
'No, we are going to the museum.'
'Oh, do we have to?'
'Yes, it's part of your education.'

So they went to the museum, they saw lots of ancient objects.
'Ah, wow, that was brilliant!'
'Ahhhh, my knee, I tripped over.' They looked at what he fell over, there was a huge hole. They took the tiles up and couldn't believe their eyes when they saw a really big tomb. They went down now, it was exciting, George had even forgotten about his knee.

They saw a coffin, they thought they would be able to keep it a secret . . . *but could they?*

*Katherine Thwaites*
*Ixworth Middle School, Suffolk*

# MAKE IT BIG

'Oh please, I am a good singer, I'll make it big,' pleaded Molly Ickle. She was sitting in one of the interview rooms at Angel Recording Studios, she had been turned down to record a song again.
'I'm afraid your voice is just not good enough to be signed on by Angel,' said the young man.

Molly stood up, walked out and slammed the door. When she got home Molly went to her bedroom and cried until she had no more tears to cry.

The next day Molly looked at her list of recording studios, 'Ten down, only five more to go,' she sighed. The next one on her list was Jive Recordings. She rang up and booked an interview for that afternoon.

Molly was sitting in the Jive waiting room. 'Molly Ickle, would you like to come through?' Molly stood up rather shakily and walked through the door. An hour later she came back through feeling much more confident. She had finally got a recording contract. Yes, she thought, I've done it.

A year later and she was releasing her debut single named 'Make It Big'. It was a hit and got to number one all over the world. Molly was overjoyed and ran around the house screaming with joy.

Five years after this Molly was married to an old school friend named Mike. So far she'd had nine number one hits and three top ten hits. She was known as the 'Queen of Pop'.

One night Molly was lying in bed thinking back to that time six years ago at Angel Recording Studios, I said I'd make it big and I have, she thought contentedly. Molly Ickle, the 'Queen of Pop' turned over and went to sleep with happy dreams.

*Anastasia Porteous (11)*
*Ixworth Middle School, Suffolk*

# GLOOP GLOOP

It was a cold night on the streets of London, the frost was dripping off the windows as the wet, dewy, frosty rain pattered on the floors. There on a doorstep stood a little girl crying as the rain dripped off her clothes. She was a very interesting figure and many people looked at her with curious eyes as they walked past.

Then came a loud *crash*, 'Gloop, Gloop,' said the girl.
Then she heard some thunder as the wet, murky ground shook, she heard some screams and shouts of, 'Help,' and 'save me,' as everyone ran for shelter of their houses, but poor little Rose just stood there getting wetter by the minute. She saw a big metal figure coming towards her. The big monstrous robot clasped a big metal hand around her, the poor little girl was being held so tight that she couldn't move.

The robot finally stopped at . . . at . . . well, it wasn't where Rose thought she was going, because she was taken to the dump. The robot hung her over a pit that was full of green toxic sludge. *Gloop, gloop*, went the sludge as her feet went in.

'Kill, fry for me to eat,' bellowed the robot whose name was Die.
'Help! Noooo,' screamed Rose, 'Gloop Gloop come and save me please!'
The huge gloopy thing appeared, 'I am Gloop Gloop,' he said in a strange squeaky but gruff voice, as he dived at the evil robot trying to save Rose, but oh no, he and Rose fell in the pit of sludgy, green, gloopy, toxic sludge.

Die was laughing his head off, until his head suddenly did come off. Rose and Gloop Gloop came out of the sludge, but they had turned into sludge monsters. Then they were the ones laughing at Die, but their heads didn't come off, instead they turned back into humans, well Rose did, but Gloop Gloop stayed as a sludge monster because he had always been one anyway!

*Frances Busson*
*Ixworth Middle School, Suffolk*

# A Day In The Life Of An Airshow Pilot

I am awoken form my 'G' induced sleep by warning alarms screeching at me for attention. One look outside tells me I'm hurtling towards the deck at twice the speed of sound in an uncontrolled spin. Not the nicest position to be in on a Sunday morning.

I wrench the controls to and fro with little response, I can see lots of people scurrying round below me observing the gentle spiralling and sharp flips and jerks that I am having to endure in the airspace above. Plumes of smoke are pouring out behind making awkward grey/white patterns against the threatening shadowy sky. The voice of a lady shouting the same command, 'Pull up, pull up!'
My eyes flick around nervously, checking my position.
'3,000 feet, pull up!' squeals the onboard computer.

A cold sweat trickles gently down my forehead as my mind ticks over all the things that could happen in the next twenty seconds.
'You are exceeding maximum speed limits, reduce thrust, pull up!'
I begin to think of who that monotone, nagging voice could belong to; some poor man's wife maybe? A doctor? A dentist?
'1,000 feet, pull up!'
Or maybe my mother!
'500 feet, pull up!'

This is the crucial moment; the meaning of my intense training is about to fall into place. With one sharp snap of the control column I level the aircraft off at 100 feet, much to the cheering delight of the airshow crowd. Relief races up and down my body, firstly from pulling off the complex manoeuvre, and secondly I am finally rid of the feeble voice of the onboard computer! Over the radio comes, 'Well done RED9, excellent manoeuvre, we're going home.'

*Benn Oliver (14)*
*Linton Village College, Cambridgeshire*

## CARS PASS SLOWLY

Hello, I am nobody, and I pretend to live somewhere that nobody's ever heard of. I don't think I'll do anything today, but wait, I never do.

I sit and drink lemonade from a glass. It's a shame, my glass is rarely full, there is usually a dry space above the lovely liquid.

A box of chocolates sits on my table. It's strange, those chocolates never hurt anybody, but we treat them with so little respect, we never have parties for chocolates or chocolate fun days.

My windows are boarded up. I don't need the light, well, really I don't deserve it, I never do it any favours in return, I just sit selfishly in its glow.

A candle nearby on the floor flutters pathetically. But, unlike chocolates I have a deep respect for the candle. Its wax that is so happy, but yet so willing to melt and move to a different place and the wick, that stands tall and proud like a true leader.

Two hundred and seventy-three ants crawl in the corner, with such deep blue concentration it makes the room seem grey.

Dust sweeps across the floor, a complete opposite to ants, moving without purpose or direction, its only goal to move a bit more. Maybe dust has a family to go to, but I think dust forgot its family a long time ago, maybe before I did.

Cars pass slowly outside. Or is it time?

*Jack Glossop (14)*
*Linton Village College, Cambridgeshire*

# A Day In The Life Of A Writer

Blankly, I sit in my dingy, old, brown chair staring up into the pitted, dirty white ceiling, which currently seems more intriguing than the task in hand. I twiddle my pen lazily, as I notice the doodle on the crusty pen holder in front of me.

Currently the room is dim and blank, which doesn't give the right sort of atmosphere to create a bright new idea. The curtains are closed and half the lights turned off. One of them is buzzing eternally. It is driving me crazy; my head is going to explode because of this subtle, yet very noticeable noise. Turn it off!

A sigh of relief as that repetitive beat has disappeared. Silence. A new tone seems to have filled the misty air in the compact room. I turn my head smoothly, over to the dilapidated window as a bird flies over the tattered wall and into the bare tree that shivers in the cold lifeless air.

*Grr!* Concentrate. My mind drifts to and from the room taking me away from the realism of the daunting situation. The more I think about it the more my mind floats into my vivid imagination which is the only thing stopping my flow of inspirational thoughts.

The room is still dark which reflects my thoughts. The lights flicker. On, off, on, off. Abruptly the room fills with light and instantaneously the lights turn on my mechanical head. An idea!

I put pen to paper and begin to write fluently, *Blankly, I sit in my brown, dingy, old chair, staring up into the pitted, dirty white ceiling . . .*

*Daniel De'Ath (14)*
*Linton Village College, Cambridgeshire*

# ON MY WAY TO HIGH POINT

Uncomfortably I sat in the dark room of guilt, the small room where you sit and guilt runs through your wondering mind, and constantly haunts you non-stop. This is the room in the police van when you're moving prisons and claustrophobia springs to mind.

The door's flung open and my first sight was the lumpy face of that extremely ugly policewoman. She stood standing and glaring at me for a while and eventually let me stand up. I held out my trembling hands for her to clamp those gripping silver cuffs to them. The next step was the worst, I had to take that long journey from the van to the glum cell. I had to walk all the way! I walked through the door of my cell to find almost complete blackness. Why am I here?

So here I am now, standing in this lonesome darkness inside a prison cell, at High Point. My brain is jam-packed with thoughts, thoughts that only I know the answer to.

I keep seeing those little children that I have taken and tortured. I'm a sick, sick woman, a woman that should be killed.

Maybe my dad made me like this, he used to hit me and torture me. I don't know.

I heard someone in another cell say my name. I heard, 'Myra?' I'm famous but for all the wrong reasons.

*Tom Davies  (13)*
*Linton Village College, Cambridgeshire*

## THE DAY THORNTON HALL BURNED

*(Based on Jane Eyre by Charlotte Brontë recounted by Mr Rochester and Bertha Rochester)*

Her hair hung in snake-like tendrils framing her hatred-sculpted face with black fire. Remnants of beauty still showed in her bulbous eyes, but lay unrealised, forgotten, for she was haunted, haunted by her mind. She had no authority over her vampirish instincts: once in an attack of violence she drew blood from Mr Mason, her brother.

But in all honesty can I rightfully condemn Bertha for my fatal blindness?

I feel caged like a bird. My mind touches fleetingly all my clashing emotions. I'm so angry, intense desperation bruises my skin purple. I remember everything, those despising eyes scorched into my memory. I need revenge . . .

I strike the match and excitement courses through me as I sway with the thought of fire destroying Thornton Hall, my prison. The sheets of Jane's bed peel black as orange fire consummates the bedroom. I run, laughing, leading the fire, feeling it burn my skin. Once again I am lost, drowned out by the crackling of choking smoke. On the roof, I look down at the hills and mock all the servants turned out to the cold by me. I turned to the rugged face of Mr Rochester.
'Don't do it!' The words mean nothing. 'Bertha.'
The dark below looks so tempting. I looked back at the outstretched arm with contempt. How could I go back to his prison? I laugh, then jump. The freedom as I plunge through the hot air is close to euphoria. Revenge is mine . . .

*Hannah Warner (14)*
*Linton Village College, Cambridgeshire*

# TEN MONTHS ON

*What Has Happened To The 'War On Terrorism'?*

It's now ten months since the dreadful attacks on America on September 11th 2001. And, amid stories about Enron and WorldCom, do you still think about the war on terrorism?

There have been the odd stories about the marines shooting Al-Qa'eda fighters, and that the CIA didn't tell anyone that they knew September 11th was going to happen. But, now most of that has trickled out. What is really happening? What do you think about the war on terrorism? Should the Americans and British have troops in Afghanistan, where they are not going to capture the world's most infamous terrorist, Osama bin Laden?

All the ammunition they, apparently, need to blow up caves, which are full of ammunition, which they could use. This uses your money! And, just recently, the Americans, apparently in 'self-defence' bombed four villages. What is the reason that almost fifty people are dead? A wedding party! They were firing small handguns in celebration. The Americans thought they were firing at a reconnaissance plane. As if small guns can bring down an aeroplane. The Afghanistan people don't want their own army. The coalition government wants to sort out its own problems. They want to set their own agenda not picking up the pieces from American accident. Accidents that have left 6,000 people dead. Twice the number that was killed on September 11th.

Is what's good for America really good for Afghanistan?

*Rachel Davies (14)*
*Linton Village College, Cambridgeshire*

## POSSESSED

Stepping into the cold blackness, I can see the untended shed peeking out from its protective cover of a tree.

Gently making my way towards the shed through the long grass tickling at my knees. I keep an eye on my parent's bedroom as I swing the maturing door open. There it is. It really does look a mess but the rusty frame and old wheels are more than they appear. On the handlebars the old bell still shines, the exhilarating ring it exploits escalating the excitement inside me.

My eager leg stretches over the seat and rests on the metal peg. A quiet push and the bike is slicing through the grass, gaining speed steadily the lengthy grass whips at my ankles. The forceful wind bashes at my face. The short bumps disappear and the smooth road melts with the wheel. Gaining yet more speed the slope of the hill soon arrives. The wheels hum in the air with the speed.

The bell shrieks out, piercing the rush of the wind. The bike begins to swerve of its own accord, each time moving closer to the kerb. I can't stop it. The sheer excitement turns to fear. The bell lets out another shrill scream, a cackle seems to blast through my ears. The back wheel locks and the bike skids, just missing a single car parked by the opposite kerb. Now at a halt I catch my breath my heart still pounding. This thing is possessed!

*James Farenden (14)*
*Linton Village College, Cambridgeshire*

## 9/11

The fierce morning sun reflected off the wing with the constant humming from the engine in my ears. Two men behind me were making a terrible fuss about something. I just turned my head and gazed dreamily out of the window, hoping for my flight to be successful. That's my problem, I always think of the worst possible situation, oh well, that's just me.

'Please stay calm, the flight has been disturbed.'
'I assume that was the pilot's voice,' I said to the people behind me. 'What was he talking about? Does this normally happen?' I said with a giggle. They didn't look quite as calm to me. Suddenly four air hostesses rushed down the aisle. They frantically gave safety sheets out. One girl dropped them and broke down. It was then that I knew that something was wrong. I turned yet again but the people behind me had vanished.

The plane dispersed the cloud cover, then the towers appeared in the foreground with a mass of thick, black smoke, which cast a shadow over much of Manhattan.

I could see debris falling from the left tower. We came very close to the tower when I realised where we were heading. The last thing I remember was a face appearing from behind the curtain. He looked at me. In a split second a flame rushed through the aisle taking everything in its way. Darkness fell.

*Tom Sargeant (14)*
*Linton Village College, Cambridgeshire*

# TUN IN THE TREE 13

A large sun was beaming its rays slowly up over the ocean of trees. A small village was awaking at that precise moment. This village was not your typical tribal village. The inhabitants were 3ft tall.

Tun was just exiting his home. He stepped out and with a moan he began to run to the café. He rapped on the wooden door and was greeted by a timid old man named Harnen. 'What do you want boy?' the bearded man snapped.
'I am famished,' pleaded Tun, 'but breakfast is ages away.'
'Listen boy, if you retrieve my spectacles from tree 13, you will receive food,' added Harnen.
'But tree 13 is dangerous,' replied Tun.
'Yes, but my leg is broken, so I can't go,' Harnen answered.

Tun set off. His destination was behind a thick thorn bush. Tun pushed his way through it, occasionally pausing to fix his wounds. Suddenly he saw the tree towering above his head. He approached the door and pulled. Looking inside, he could see only black. He stepped into the dark room and began to search for the spectacles.

A bright light flashed and a voice boomed, 'You must leave.'
Tun turned around and sprinted from the room. He fought back through the thorns, not looking back.

He reached the old man who was standing wearing his spectacles. 'I forgot I had them in my pocket,' he called.
Tun looked at him. 'Wha . . ?' he grunted and sat down with a thud. 'I need food.'

*Ed Bonsey (14)*
*Linton Village College, Cambridgeshire*

# ROBIN HOOD

Robin is the leader of the recently formed 'Robin's Band Of Perky Pikeys'. (He came up with the name himself.) You see, Robin has an unfortunate 'vertically challenged' half-brother, Rodney, who had an embarrassing accident with a monkey, a banana and half a traffic cone. (But that's another story.) Robin made a promise to Rodney to try and make it up to him in any way he could.

As Robin was a pikey, and did not have an extremely good education, he decided the best way to help Rodney was to form a group of outlaws and steal from the poor and give the money to midgets like Rodney. Later, Robin decided that stealing from the poor would be both harsh and pointless, so he decided to steal from the tall instead, for Rodney did not like tall people.

One morning, in their trailer park, Robin had called a meeting. 'Is everyone here yet?' asked Robin slightly frustratedly.
'All except Maid Martin,' replied Little Johnny.
'Okay, Rob. Martin's here now.'
'Right fellow pikeys, it has come to my attention that we have some rivals, some do-good hillbillies have started doing some outlawing of their own. However, they have decided to steal from midgets and give to the tall. It's time we showed 'Harry's tribe of Happy Hillbillies' what the 'Perky Pikeys' are made of! Big Dave, brief the troops so they know what to do.'

Next morning, Harry woke up with no legs!

*Will Woodgate  (14)*
*Linton Village College, Cambridgeshire*

# An Hour In The Life Of A Passenger In September

The rumble of constant conversation. The roar of ever-turning engines. Things never change. Bodies walking up and down the aisles, bodies sleeping and bodies talking.

I fidgeted in my scratchy seat and twisted to see an Arab man shuffling his way towards the front. As he passed me I settled back, thinking nothing of it.

A great gasp filled the regular rumble and screams shrilled through my now shocked body. I looked up, to my ultimate horror, to see this man holding a gun to an absolutely terrified air hostess.

One extremely brave man raced towards the gunman and attempted to challenge him . . . An ear-bursting *bang!* Silence! I turned away and winced! His bravery rewarded with a painful death under awful circumstances.

The sinister gunman forced the trembling hostess to open the hatch to the pilot's cockpit. Horrible thoughts passed through my petrified mind. The hatch slammed shut. What was he going to do?

Another eerie silence prevailed. Then the vast plane slowly banked.

Panic spread! I stared anxiously out of my confined window to see the approaching skyline. The plane plunged down and my heart sank. Our new worrying destination: New York . . . 8.58 . . . my time was up . . .

*Luke Little  (13)*
*Linton Village College, Cambridgeshire*

# 'P' Is For Pig

The three pompous pigs, paunches protruding through their gaudy waistcoats, sat at the petitioners' bench in the council chamber. The council leader nervously announced his decision on the planning application submitted by P Pig & Bros for a housing estate in the church grounds. 'I er . . . see no good reason to object.'

'Maybe you can't, but I certainly can!' exclaimed Mr Wilf Wolf, the local environmental pro-activist. 'Church land should not be ransacked for private profit.'

The eldest pig, Percival, addressed his reply to the council leader. 'As you already know,' he condescendingly proclaimed, 'the church is in financial difficulties and our proposed action would relieve their pecuniary embarrassment.'

'That's just a load of sh . . . allow words,' retorted Wilf.

'My decision is final,' stuttered the council leader. 'Proceed.'

At the naming ceremony of the new estate, *Porkers Park*, Percival pig was pontificating about his propitious use of environmental materials. He did not notice Wilf lean against the straw starter home and knock against the stylish stick chalet. Both collapsed and so did the expression on the mayor's mercenary face.

'You tried to increase your profit by using substandard mortar to build this brick house,' bellowed Wilf. 'Building regulations have been contravened and it should be demolished.'

Before the pigs could protest there was a thunderous noise, the chimney quivered, sending bricks cascading to the ground and the pigs were buried alive.

'Justice has been done,' proclaimed Wilf. 'This land must be returned to its rightful owners and used as an environmentally friendly burial ground.'

*Anna Tumber (14)*
*Linton Village College, Cambridgeshire*

# A DAY IN THE LIFE OF . . .

I strolled calmly home late this Friday night. The sun had just set and the only thing that lit my way was a flickering street light every so often. The sun may have dissolved, but it was not any cooler, the humidity made me stop and find my breath.

There it was, it had been a struggle to find, but now I was there. I was home. I eagerly crept through the door desperate to see my wife and my two beautiful girls. Suddenly, a note appeared on the floor. I picked it up and read it. I had a sinking feeling inside and again struggled to breathe.

I slumped to the ground, I just couldn't come to terms with it, surely not, surely I was too young, had they not thought about my wife and children? I threw the paper to one side and tried to make sense of it all.

For the emperor, all for the emperor, everything always for the emperor and now me. My life for the emperor. I kept asking again and again to myself, why?

Fear had now displaced the anger. What was to come after this life? I played round several ideas in my head, but just couldn't make sense of any of this. I was being sentenced to death, not with an executioner, but with a plane. I would die for my country.

*Euan Corrin  (13)*
*Linton Village College, Cambridgeshire*

# THE HELL OF HIROSHIMA

Turning back now, I remember, upon opening my eyes, I realised I was in intense pain both physically and mentally.

My battered, bruised, broken body crawled from the confusion of bricks, concrete and bodies. I staggered to the next street expecting to find help and medical aid, but rubble and a thick dust barricaded the roads. I joined the frantic crowd. Dazedly I spun round, noticing the ripped flesh, mutilated faces, serious burns and as I looked back, hundreds of faces stared back with empty, blackened eye sockets.

I lurched through the streets. Each one looked as though ten enemy bombs had hit it. Realisation was slowly registering in my mind. The bomb had not just hit these few streets, it had hit the whole of Hiroshima.

Even now, years later, I walk through the abandoned streets, in the centre of the city shadows, on the walls, haunt me and the agonising screams ring in my ears. Thousands of strange cases have been happening; people are still dropping dead for unknown reasons, wounds and burns have not healed and most of all, people's grief and pain has not healed. Hiroshima is still a dangerous place to live.

Nobody can even imagine the effect of a nuclear war weapon. And when I walk through these very streets the same thought runs through my mind as it did on the 6th August 1945; America, what have you done?

*Jasdeep Rai (14)*
*Linton Village College, Cambridgeshire*

# A DAY IN THE LIFE OF GUY 'INCOGNITO' THATBLOKE

Do I know you from somewhere? I'm Guy Thatbloke and it's my occupation to tell the Prime Minister what to do. In most of the pictures of Mr Blair, I am standing in the background, looking handsome and wearing a toupee and brogues. Yes, he receives all of 'his' ideas from me. Nobody has heard of me as I am always sitting at my desk, nibbling Snack-a-Jacks pondering over the minutes of the last cabinet meetings that Mr Blair took the liberty of texting me. You will know that Mr Blair has increased stealth tax. That was my idea! I had to tell him, my pocket needed it (I gain 'brownie points' for each of my ideas I put forward to him).

Mr Blair is not sophisticated in any conceivable way. All he does is lounge around in his *luxurious* office, scoffing biscuits and milk, playing with his executive toys. He wangled his way into being the PM by gangsters known only to themselves and their victims. Mr Blair, I think, is like the Guy (no pun intended) on Fireworks Night, like a symbol of the actual event. Please do not get me wrong; I despise Mr Blair. I'd rather be the man with the packet of Swan Vestas.

You may be asking yourself how I ended up in my job instead of a famous boffin. Well, I simply rose through the ranks. From a desperate job scraping together a living to being tied up in the brambles of politics.

*Edward Dickinson (14)*
*Linton Village College, Cambridgeshire*

# ON THE BEACHES

There was a severe jerk, a dull rattle of pebbles, then the doors opened. The men stampeded out, fuelled by adrenaline and fear. They were charging blindly into the unknown.

As they left they were bombarded by a hail of metal and lead. They all dived at the nearest rock, or solid object that could provide comfort for a short while.

The men were petrified. There was sand flying in all directions, shouts coming from everywhere, and the zinging of those little pieces of death.

The order was given, the cover was left behind and the advance began. Men on both sides of the bridge of prospect hit the ground. The men were advancing fearlessly towards freedom, or death. The heroic warriors of the beach were running in all directions, stopping only to take aim at the grey coats at the top of the sands.

The golden sand between the pebbles appeared to be dyed crimson with the life of fallen men. The rocks were becoming a muddy brown as more and more soldiers trod on them in their quest for domination.

The greatest battle of all time had just begun and thousands upon thousands of ordinary men were fighting for their countries to secure an honourable standard of living for those back home.

This was war, this was history in the making, this was D-Day.

*Callum Mayfield (14)*
*Linton Village College, Cambridgeshire*

# PAST THE SUN

Every pearly hair on its back glistened in the sunlight, like tiny diamonds covered it. A bright light shone above its head illuminating its handsome features. Wings swept through the warm air, spanning metres into the silvery clouds.

The creature soared through the sky towards the golden sun. The heat was intense, droplets of sweat fell from its forehead. You could see frustration in his bright eyes. All it had to do now was cross the sun!

Away from this world the creature flew. From a place of pain and discomfort to anyone who approached it. Past the sun was a new world, a land filled with beauty and elation.

As the animal passed the sun, the new land came into view. The excitement grew greater and the expectations prospered.

Thud! The creature landed amongst a poppy field. He lay there for a moment, to catch his breath and take in the beauty. In the distance, there was a cluster of small buildings.

He made his way into the town where creatures walked and talked together. Humans. The creature was anxious. Many humans ran in fear of him, shouting and screaming. One exception grabbed a metal bar and hit the animal over and over, until it could not stand. Others joined and began taunting him. Tears fell from his once bright eyes and pain smothered his body.

This land of beauty and elation was actually a world of suffering, violence and unhappiness. Nothing is quite what it seems.

*Emily Durley (14)*
*Linton Village College, Cambridgeshire*

# TWO HOURS TO LIVE!

'Phew,' I sighed with relief, we were airborne at last, after a two-hour delay. I sunk into the padded seat, I was in paradise. I was finally moving out of my parents' house! In two hours I would be the other side of America starting up my new life.

I had been glaring out of the window at the heavenly clouds floating into the unseen, when two Arab men rose from their seats behind me. The one on the left had a shifty look about him so I analysed him carefully until he was out of sight.

A terrified screech rattled through my bones, as I jarred my neck throwing myself in the direction of the noise. The pilot's cabin door flew open with rage. One of the men I had seen earlier insanely dived to the middle of the plane with a revolver placed firmly in his hand, his finger on the trigger.

My body transformed into a raincloud, dispersing nothing but beads of sweat. Then he spoke, his words flew into each other and span round and round in my head, but I just got the gist of it all right. We were on a hijacked plane; we were a few yards from obliterating the Twin Towers. We were going to kill thousands of innocent people, devastate the world and America for life.

I pinched myself to reassure myself I was dreaming, but to my absolute horror it was real.

This was it, goodbye Mum, goodbye life.

*Laura Dickens (14)*
*Linton Village College, Cambridgeshire*

# FEAR!

I was so cold. In fact, I had never been as cold as I was that morning. I was on my way to the injury that would ruin all enjoyment in my life. However, I was one of the lucky ones. Out of the twelve other men in my team, four came out alive. I was one of them.

I was on a small amphibious vessel that swam its way through the debris from previous trips that ended before they began. I was on my way to fight Nazi Germany. As soon as we hit the beach the huge steel door that had been shielding us from the bombardment of machine-gun bullets, dropped. We were open to enemy fire. The front four men were annihilated instantly. This was the beginning of a massacre.

I leapt over the perished corpses, and hared across the beach, scattered with carcasses. I hid behind a strange looking steel structure. It had huge steel girders like arms reaching out as if it was also in pain.

As I sat there I was thinking about my wife and my two little boys. I began to wonder, what if they had to go through this? I was aroused by a loud scream of pain. It was another of my team, dead. All I could hear now were cries of pain and bullets flying through the air around me.

I clambered to my feet and ran directly into never-ending pain.

*Lewis Cracknell (14)*
*Linton Village College, Cambridgeshire*

## MURDER HUNT

The side walls of the basement of the Houston hospital for the criminally insane trickled with stagnant water. The steel door at the top of the stone steps was slowly rusting away. The door creaked open, lacerating the stone.

Inside the doorway stood special agent Maloy. Maloy had worked for the behavioural science unit for ten years but never on such a dangerous assignment. Today he had to interview the world's most dangerous killer, Dr Fell.

Several years before, Dr Fell had attacked Jason Verger. After the assault, Jason was left with deep trenches in his face and the bottom half of his nose missing. The surgeons had tried to cover the gauges the best they could with a skin graft, but you could still see the blood flowing through his pulsating veins.

When Maloy reached his cell there was blood on the door. When he entered, two guards were laying dead on the floor. Dr Fell had escaped and was as dangerous as ever.

As Maloy left, he saw a poster for Dr Fell. The Verger family were offering a £500,000 reward plus more if it led to his arrest.

Maloy was sitting in his kitchen listening to a news bulletin. Dr Fell was said to have killed another man in the city of Dallas. He grabbed his wallet and went to book a flight to Dallas. The hunt for Dr Fell had just begun.

*Chris Negus (14)*
*Linton Village College, Cambridgeshire*

## WHAT IS IT?

Over the past five days numerous reports have been coming in from Norfolk of 'weird, unexplainable' happenings . . . Are they just coincidental or is something much more sinister or supernatural going on?

Around 8am yesterday morning, a retired man living in Cromer insists that for an instant he was momentarily blinded by an intense indigo flash of light . . . What is the explanation for this? This was not all though . . . six other people in the same area have reported having a similar experience, but each person seeing a different coloured flash!

A young lady from Sheringham revealed on Tuesday that when she was taking a walk as she usually did, for a split moment she saw an illusion. In this short time she noticed that everything around her turned to rubble and dust; the houses on her left and right shook silently then crumbled to a heap on the green, now brown, grass. The trees blew over without any wind, and all the pretty plants' flowers shut, curled up and died.

The woman that claims that this is what she saw, was described by her friends and family today as being 'mature, considerate and conscientious to those around her'.

Scientists and a leading psychiatrist are working on both of these particular incidents that these unfortunate people have experienced . . . They have said that they have so far come up with two theories as to what has happened, but they will announce them when they are more certain or they have more information on what happened.

*Catherine Orgee (14)*
*Linton Village College, Cambridgeshire*

## AN UNSEEN AUDIENCE
*(A short chapter in the style of J R R Tolkien)*

Bilbo awoke with a start. As he strained his eyes to adjust to the intense darkness that surrounded him, he began to make out the glittering red pinpricks of light from thousands of eyes, all staring intently at him, watching every move he made.

A muttering, a shuffling broke out among this unseen audience, and soon the entire chamber was filled with strange echoing whispers. The whispers were close enough for Bilbo to catch the odd sentence, and what he heard struck fear into his very soul.

Bilbo's mind was racing. How had he got into this frightful situation? He could barely remember anything. He vaguely recalled crossing the Edge of the Wild, but that was ages ago! He remembered the dwarves. Where were they now? And Gandalf?

Once again, Bilbo came close to tears as he thought of his cosy home, and wondered for the umpteenth time why, oh why, he ventured to leave it. Nothing made sense anymore. His head was throbbing and he hadn't eaten in days. And now he was suddenly a prisoner, trapped underground in a darkness so thick and palpable he felt he might choke. What was he doing there? And what on earth did his captors want with a small, insignificant hobbit like him?

Suddenly the whispering stopped and the room became silent. Then from the depths of the gloom, he heard a plaintive, sorrowful little voice cry, 'Help me. Please help me.'

*Helen Jedrzejewski (13)*
*Linton Village College, Cambridgeshire*

## MORTAL LAW

Lee flung the giant man over his shoulder and forcefully flattened him onto the floor. Lee was fighting a member of the Yang terrorist organisation on behalf of the Tokyo police and had just run up against a corrupt group.

Lee jumped up and swivelled around to see his partner, Yag, being pummelled by two of the gang. He briskly vaulted himself over to Yag's assistance and, with two jabs, knocked them to the floor. Rashly, another member ripped a gun from his holster and shot.

Lee grasped his throbbing arm and yelled out in pain, sharply striking in the hope of knocking the man out. Luckily, instead, he smacked the gun from the man's hands. Then, as the man reached and grasped for the gun, Lee booted the Yang gang member in the face, knocking him out cold.

Some of the terrorists scampered away, whilst some lay paralysed on the floor. As Lee wrapped his shirt around his arm as a bandage, a tall terrorist appeared. He grabbed a small object from his pocket, pulled the top off, quickly rolled it into the room and then sprinted in the opposite direction. Lee quickly got to his feet, grabbed his partner and the knocked-out man and dragged them as quickly as he could to the door. The house suddenly exploded and crashed down as Lee dived out of the way.

Hopefully Lee would be able to get information from the criminal and break through in the case.

*Tom Miller (13)*
*Linton Village College, Cambridgeshire*

# A DAY IN THE LIFE OF . . . A SOLDIER AT WAR

The reverberation of the waves beating against the boat was as if someone was beating against a door, desperate to enter.

As the bandits flew overhead, I thought to myself, what have I let myself in for?

I caught a glimpse of Omaha beach. It was swarming with enemy soldiers, inclined to pounce like lions on their prey, and we were the prey.

Another thirty seconds later, I heard the *clunk* of the boat colliding with the seabed. That was the sign for my adventure to begin.

I ran from the boat and sprinted, straight towards the nearest cover. My captain met up with me, giving me my orders. 'Take out the machine-gun,' he roared at me, like a police car after a suspect.

I left my cover after a minute of contemplating the actions and precautions I would have to take for my mission. The scream of bullets whizzing past my ears was enough to wake Sleeping Beauty, it hurt!

I found a suitable place for cover to empty a round of my rifle bullets towards the enemy, killing someone with my last bullet.

I darted from my cover to the empty machine-gun post to take out the main turret. I opened up and felt alive as the bullets poured from the barrel. The explosion of my target filled me with passion and a sense of achievement.

I turned around and the pain was immense. I thought I was a gonner.

*Daniel Fletcher (14)*
*Linton Village College, Cambridgeshire*

## CELEBRITY DEATH MATCH:
## THE SEVEN DWARVES VS THE LOCH NESS MONSTER

'Ladies, gentlemen, fairy tale and mythical creatures alike, welcome to the biggest ever Celebrity Death Match. I'm your commentator for tonight, King Arthur of the Round Table, here to help me is respected, hard, um, man Collin Jones, aka 'The Big Bad Wolf'. Mr Wolf, who do you think is going to win?'

'Personally, I think . . .'

'Sorry, I'm going to have to stop you, here come the competitors. They're stepping into the ring, with the announcer.'

'Ladies, gentlemen, fairy tale and mythical creatures, welcome to tonight's fight. In the red corner weighing 4,500 pounds - The Loch Ness Monster. In the blue corner, with a combined weight of 625 pounds - The Seven Dwarves.'

'There's the bell. Nessie whips her tail, catching Dopey and Sleepy, launching them into the crowd. The Dwarves don't like that. Grumpy's about to explode. He's got a pickaxe and he's running at Nessie. He's buried it in her side. Nessie looks in crippling agony. Wait, she's getting up again. *Slam*, she's down on top of Bashful, Doc and Grumpy. That leaves Happy and Sneezy, what'll these two conjure up? Happy's pulled a book of bad jokes from under his hat. He's telling them to Nessie, she doesn't like it one bit.

She's hawking and snorting, oh no, she's blasted Happy with a grotesque blob of phlegm. Folks, I think we can say Nessie's won.

What's this? Sneezy's sniffed up some dust and looks like he'll erupt at any . . .'

'Aaaaccchhhhhooooooo!'

'Oh my, Sneezy's blasted Nessie all the way back to Scotland. That's it folks, we have new champions - The Seven Dwarves!'

*Simon Blackman (14)*
*Linton Village College, Cambridgeshire*

# THE WINGED MYSTERY

It first caught my attention by perching upon a leaf, flickering in the pale moonlight. I went to take a closer look, but it cheekily flew away before I could see what it was.

I went back to the same secluded spot every night. I couldn't help it - I needed to know what it was. Every time I saw it, its fragile wings were gleaming under the moonlit sky, but that was all I witnessed.

Then one night while I was relaxing under the stars, heavy rain started to fall. Then I saw the most extraordinary sight in the world.

As the rain fell harder, the diminutive luster twinkled faster. Without warning, the winged creature fell with a light thud. I knew this was my chance to see what had been so enticing.

I cautiously walked towards it, taking deep breaths along the way. The rain had lightened up a bit, but the earth was pulpous and my feet squelched as I moved.

There was the mysterious creature. It had the most petite features I had ever seen. It had a precious figure covered in a pink petal dress. Its head looked as though it could snuggly fit into the palm of my hand, and it was covered in silky, curly brown hair. Its legs were as long as my fingers, and had miniature feet. It suddenly woke up and just flew away. I knew that that was the first and last time I would ever see a fairy.

*Kayleigh Orloff (14)*
*Linton Village College, Cambridgeshire*

# A MORTAL LOVE

Many believe that mystical creatures are a fairytale, a fantasy, even a lie. But this is a story to open even the eyes of rationalists, a story of hatred, beauty and most of all, love.

It begins with three of the most extraordinary creatures, those of which you yourself may find hard to believe truly exist, but then who are we but mere animals of the dust to argue with the existence of such enticing creatures.

So now I must draw you in deeper. I must reach your mind and clutch it as I now attempt to pass on this most ensnaring memory, recalling the day when it all began.

These three creatures were none other than the notorious Fletch, Goblin and Fawkes. But who could have known that a unicorn, an elf and a phoenix could be so different and yet so alike. Each prioritises their different needs in life and so uses their abilities for their own purposes.

If only they had known what was racing in their direction. If only they had never discovered what it is that lies in all our hearts, that which changes the path of time forever and unlocks that which should never have been opened. The deepest, darkest secrets of those which shall not be named. Secrets of hatred, beauty, and most of all, love.

How this would never have been such an enticing tale if their paths had never crossed. But then again, always and forever time will come.

*Jessica Plumb  (14)*
*Linton Village College, Cambridgeshire*

## THE KISS

Once upon a time there lived a very vain prince. He lived in an enchanted castle. The castle had a creeper with rainbow-coloured flowers sprouting everywhere. Doug who lived near the castle was the only friend of the prince, but a loyal one.

One day Doug thought he would teach the prince a lesson. He organised a party for the prince but didn't invite anyone except a frog who was actually a princess.

The princess had a godmother who was a *witch*. She didn't like the princess so she put a spell on her. The only way the spell would be broken was to be kissed by a prince. Doug thought that if the prince and the frog were the only ones at the party, then maybe the spell would be broken.

When the party came, the prince was waiting for his guests, but little did he know that the only one guest that was going to arrive was the frog. Doug dressed the frog in a handmade pink dress and a tiara placed on her sluggish green head.

The party was a great success, the prince danced with the frog and didn't suspect a thing. As the frog left, the prince kissed her goodnight. Before the prince's eyes was a flash of light and a puff of smoke.

As the smoke cleared, there stood the most beautiful princess. They married the next day and lived happily ever after.

*Laura McCann  (14)*
*Linton Village College, Cambridgeshire*

# FIRE!

Reflected in his eyes the flames were burning bright, roaring as fierce as they did on TV, but this time it was real and it was all his fault.

He never wanted this to happen. He was just having some fun. His thoughts were lost in his fixed gaze as he stared at what he had done.

He never thought, not for a moment, that this could happen. If he had, he would never have left it. Never. The bonfire was gently smouldering when he left, when he returned, two minutes later, the whole house was ablaze.

He was overcome with a feeling of guilt, which later turned to utter devastation as he realised the severity of the damage done.

It was irremediable, the house could be re-built at a cost, but the lives of the people he saw being recovered from the burned wreckage would never be the same again. They were still, unconscious or maybe even dead, it was impossible to tell.

He watched from a distance, far away enough for him not to feel the immense heat and he told himself he would become a fireman. At least he might find some way to mend what he had done. In the meantime he had to live with himself, carrying such a huge burden.

The investigating fireman stood among the debris, the still hot remains of the house, as he prodded it with a stick - the mangled remains of a chip pan.

*Katherine Wright (14)*
*Linton Village College, Cambridgeshire*

# RED AND FAMOUS

The brass pendulum swung lazily back and forth and a lazy click emitted from the worn clock. The image shimmered in the heat and it seemed even the sound was muffled by the simmering haze. It was abnormally hot in here. Red didn't appear to mind, he sat in a blemished dark brown chair, his feet laid heftily on a heavily singed wooden table. He yawned and started to play idly with the pen in his left hand, was focused intently on the ceiling, it shimmered back.

'Hey Boss,' a coarse voice rang out.
Red pivoted to face its rough direction.
'Where do you want me to take the 'employees'?' it rasped.
'Oh, the usual, down the mines today.'
A dull grating moan issued, followed by the sharp snap of a whip, the contingent of callused, unshaven labourers shuffled past lugging crude digging implements in a familiar hunchback pose all the while groaning solemnly.
'Thanks Boss,' the rough voice returned.

Red yawned and watched them limp off into the distance, eyes glazed. He settled back into his chair, distant screamed echoed, stifled by the (for anyone else) unbearable heat. It was actually quite a big chair, almost a throne and if you looked at the surface closely, it gave a grubby sparkle, like a million slightly tarnished diamonds. The desk, that too was in its own special way highly rococo, edged with dirt-tainted brass, thousands of highly complicated patterns singed delicately into the wood and in the middle, a large pentagon which shone an unnatural crimson.

Red stared at the ceiling, it was hard work being the Devil. The ceiling shimmered its agreement.

*Bob Read  (14)*
*Linton Village College, Cambridgeshire*

## PEACE AND STRAWBERRY SMELL

With a satisfied grin of grim satisfaction, a tall, thin woman with high cheekbones paces out of Addenbrookes. She doesn't walk as you would expect a normal woman to walk though, her movements sort of flow and blend into one. Like . . . like a cat, a machiavillian cat.

In one swift movement she leaps on her motorbike and speeds off to the city centre, her blonde hair flailing out behind her.

Down in the city centre, the Grafton Centre to be precise, an old Hindu grandmother is being pushed along by her devout son-in-law. Even I, the narrator, can sense the warmth and love that bonds them.

She is there (if you are curious to find out) to buy a new stick of incense for her small statues of peace and strawberry smell back at home. At home, where her daughter is waiting with the baby she bore just a week or so ago. Oh the joy, the sweet, mellow joy that he bought with him when he did arrive.

Wait, she shudders, does she feel that little, fatal touch on her shoulder? I wonder, does she feel the icy fingers touching, stroking, soothing every limb of her body with the flow of her blood? Her blood which has stopped its flow.

Does she see in those last precious seconds of life the tall blonde woman moving stealthily away into the crowd and yet staying relatively close so she can spectate?

Does she realise that the woman has got out her note pad and is ticking off a name on her list, watching her dying with a sardistic smirk?

And as she is no longer there to realise anything any more, the Grim Reaper turns upon her steps and moves with ravaging strides to her next victim. All in one swift movement.

*Niels Meissner (14)*
*Linton Village College, Cambridgeshire*

# A DAY IN THE LIFE OF . . .

For days I'd been watching what you'd said and done. They claimed this ship was 'unsinkable' and naively you all believed them. If only you knew you were all going to be part of one of the biggest tragedies of the twentieth century.

Just four days into our maiden voyage, something massive happened.

It was a new day, just like yesterday and the day before that. The fascinated were up early to see the magnificent sunrise, and then there were the overpaid journalists who didn't wake until midday. The most talented violinists were performing beautiful music and the gamblers crowded the casino.

As the evening approached, the banquet halls filled with the sound of clattering plates and ching of silver knives and forks. Caviar and salmon strangely complimented smells of sea air. Roast beef dinners and fresh English salads are followed by exotic fruits and Pimms No 1. As the popping of champagne corks rescinded, the captain bade goodnight to his table guests and returned to the bridge. Then what should have been a famous voyage to New York turned infamous as the 1st Officer shouted, 'Ice! Dead ahead! A big berg!'

Now the ocean is about to swallow me, only the stern and funnels remain above water. Am I saying goodbye to the world forever? Will they ever find us? Will they ever find me? Who am I? I'm the chandelier in the Great Hall of the 'unsinkable' Titanic.

*Natasha Withers  (14)*
*Linton Village College, Cambridgeshire*

# A DAY IN THE LIFE OF A . . . WITCH

The rough rope irritates my wrists. The stake holds my back upright. I look down at the heartless people of my village.

They whisper to themselves and give darting glances in my direction, keeping well away. Keeping well away of the dirty, foul and sinful dark silhouette, crippled in rags, tied up. Me.

My pained eyes sadly stare at the only place where I had found happiness, the forest. My heart is throbbing to go back, so I turn the hands of time backwards into my memories of the forest.

The sun's rays reflect off my golden hair and the smell of honey sweetens the air. The colourful flowers sway in the wind and the glistening grass refreshes my mind. The buzz of the bumblebee and the twittering of birds are music to my ears. A silvery melody weaves itself out of my mouth as I pick ripe berries. The forest is my only home. The fatherly trees don't stare or insult me. As soon as I was born, I was rejected.

Suddenly, a clanking sound echoes round the forest. Terrified, I scramble round a bush to hide. The wicked hunters are within the defenceless forest. The black hunters kill the innocent creatures. They play with me and abuse me. Tears well in my horror-struck eyes.

I flinch, as I remember the sting of the whip on my soft skin. The cruel words they used on me.

My memories fade away, as I feel blaring heat. The yellow flames lick at my fragile body. My weary eyes shut with my life, glad.

*Ines Collings  (14)*
*Linton Village College, Cambridgeshire*

## END OF SHORT STORY

Horror echoes round the room as I slowly walk in. I can still remember the dusty smell, which I now choke on.

Still the vision is clear in my awful memories - screaming for help, I just watched, just as a child - weren't we all?

The night was still, and the attic creaked loudly. By candlelight I flickered over to the corner of the damp room, settling myself down. Placing the candle on the wooden floor and securing itself with a moat of wax.

Alone: I muttered along with the wind, but then the wind smothered the candle, leaving total darkness. My heart grabbed my lungs as I hesitated to breathe. The door was opening, slowly enough for me to escape, but I couldn't. I just sat there paralysed, staring where something might stare back, or she would stare back.

I started to move, I leapt over to the door, slamming it shut, imprisoning myself in a small damp room which I used to think was the attic.

Now I'd started, it wouldn't end. It wanted me like it did my friend. Light shone through the cracks in the door, it was getting brighter and brighter. Gusts of wind smashed the door open. The glare, I held my hands to my face and turned away.

Slowly gliding in was a little girl, or should I say a ghost of a little girl, who I used to know. She was my friend when I was younger. It all went wrong.

She whispered to me, talking with her blurry eyes echoing round the room.
I screamed, 'No.'
Calmly she looked at me, 'You're all going to die.'

*Samantha Green  (14)*
*Linton Village College, Cambridgeshire*

## THE RAINFOREST

Cautiously I traipse through the deep leafy bed of the dignified rainforest. Each breath I take, louder than the previous, everything around a potential danger.

In the distance, I hear the shrill call of the Howler monkey, chatting loquaciously to his companions the other side of the rainforest. Insects hover in abundance in concise swarms, producing a collective buzz.

As I peer around the lofty trunk of a tree, I am unable to hear anything but the sound of the enraged water, crashing down on the jagged rocks at the foot of a truly captivating waterfall.

I can almost feel the wary eyes of inquisitive creatures, peering from behind bushes around the lagoon. Who is this intruder? they must be thinking. My eyes slowly adjust to the shock of the sudden brightness, as I step out from the shadows of the looming trees.

A twig snaps behind me and as I swing around in alarm, I am relieved to see it is only an anteater, who scurries away, startled by my sudden movement.

The decomposing leaves in front of my feet, rustle and move. My pulse begins to race around my apprehensive body, as the moving tunnel of foliage bypasses me, and continues its journey.

A band of heavy clouds block out the intense heat of the sun, and spots of rain begin to trickle down my tense neck. To start with, this shower is refreshing, until the heavens open and I experience a mini monsoon. As I shelter under the large leaves of the forest, I feel that I have now experienced everything the rainforest is renowned for.

*Hannah Norman (14)*
*Linton Village College, Cambridgeshire*

## THE UNLIKELY WARRIOR

'Why, oh why?' the unlikely warrior murmured, scraping the large gangly sword along the gravely labyrinth floor, every now and then stopping to retrieve his belt that had the tendency to slip down round his knees.

While attempting to peer through the utter darkness and avoiding becoming the 'Roman fool', he managed to trip on the floor, coming too close for comfort with the hollows of a skull, most likely one of his less fortunate predecessors, who had failed to slay the infamous Minotuar. 'Poor bloke,' he said, clumsily reattaching the head to the rest of its crumbling body.

Ambling on, he pondered on why exactly he'd let that irksome barman persuade him into accepting this ridiculous bet, and why he hadn't just blown the last of his pride to live as a hermit instead.

Puffing himself up to a grand height of five foot seven, he lumbered on until he reached what he thought was the centre of the labyrinth, as it appeared every passage led to this room. Peering into the gloom of one particular tunnel, he caught a glimpse of hazy green light, and with it tendrils of grey smoke emerged. Listening, he could hear the soft grumbling of a sleeping giant.

'Uh oh,' he whispered. Suddenly the breathing stopped and a huge emerald eye flashed open. His oversized sword was flung to the floor and the contender fled, but the beast was not far behind. The Minotaur's huge feet stretched out before it, the noise echoing in the halls, and with one foul swoop the unlikely warrior joined all the others before him.

*Sarah Smith (14)*
*Linton Village College, Cambridgeshire*

## SUGAR-COATED MOUNTAIN
*(Part of a short story)*

You are walking cautiously, following the small narrow path which is slowly diminishing under the little buds of cotton-white snow. As you walk you leave deep prints in the thick blanket of snow. You can hear the red-breasted robins chirping a sweet melody on an early spring's blossoming tree. Feeling the cold, wet snow slowly penetrating your dry, clean socks, you walk on into the deep, smothering fog.

Higher and higher you climb and you can feel the change in altitude, the flakes of snow are becoming smaller and more insistant and you're constantly sniffing as your nose runs like the rapids.

You're blinded by the depth of the fog you wade through, feeling for rugged rocks to guide you onwards. The sound of your footsteps is echoed, creating a staccato effect. The sloping mountainside makes your tall legs feel like jelly; you stumble forward, every step taking an emormous effort.

The blinding is only temporary; the dense fog, like the tide, soon goes out. You feel the bitter cold strike you once again, hurting your entire body this time. The bellowing wind screams out at you, knocking you to the hard ground while you clutch your bruised body.

Minutes pass and you lie motionless still nursing your tired and numb body. Then suddenly you pick yourself up and urge your body to keep going. You see the mountain top in range, you use all your remaining strength and energy to try and get there. Out of breath and half dead you make it, gasping for vital oxygen. You pull out your windswept flag and hammer it into the thick, frozen ground.

*Jo Malins (14)*
*Linton Village College, Cambridgeshire*

## DAY IN THE LIFE OF SUSIE

Ever been so lonely that you have cried? Ever been so alone you have shook? Ever felt like dirt and been looked at by strangers day in, day out? No, I doubt you have, and I hope that you never experience the pain and loneliness I feel every minute of every hour of every day. Yet another person walks past me without the slightest care in the world.

I sit on my tattered rug with my rucksack beside me, holding only my most prized possessions. People say that we are here on these slabs of concrete because it's our choice, but people know nothing as I soon found out on my first week of this eternal nightmare! Once you are in this, it feels like a never-ending hurricane spiralling down and down and never stopping. I hold no control over my life whatsoever.

I can't ever remember being warm and content with life, or ever feeling ready to burst because you have eaten so much. My usual food consists of a hot cup of tea to stop my frostbite getting any worse, and a bread roll. I save the change for some alcoholic substance. I hear people tut as I unscrew the cap on the inviting bottle and say, 'No wonder she is in that state,' in loud voices. I wish I could stop, I really do, I wish . . . I wish the pain of this eternal nightmare would stop somehow, somewhere.

*Rachel Kiddie (14)*
*Linton Village College, Cambridgeshire*

## THE THREE WOLVES

Once upon a time there were three little wolves that lived with their mum. One morning she said, 'Today you must go and never come back.'
The little wolves walked off with their tails between their legs.

One met a man with some straw. The wolf asked, 'Nice man, how much is your straw?'
'To you,' the man replied, 'it's free.'
The little wolf took the straw and built a house.

That night the evil pig came. He banged on the door and shouted, 'Let me in, or I'll snort and grunt and smash your house down.'
'Not with the hairs on my chinny-chin-chin,' the wolf replied cockily.
The evil pig snorted and grunted and smashed the house down. The little wolf ran to his brother. They met a man with some sticks, they stole some and built a house.

That night the evil pig came. He slammed on the door and yelled, 'Let me in, or I'll snort and grunt and smash your house down.'
'Not with the hairs on our chinny-chin-chins,' the wolves replied icily.
The evil pig snorted and grunted and smashed the house down. The two wolves ran to their clever brother who had built a house made of bricks. They made themselves comfortable.

That night the evil pig came. The little wolves shouted, 'You can grunt and snort but you won't smash this house down.'
The evil pig snorted and grunted and smashed his head on the wall. The wolves dragged the evil pig in and had pork chops for dinner!

*Stephen Orriss (14)*
*Linton Village College, Cambridgeshire*

# WAR BOY!

I sit listening to the sound of the murdering bombs, and the sound of soldiers calling names out and praying.
'Our Father, who art in Heaven, hallowed be thy name . . . '

As I look around all I see are rotting bodies. Beyond the billowing clouds of smoke, I see a familiar face smeared in dark, dried mud. As he walks closer, I soon start to realise who this stranger is. It is my father. 'Father?' My attempt at a shout carries out as just a faint whisper.

Painfully I reach out my bandaged arm and this time my father turns round, with one eye covered and an arm hanging in a piece of ragged, grubby cloth.
'Son, four years it's been,' he says as he kneels down slowly and smoothes my rough skin on my suprised face.

The sound of the bombs and deathly gunshots begin to die, as though the tragic war is coming to a welcoming end. The sergeant major emerges from behind a mound of lifeless men. 'Look, I have come here to tell you the best news you've ever heard in four years. I have just received a phonecall from the head office.'
A slight gasp of delight comes from all the brave men lying in what I called 'Death Alley'.
'The war - my men - has come . . .' A salty tear begins to fall from his bloodshot eye, 'come to an . . . come to an . . .' he repeats, 'end.' He lets out a relieved sigh.

As I look up in happiness to my much loved father, a dramatic shell explodes violently behind him. 'No, not now, please,' I cry to him.
He collapses into my arms and murmurs to me, 'Look after yourself and your mother.'

*Annabel Palmer  (14)*
*Linton Village College, Cambridgeshire*

# KILLER INSTINCT

Whispy clusters of fuzzy pastel cloud spat across the crisp azure morning sky. A forest of snow-hatted stick-men trees on a Lowry landscape. Zooming in I see a small secluded cave. Savaged with pessimism, I assume it's preoccupied, but with no other place to venture I proceed onwards towards the spot, dragging behind me a large sack that contains the changer of my life. On entry I sit and ponder over my new-found sanctuary, with its scintillating, pale blueberry poles of diamond ice.

A cloud of snow rushes past, sweeping its frozen cape across my face. Shivers are sent sprinting down my spine.

Solitarily she sits, uttering magical words of wisdom under her rasping breath. On her lap lays her book, a book full of guilt, remorse and sorrow. She cannot turn back time. What's done is done and cannot be undone.

The cold body lies on the cave floor with icicles over its head. The snow around the sack begins to melt, creating an oasis of fresh, pure water in which the body is being emerged. Reluctanly I straighten up and drag the sack over to a fresh patch of snow. Again and again I move the sack, each time becoming more weary and tiresome.

My life revolves around the sack, well not the sack, its content. The innocent body now lies cold, almost frozen, as is my life. I spend my only time protecting my identiy, myself and the body. The body, that is my wife's. Yes me . . .

I am a killer.

*Ella Prior  (13)*
*Linton Village College, Cambridgeshire*

## A Day In The Life Of Anne Boleyn

People lined the dusty street as I walked slowly to my death. Towards the town square I could see the platform with three figures on it. I glanced at the crowd. Some people were weeping silently, others just gazed at me, showing no emotions at all.

The silence was empty. The air was dry and my stomach was twisted in knots. I was afraid. Since I was a little girl, this was the first time I had shown fear. My dignity was being crushed. My heart was pounding.

As I approached the platform, I felt the sun warm my face. It didn't seem right to die on such a peaceful day. I stepped up the steps and saw my mother, my friend and my killer. My mother's eyes were red from crying and she had crystal tears shimmering on her slightly wrinkled rosy cheeks. She handed me a pouch of gold coins and as I took them she held onto my hand, smiled weakly and said, 'I'll love you forever.'

I turned around and handed the masked axeman the money so that he would sharpen his axe. My friend stepped forward and hugged me. Her tears were running ferociously down her face as she told me to turn around so she could put on my blindfold.

I felt sick. The sun was smothered by the cloth and I was guided down to the harsh coldness of the wooden block. The world around me seemed to quieten even more. What will happen to me after I die? Is there anything after death? Heaven, Hell? If so, where will I go? All I have to do is wait to find . . . !

*Amy Dockerill  (14)*
*Linton Village College, Cambridgeshire*

## A Day In The Life Of No 603, The Soldier

Thoughtlessly machine guns are fired, mowing down life upon life, number after number. The fatal thud of shells echo around in my body as I hide, like a coward, in a dark corner of this bunker.

I can hear foreign voices from outside as soldiers run past. My heart beats heavier all the time. As a woman's scream shatters the air, images of my wife and family fall like lead upon my mind. My thought is broken as shards of metal slice into the wooden door, sending splinters of wood hurtling through the room. I huddle into my dark corner and close my eyes to the anarchy war.

My wife's last words; 'Be back soon,' as she had said, rattle amongst garbled memories. Every second is stretched into minutes and for a moment I lock eyes with a soldier through a gap in the door. His flesh as white as mine. Full of fear, scared like me. In a blink of my eye he was lying dead on the ground, blood pouring from a hole in his helmet.

Armoured vehicles thunder past, firing streams of bullets that bite into the flesh of more soldiers. The moans and cries of death fill the air. My blood runs cold with fear then boils with anger and as I clutch my gun, my finger curls over the trigger.

*Nathan Lumby  (14)*
*Linton Village College, Cambridgeshire*

# A DAY IN THE LIFE OF A SQUADRON PILOT

During those dreary, doubtful, waiting hours, before the brazen frenzy started, men drunk with fatigue lapsed into worn deckchairs. The heat of the summer sun beat down on the weary, hanging faces of the squadron pilots. A lapse of concentration, priceless. The scramble sounds and the thundering line of battle sailed through the air, death moaned and sang.

Entering the melee of twisting planes and smoke, I had little trouble finding an enemy and opening up, with the distinctive shudder of the aircraft's body as the machine-guns spitting tongues of fire, ripped into the flesh of the bomber's metallic skin, shafting it with bullets along the length of its fuselage. Bursts of ammunition erupted from inside the plane as it turned into a bright orange and red fireball, becoming a death trap for the helpless crew.

Watching it go down, I didn't see the blazing guns of the aircraft behind. In seconds the narrow cockpit was a mass of leaping flames; instinctively, I reached up to open the sliding hood. It wouldn't move. I tore off the straps, which were tying me to the chair and managed to force back the hood . . . I remember a second of sharp anguished agony, remember thinking, so this is it! and putting both hands to my eyes. Then I passed out. When I regained consciousness I was free of the burning machine and falling rapidly. I pulled the ripcord of my smouldering jacket, checking my descent with a jerk. Looking down I saw that my left trouser leg was burnt off, that I was drifting down towards the sea and that the English coast was deplorably far away.

*Jake Weston (14)*
*Linton Village College, Cambridgeshire*

## CHASING THE DRAGON

You fear me, you fear my scales, those fiercely varnished living slates that cling upon my inner skin. You hate me, you hate my chiselled, emerald eye. It's watching you with malice for the mirage you cast and the distant hope you project to all who hear your flaming cries of anguish and rage against the darkness.

You can smell my musty fog that airs itself around me, and the taste of brimstone in the roughage of the night. You need me though, you need my smell of radiant death and crave my sniff of nightmare. I can guide you with demand.

Come, follow me, I'm flying with canvas wings of green parchment and crystal-studded claws embedded in the soft, icy sky, draped from the heavens by golden thread. Come ride, ride on me, come on a trip of billowing air and vanilla drips of sun that loosely freckle the way we go.

But now to home as I expire with time and dissolve, for fulfilling your thirst has aided my need and pacified my vivid desperation, but you are to return to my dismal cave. A vague want awakens with colourless silence and drained harmony. You crave me, but you must get me. Come, hound me, follow me, track me. You must get me. You're chasing me, you're chasing the dragon.

*Chris Cornwell (14)*
*Linton Village College, Cambridgeshire*

# A Day In The Life Of A World War II Soldier

Wearily I stand, bent with fatigue. All around me is a deep sea of limbs. Dead fish are interspersed among the corpses, their souls washed away by the tide. Few men are with me standing, many of us missing limbs and clothing. No sand is seen, it is covered by a carpet of bodies.

Embracing the terror, I pull my chipped helmet over my eyes, blocking out the vivid images of death. I can hear the fear in men's voices. I curse through the burial ground of my comrades.

I am alone in this black landscape. The Earth's jagged teeth grip the sky and grin back at me. Death tramples, as each soldier is a victim to the onslaught of bullets.

The monstrous anger of the tanks give us hope, as they anchor into the sand. Hungrily, they move up the beach, clanking and throbbing in the air. Slowly, stubbornly, I fall. The strength of the silence traps me.

I discard my backpack, slinging my rifle over my shoulder. I defiantly walk forwards to the unknown. The fog of dread hazes around my soul. Grasped by a cold hand, it is lifted. I see more clearly.

The mourning wind blows, crying for the millions dead. I am one.

*Francesca Elliott (14)*
*Linton Village College, Cambridgeshire*

## YOUR WORST FEAR

He glided gradually across the floor to her bedside. Darkness followed him. He was black, dark, all of your fears put together. His dark cloak concealed his pale face and his grim smile, his colour-drained hands down by his side.

As he stooped high over her, she tried to escape, but fear held her rigidly down. His elongated, colourless finger stretched out to touch her heart and extinguish the weak flame that was her life. Fear grew, getting more powerful as he got nearer and nearer. Darkness closed in.

She tried to scream, but Fear clamped her mouth shut and Darkness was on top of her now. She started to slip into Darkness. His bony finger was now only millimetres away from her body. He let out an echoing, corrupted laugh as he blew out the remnants of her life.

She had now fully fallen into Darkness and Fear had overcome her. Pain shot like a bullet around her body. She had lost the war against death and then she was a prisoner of war. She was gone, lost, untraceable.

It was time to move on. He glided forward to his next victim. His followers advanced to proclaim his coming, for his coming means Darkness, Fear and Pain. He will overcome you and you will fall to the will of him.

For he is the difference between life and death. He is Supreme Darkness. He is the last thing you'll ever see. He will end your days. He is . . . *The Grim Reaper*. I know this all too well.

*Sam Penfold  (14)*
*Linton Village College, Cambridgeshire*

# A Day In The Life Of . . . Fear

The hungry shadows from which I view him begin to advance. Stealthily, we creep, longing to consume him, absorb him.

The light from the single, solitary candle he grips, wavers. My face is not reached by it. I am unreachable to all but those whom I prey on. We continue to close in, ever close to enfolding him. He has not yet begun to squeal.

My claws reach out, grasping at his soul, waiting for the moment - my right to possess him. He will then belong to my master and me for all eternity. Another soul to add to our blazing lake of fire.

My hunger is overpowering! Those impatient claws search. They ransack his body and then clutch his soul. I am allowed to feed. Exchanging his self for my self. Through his eyes I now see the strength before us.

The outline of the man I peer at is radiantly glowing, yet, to me, a threat. His lips move, but I close my ears to the command. Again they move, and expel the simple word 'go'. I feel the ripping: the claws beginning to lose their grip . . .

No! He's mine! I am one with him: a part of him. He belongs to me, but I cannot overpower that word. Pain surges through me and I recoil. Now, without my prey, I am weak. I know I can never return to him: he has been taken by the other side. I will never possess him again: *fear* will never possess him again.

*Rachael Newton  (14)*
*Linton Village College, Cambridgeshire*

# A Morning In The Life Of A Teacher

It's 6.00am and I have stirred from my slumber, only to realise what day it is.

I open my sleep-locked eyes and feel the duvet of dread slowly rise over me.

Clumsily, I lumber towards the bathroom and fall into a bath of welcoming warmth which symbolises the first and last pleasure of the day.

Crashing down the stairs, I grab a croissant and collapse in a heap on the sofa, slowly reaching for the remote. *Ping* and the TV booms out.

My eyes begin to wander, wander over to the dust-ridden cabinet which contains the whisky. Very tempting!

My eyes focus on a journalist bouncing around in the background, getting ready to pounce on a fresh story.

Realising the time, I gather my things and run out of the house.

As I'm driving, I feel like my fate is looming. The tunnel that usually took 10 minutes to get through is over in a flash.

Cautiously, I pull up to my usual parking space, check to make sure none of them are there and hurry off.

Like a spy, I dodge around them, trying to be invisible.

I'm in and have slammed the door.

I look around and see the gum stuck to the ceiling, the gossip magazines and mobiles on the table. Ah, the staffroom.

As I make a cup of tea, I glance out of the window and see the gaggle of my tutor group scattered around, shivering in the rain, waiting outside the classroom.

I turn around.

Maybe I'll leave them there for a few more minutes!

*Emma Laidlaw (14)*
*Linton Village College, Cambridgeshire*

# A DAY IN THE LIFE OF ANNE FRANK

The repetitive drone of the thunderous banging goes on and on. I crouch down in the small attic room, my heart roars around in my chest at a desperate pace, like a lion raging around in its small, cramped cage. The darkness swallows up my pale, trembling body. I am not allowed to move a muscle or make a sound in case they hear me . . .

I've had to leave my friends and my school. I've had to leave the teachers that discriminate against me for who I am. They'd squeal at me from across the classroom, their beady eyes locked on mine.
The pounding drones on . . .

I am a Jew; the most low and dirty creature ever to walk the streets of Nazi Germany.
Just imagine:
A warm sunny afternoon, you're strolling down the road. All the Jewish shops are boarded up, the paint peeling gently at the edges, the windows shattered, shattered like the lives of those who no longer share a place in humanity. On your woollen jumper, the six-pointed star pinned against your chest, like a knife digging into you, each point burning a hole into your soul. Then a group of blond-haired, blue-eyed boys are buzzing round you, waiting for the right moment . . .
'Jewish scum!' It happens in an instant, the hard shove in your back, it feels as if the whole world has pushed you down, falling, falling for eternity. Then smack! You land, your bony face hits the dirt-ridden ground. The echoes of torment whirl around your scrawny body. Everything stops, the silence deafens you.

Suddenly, the splintering crack of the warped door smashes. Thud, thud, thud. The sound of the mighty boots on the hidden stairs. The giant, bony hand on my shoulder. 'Time to go, little girl.'
Goodbye dearest diary.

*Hannah Burns  (14)*
*Linton Village College, Cambridgeshire*

## THE CHIMNEY SWEEP LION

There once lived a lioness named Aroara. She lived on the hot island of Tarkata, which was 20 miles off the coast of Africa. She spent most of her time parading in front of the other animals, shaking her tail in the air. She was always looking in the mirror and called herself the queen of the animals.

One day Pogo, the little white mouse, spoke up. 'I'm sick of Aroara parading and dancing in front of us every day,' he squeaked. 'Something must be done.'
All of the animals agreed and wondered what they could do to stop Aroara's boasting. Soon Illeus, the wise macaw, came up with an idea. All of the animals listened carefully as he told them his wonderful plan. The animals all at once got to work. Illeus built a small, wooden shack in a clearing in the forest and Pogo helped him to construct a large, sooty chimney right in the centre. The plan was ready.

The next evening all of the animals gathered in the clearing. They took care to hide themselves in the undergrowth - here they would see what was going on, but wouldn't be seen themselves. Illeus went off to find Aroara. At last he found her near the lake, smiling and pulling faces into the water and stroking her ears. He silently crept up. 'Aroara!' he screeched noisily, 'I have a surprise for you.'
Aroara leapt around. 'Who's there?' she roared, scanning the landscape. 'It's me,' said Illeus 'and I have a surprise for you. Just follow me.'

Quietly, Illeus led Aroara back to the shack where all of the animals were waiting cautiously for her arrival.
Illeus led Aroara into the hut. 'Up there,' he pointed to the chimney, 'is a powerful powder for making you prettier.' He paused. 'If you go up there, you will come out looking like a queen.'
'Really?' cried Aroara. 'Let me go now.'
She scrambled over to the chimney. She lifted her paws onto the mud surface and pulled herself into the black darkness. Inside it was cramped, dusty and smelt weird. Aroara didn't like it at all. She scrambled all the way up, through the narrow tunnel, until she reached the top. She pulled herself out and scrambled back onto the ground.

Illeus ran over to her. 'You look lovely,' he cried, handing her a mirror. She gazed into it and shrieked in terror. 'I'm black,' she screamed, 'completely black. There's no tan left.' In horror, she ran off to the river and plunged into it. Try as she might, she just could not remove the soot. Aroara was very upset. She apologised to the animals for boasting and promised she would never be selfish and full of herself again.

Well, Aroara is still black to this day. She has now got a new name - panther. Hopefully, soon she'll realise black can be just as attractive as tan.

*Annabel Walker  (13)*
*Margaret Beaufort Middle School, Bedfordshire*

## WRITTEN IN THE STYLE OF ARTEMIS FOWL

Captain Root of the LEP Recon - Lower Elements Police - groaned and sat up from his position on the floor where he had slumped last night. He had a thumping headache and he was feeling woozy. He cursed himself for drinking so many nettle and slug-juice smoothies the night before. He knew they were alcoholic, but he had had to have something to take his mind off the embarrassment. Why did he have to have the only female fairy in LEP Recon assigned to his squad? It was a man's job, he thought.

Captain Root was a fairy. He had green mottled skin, slit eyes and a hooked nose. But, contrary to popular belief, fairies have no wings and Root was no exception. Root lived in Haven. It was built in the only place humans hadn't got to yet - underground - and was strictly a fairy town. But, because of this, it was overcrowded and had way too much traffic. That was why there was a whole traffic department and that was where the test case had come from. Her name was Holly Short and Root thought she had a bad attitude.

Holly kicked a chair and it went spinning off across the room, distributing the last night's celebration feast for becoming a Recon officer. Holly was in a bad mood - bad even for fairies: which is very bad. Now she was going to be late . . .

*Sean Houghton (12)*
*Margaret Beaufort Middle School, Bedfordshire*

# REWRITE OF GOLDILOCKS

There was once a family who lived in a modern flat in the centre of London. The family consisted of Mum, Adele, an enthusiastic writer; Dad, Peter, an ordinary business man and Nicole, their daughter, an 11-year-old dancer.

One morning the family got up to their usual breakfast of hot croissants and fruit. As they sat down to eat, they found that the croissants were too hot to eat. The family decided to go out for a ride in the car while the croissants cooled down.

Meanwhile, a nasty man came into the family's flat and ate all of their croissants. He then sat on their chairs, went into their bedrooms and went to sleep.

By this time, the family had returned, expecting the croissants to be just the right temperature, but the whole house was a mess. All the chairs were broken and there were footprints all over the floor.
Nicole screamed, 'Daddy, someone's been sitting on my chair.'
'Well, it's not me!' said Adele and Peter.
'Yeh, and someone's been eating my croissants,' said Peter crossly.
'Oh my goodness, someone's sleeping in my bed!' said a very shocked Adele.
The whole family stood there in shock. Someone was actually sleeping in their bed! The family immediately called the police who came to take the nasty man away. Mr Constable Smith said, 'Oh yes, we've had problems with him before, causing trouble. Well, he's safely locked inside now.'

*Martha Hodgson  (13)*
*Northgate High School, Norfolk*

## GOLDILOCKS AND THE THREE BEARS
## FROM GOLDILOCK'S POINT OF VIEW

I was taking a stroll through the wood on one very nice sunny day, when I came across a very nice little cottage. I just couldn't resist taking a look inside. The door was open, what damage could I do? It was deserted anyway.

I went inside. It was a very cosy little cottage. I was feeling a little hungry, as I had forgotten to have some breakfast that day. I was lucky that there was a big table in front of me with three bowls on. One bowl was huge, another wasn't as big and there was one bowl that was just my size.

Inside the bowls was porridge. I love porridge, I could eat it for breakfast, lunch and dinner! But anyway, that's not the story. I tried the porridge from the biggest bowl, but it was so hot that it burnt my tongue. Next, I tried the porridge out of the medium bowl. It was stone cold! The last bowl of porridge must have been the right temperature because I had eaten the whole lot.

I went on exploring the little cottage. I came across three chairs. I sat on the first one. It was huge and so hard that there was no way that I could get comfortable. I sat on the second one. It was still a bit big for me, but it was too soft. I couldn't get comfortable on that one either. The last chair was just my size and it wasn't too hard or too soft. I have a bit of a habit. It's rocking on chairs. I couldn't help it. I was rocking on this chair, when all of a sudden it broke and I fell on the floor. I got up and then went into the next room. There was an enormous bed in it, a smaller one and one more, like the one I had at home. I got up on the biggest bed and laid on it. I could not get comfortable. It was too hard. I got up and tried the next bed. I just couldn't get comfortable on that either. It was too soft. However, the next bed, which was my size, was like my bed at home, but it was a lot more comfortable. I wasn't feeling particularly sleep at the time, but I somehow fell asleep.

The next thing I knew, there were three bears crowded around me. A big dad bear, a smaller mum bear and a little baby bear who was crying. I got up and ran away. They looked very scary and were growling at me. I couldn't see what I had done wrong.

*Amy Young  (13)*
*Northgate High School, Norfolk*

## KYLIE CONCERT

'Of course I'll go with you!' Becky screamed down the phone to her friend, Elsa, excitedly, because Elsa had just asked her to go to a Kylie Minogue concert with her.

Elsa had just been listening to the radio and heard two free tickets to the concert being advertised. All you had to do was phone in and answer three questions about Kylie correctly. Elsa phoned in and luckily, she managed to correctly answer all three questions.
'Well, it's on the 17th of August, so we'll have to take the day off school. I'm so excited! I just can't wait!' exclaimed Elsa.
The two girls then spent the next hour talking on the phone, planning every single detail, so the day would be a success.

On the morning of the concert, Elsa knocked on Becky's door early in the morning and they set off to the bus stop. As they stepped onto the bus, all they could hear was people singing Kylie Minogue songs. These people obviously loved Kylie as much as they did.

When they arrived at the stadium, they managed to find their seats and were glad to know they had a perfect view. They were in the middle and seven rows from the front. When Kylie came on, they both stood up and cheered and spent the night singing along with Kylie and the rest of the crowd.

They were so tired when they finally got home, they walked in and collapsed on the sofa and fell asleep.

*Holly Buckingham (13)*
*Northgate High School, Norfolk*

# VIDEO BUST-UP

*Monday, February 6th 2002.*

Latest reports see the sad story of Kerri Morton, a 16-year-old Brandon High School attendant, killed in a bust-up at the Marina video store on Orchland Street, Norwich.

Kerri was attending to the last customers of the evening, when three white men, said to be quite young, ran into the store and asked for the till money, while grabbing some videos which were for sale from the shelves. Kerri bravely stood up to them, but was shot 10 times in the stomach and chest areas, dying of punctured lungs. Police were called out by a pensioner witness, Mary Scottburn, who was badly shaken up and horrified at the scene. She said, 'After the young men had shot the young assistant, they smashed up the till, took all of the money and rushed out'.

There were two other witnesses, but the men had clearly disguised themselves. Police are appealing to any other witnesses who may have seen the getaway or the vehicle that may have been used.

If you do know anything, please get in contact with the local police as soon as possible.

*Shannon Fuller (13)*
*Northgate High School, Norfolk*

73

## SCRAMBLED EGG AND SOLDIERS

One midsummer's day Humphrey D Eggsmith was slowly ambling along the country paths. He had just stopped at a café and had a bacon sandwich, when he heard a loud scream, 'Aarrgghh!'
Suddenly a young woman ran from the trees. 'Argh! Spider! Spider!' The young girl was clutching a plate with curds and whey round the edge.
Humphrey went up to the girl and said, 'Whatever is the matter?'
'Well, I was sitting on a stump eating my curds and whey, when along came a spider and sat down beside me and it made me run away.'
'Oh well, as long as you are alright now that's all that matters. I have to go, maybe I'll see you around.'
'Bye!' The young girl walked away and Humphrey carried on along the path.

About quarter of an hour later, Humphrey saw a house that looked like it was made of biscuits and sweets. He went up to the house and looked through the window. Inside there was a small girl and boy and an old woman. The woman seemed to be in a struggle with the children. Suddenly the children pushed the old woman and she fell into a cauldron that was placed over the fire. Humphrey was gobsmacked. The front door flew open and the two children ran into the forest.

Humphrey decided to carry on the path. Soon after that he saw a small flock of sheep running free. The sheep ran into a field and a couple of minutes later, a lady came running towards Humphrey. Humphrey said, 'What's the matter with you?'
'I've lost my sheep and I don't know where to find them!'
'Don't worry, just leave them alone and they'll come home wagging their tails behind them.'
'You think so? I tell you what, I'll try it, thank you.' The lady turned around and walked back the way she came.

Humphrey came to the outskirts of a town where there was a low wall, he sat on it. After a while he became dozy and fell asleep and in doing so he fell off and smashed.

Not long after, all the king's horses came to the rescue but failed to help the poor, poor Humphrey.

*Lee Tomlin  (13)*
*Northgate High School, Norfolk*

## FRIGHTENING FAIRIES AND PETRIFYING PIXIES

Fairies and pixies are small creatures whom many believe to be fictional until about a day or two ago.

Mrs Zackerson and her daughters were among those who believed them to be fictional. That is, until a group of them turned up at their door asking for a job . . .

Last week, thought to be Wednesday, during the late afternoon in the town of Wadeham, about seven fairies and six pixies came knocking on the door of Mrs Zackerson, asking for jobs to do about the house as they had no place to go, or so they said.

Everything seemed to be normal (or as normal as it could get) that day until late that evening. The fairies and pixies had been doing the washing and the ironing, gardening and vacuuming. After they finished their jobs they went a little quiet and Mrs Zackerson decided it was a tad bit too quiet for her liking. They had found the alcohol cupboard and emptied it. When Mrs Zackerson tried to leave the house they

would not let her go and got really nasty, almost knocking her out. Luckily her daughters arrived back from the shop and found what was happening. They phoned the police. The police arrested the pixies and the fairies but let them out on bail after they would only say, 'Shakespeare'.

Mrs Zackerson and her daughters got away lightly.

Police are appealing for anyone else who has had experiences of this kind recently, or witnesses to come forward.

*Elizabeth-Rose Matthews (13)*
*Northgate High School, Norfolk*

# THE LOVE OF THE PRINCESS

Once upon a time in a far and distant land lived a princess. She was the prettiest and most intelligent maiden in the land. She was married to a prince. He was handsome, loving and kind. He adored everything the princess said and did.

One day, on her twenty-eighth birthday party, she became ill. She was dying. As the princess laid in her bed a quaint looking fairy appeared at the end of her bed and said, 'I have heard you are ill, I believe I can help you.'
'How can you help me?' she said.
'I will put a spell on you to make you well again.'
How could the princess refuse, she agreed.
'There is one thing though, when you have been made well again you will lose everything apart from one thing.' The princess wanted to know what she would keep so she asked the fairy. 'You will soon find out.'

The next morning the princess woke up on the street outside her castle. She had nothing except the clothes she stood in. She walked down the street where she saw her reflection in a puddle. She had turned into the ugliest thing in the world. The prince walked over to her. 'I heard that you were laying in the street, I had to find you. What has happened to your face?'

She sat him down and explained her story. At first he didn't believe her but then he started to understand.

He took her into the castle, fed and clothed her. He told her she would stay with him forever, together. Although she may have lost everything, she hadn't lost what truly mattered - love!

*Hannah Creed (13)*
*Northgate High School, Norfolk*

## KELPIE IN THE MARSH

Jessica was a young girl from Ireland. She lived with her mother and father in a quaint little cottage near the coast.

One day Jessica's mother told her to go to town to buy some milk and some jam from the market. She gave her three coins and sped her on her way.

For Jessica to get to the village, she had to pass through a wet marshland area. There was a path through the marsh and Jessica knew it well. She set off, humming as she walked. She came to the edge of the marsh when she heard the snort of a horse. She turned to see a great stallion, with a mane and tail of bulrushes; and eyes as black as coal. It was a Kelpie.

'Hello little girl,' snorted the Kelpie.
'Hello,' Jessica answered. 'I'm just going to market.'
'You are not afraid of me?' asked the Kelpie in a puzzled tone.
'No, you're only a horse.'
'Only a horse! I'm a Kelpie. I can turn into anything I want - a fire-breathing dragon, a poisonous snake, a raging bull, anything.'
Jessica already knew this, she was stalling for time. 'Oh can you show me?' she said eagerly.

The Kelpie transformed into a three-headed dog, with razor-sharp nostrils. 'Any monster can turn into something big like that. Bet you can't turn into little things?' she asked, with a some what mocking tone in her voice.
'Like what?'
'A piece of cake!' she said.
'Easy,' and with that it transformed again, this time into a piece of cake. Jessica ran up to it and ate the cake whole, thus destroying the Kelpie forever. And from that day forth, no Kelpie was ever seen by man again.

*Andrew Stevenson (13)*
*Northgate High School, Norfolk*

# EVERY DAY IN THE LIFE OF THIS TEENAGER

Heya, I'm Rebecca - Becks for short. I have a little brother, Ben. He's only five. He doesn't remember anything, I don't think he does anyway. Ben is the closest thing to me, I suppose it's because he's my only family, but when I look at my friends and their brothers and sisters, me and Ben are just different. Amy, my best friend, has two brothers. She hardly sees James because he's 19. She is forced with Thomas. She gets annoyed with him, calling him names and hits him even. I'd never hit Ben. It would be like he was a pest.

It's lucky, Amy and me are going to the same school, which means we can walk there together. It's five miles to Thorpegate High School. Sometimes we catch the bus, but sometimes we miss it because we have to help with breakfast. Mrs Breaker waits for us outside the gate every day, waiting for us to be late. The lessons are okay at school. I'm not bright, but the teachers help me. Sometimes it's hard when the other kids have the new stuff. I go back to the home.

It's hard here, but it's hard to think back when we weren't in there. Whenever I think of that, I think of Mum, not so much dad. It was his fault we don't have Mum and that's why we're in here. That's my day, every day.

*Rachel Rayns  (13)*
*Northgate High School, Norfolk*

## THE DREADFUL DAY!

'Jenny!' I called in vain. I sat back down scared. If only I hadn't agreed to go into the cave. Jenny always had been adventurous.

We'd been exploring near the camp. We'd gone past these caves and Jenny had persuaded me to go in with her. I'd followed her in, but when I stepped forward I'd slipped and ended up in a hole on a small ledge above a deep drop. Jenny had left to find help. Camp was over an hour away. It was cold and damp but the only thing I could do was sit and wait.

After an hour I heard footsteps. I shouted out and to my relief Jenny answered back. Her face appeared at the top of the hole. 'I've found some string, it may not be strong enough but it's worth a try!'

I grabbed the string and slowly climbed up. I was nearly there but the string was snapping, if I moved, it would break and I would fall.

'Don't panic!' Jenny shouted. 'I'll try to pull you up.' Jenny started to pull. I was nearly at arms' length from the top when the string snapped. I clawed at the side and managed to grab a small ledge. Jenny quickly reached down and helped pull me up.

I was out at last! After gaining our breath we started making our way back to the camp both unable to say anything from exhaustion and from shock and relief. We never went exploring again.

*Harriet Brandwood (13)*
*Northgate High School, Norfolk*

# LIFE IN THE BLACK DEATH . . .

*11th June 1349*

It was my birthday today. I got a chicken and named it Marjorie. Just lately I've heard of a bug going around. I'm not worried as I live in the clean part of London, though I did hear a person died.

*12th June 1349*

My thoughts are that a Jew is poisoning the water. My husband said he felt feverish. I made him go to bed, hopefully this bug will pass.

*13th June 1349*

I know that there isn't a Jew poisoning the water. The planets are in the wrong order, as when Saturn and Mars join they cause death. I'm worried as my husband is developing black spots and now at night a man is coming with a cart saying, 'Bring out your dead!' My husband sleeps outside with blankets, I don't want the disease spreading.

*14th June 1349*

God is the reason, but I can't think of anything I've done. We went out and people were whipping themselves. I asked them to stop but they claimed they were doing it for God.

*15th June 1349*

My husband developed swells in his armpits. I made him wear manure and sit above the sewers. Unfortunately he died and I had to put his body in the cart.

I must gather myself and be strong for my children. I know I can do it and they will give me all the support I need.

***Emma Hall (13)***
***Northgate High School, Norfolk***

# A Day In The Life Of A Laundry Van Driver

It was just another day at work, or so I thought. I deliver laundry in a van for *Mr Wong's Laundry Company* in New York you see.

One Friday I was delivering the laundry to one of our regulars named Joey. I had just turned off the freeway and had stopped at traffic lights when I saw the menacing shape of a Mafia car zooming towards me.

The Mafia ran this part of town and unfortunately for me, my family had old connections with a rival gang. Of course, I had never been involved with gang fighting, but it was well known around town that if anyone messed with me, then I could always get one of my big brothers to go and sort them out. This time there was no one and I was terrified.

I tried to get out of the way but they were going too fast and they smashed straight into the side of my van. It tipped over onto its back. The seat was crushing me. The pain was excruciating. I tried to climb out but I couldn't. I started to spiral into fuzzy darkness . . .

I woke up in the hospital. They said I was fine. I was, but only physically. In my mind, it was torture. I would  never go on the streets again.

*Samuel Braysher  (13)*
*Northgate High School, Norfolk*

# THE LIFE OF A HOLIDAYMAKER

Charles and his brothers were on holiday in a nice caravan in Great Yarmouth. Charles got up earlier than normal one day and walked into the living room where he found his brothers still asleep.

He was out last night and this morning he had a hangover. He decided not to have any breakfast as he had a horrible taste in his mouth, so he went to the bathroom to clean his teeth. He looked in the mirror hanging above the sink. He saw not his reflection, but someone else's. It was a woman with her child, they were gypsies.

Charles quickly splashed water on his face and looked back at the mirror and saw his reflection this time. He thought it was just the drink he had last night.

Charles got himself dressed and decided to go for a little stroll through the campsite and had a chat with the manager.

'Did you hear about the two gypsies who got killed exactly a year ago today?' asked the manager.
'No, why?'
'Oh because they stayed in the caravan you are staying in.'
Charles felt shivers go right to the bottom of his spine and said, 'Sorry, I have to go.'

He went to the café to warm himself up with a nice cup of tea. Before he ordered he saw the headlines of a newspaper which said, 'A year ago today the victims of caravan number 71 at Great Yarmouth died'.

Charles then got flashbacks from a year ago when he came on holiday here and remembered himself in the caravan, then going round to ask how the boiler worked and then he remembered when he . . .

*Chris Dewing  (13)*
*Northgate High School, Norfolk*

## TRAPPED

Sarah, a young girl who loved to read, didn't fit in and in turn had no friends.

One Saturday morning, in a nearby field, Sarah found a nice spot under an oak tree to read. She had a story with her about fairies. The first few pages told of a girl sitting under a tree who looked up at it and saw something flickering. Hopeful, Sarah looked up at the tree she was under and to her amazement saw something.

She hurried up the tree and in the thick of the leaves sat on the branch. Looking up she was dazed by thousands of colours. After her eyes had adjusted, she could see silhouetted shapes of the fairies. One came in front of Sarah's face and asked if she wanted to be a fairy. Without thinking, Sarah immediately replied yes. Suddenly she shrunk and sprouted wings.

Sarah told the fairies of her book and then flew down to get it. As she approached it a line stood out about the girl in the story climbing the tree. Sarah read on and found the girl was turned into a fairy and then came out of the tree to find her book. Sarah panicked; was it coincidence or was she trapped in the story?

Sarah told the fairy to change her back but it didn't know how to. She was trapped and what would happen to her? What did the ending of the book she was reading have in store?

*Stephanie Kemp (13)*
*Northgate High School, Norfolk*

# A TRUE LIFE STORY

One day a boy, just like any other boy, was diagnosed with diabetes. He only went for a check-up and one prick of his finger told his whole future. The GP sent him to the hospital just to confirm his diagnosis. When he arrived at hospital he went straight to the children's ward to have another blood test. He was checked every hour to see if his blood sugar had changed.

The next day the diabetic liaison nurse, the doctor and the dietician came to speak to him about diabetes. The dietician talked to him about the things he should and shouldn't eat or drink. The doctor asked him what he thought diabetes was about and explained a bit more about diabetes. The diabetic liaison nurse showed him how to inject insulin and test his blood and he gave his mum a fake injection, which made him feel much better because he absolutely hated needles and injections. She then told him what to do if he felt queasy and dizzy. After this he had dinner then he went home with one big change in his life.

When he got home he couldn't inject himself with the insulin because the needles scared him, so his dad gave him his injection instead. He now goes to the hospital every two months to have a check-up, to see what's happening to his body. He has yearly tests because if you don't take care with your diabetes it has long-term effects on your eyes.

*Matthew Barley (13)*
*Northgate High School, Norfolk*

## Ten-Year-Old Attempts Time Travel

Yesterday, ten-year-old John Thompson announced to the world that he has built a fully working time machine in his garden shed.

At first it was believed to have been a wind-up, but John was adamant that the famous time machine was real. 'I am absolutely certain it works. I have had several attempts in the past but they haven't worked out right. This time though I am definitely going to travel through time.' We asked the parents for their opinion on their son's discovery. 'We are so proud of him. He is an inspiration to us all and we will support him all the way.'

We also asked the general public on what they thought of the time machine. 'I thin it's awful letting a ten-year-old boy travel through time. For all we know he could never come back.'

'I think it will be a wonderful experience for him. It will expand his mind and help him do well at school.'

The day of the 'adventure' will be tomorrow at 10.00am in Mattishall near Dereham. The public are also welcome to watch.

*Rachael Herman (13)*
*Northgate High School, Norfolk*

# A DAY IN THE LIFE OF A VICTORIAN CHILD

Hello, my name is James and I am five years old. I am now old enough to work down in the mines and today is going to be my first day. My mother is going to take me to the mines just this once and after that it's up to me.

I am now at the top of a very deep hole and I am being instructed to climb down the steps. I have climbed down, there is a man following, to show me where to go. I am scared by the darkness. I imagine all kinds of monsters, but say nothing for the fear of being fired. I am shown to a hole in the wall and told to climb up and sit in it. I am then handed a rope. I have to listen out for mine carts and when I hear them coming I have to pull the rope to open the door, when the cart has gone, I have to release the rope to close the door.

I have now been here for what seems like hours and hours. The only light I have is a single candle and all the muscles in my arms hurt badly. The one thought I have to keep me going is the thought of going home although I know I still have many hours to go. My arms are now so painful I don't feel I can pull the weight of the door any longer. I am so relieved when the man tells me I can finally go home.

*Jessica Kipper  (13)*
*Northgate High School, Norfolk*

## I JUST WANT TO PLAY FOR ARSENAL

The game had been good - less than five minutes until the final whistle, suddenly things quickly changed.

'Hey, I'm not getting any service here!' Joe bellowed.

'Well if you get in good spaces, I'd pass to you,' Trey replied before a big strong guy called Mark dispossessed him.

Woodsen FC were on the counter attack. Mark had the ball at his feet with lots of teammates ahead of him. But he went for glory . . . *Goal!* Woodsen silenced the crowd. The referee looked at his watch and ended the game.

The Rushford FC players had a long talk with their manager when the team left; a scout had a quiet word with the manager.

At the end of their next training session, the manager had some good news for the players . . .

'A scout asked me to select the best players for the Arsenal trials in two weeks time. You'll all have a chance to prove yourselves in the next league match.'

Two weeks went by and the Rushford squad had been training hard. They were all desperate to know if they had a chance to play for Arsenal.

It's the final match of the trials and Joey and Trey are playing against each other for the last place in the Arsenal team. The first of the two to make an impression gets the last place.

Trey tracks back into midfield to pick up a loose ball, he dummies the first player and nutmegs the second as he sprints towards the goal. He spots the keeper off his line and chips him instantly. He celebrates in 'Klinsmann' style as he realised he has made the squad.

*David Okusi  (12)*
*St Mark's School, Harlow, Essex*

## STRANGE CREATURE

It was one summer's afternoon and everyone was hot and sticky and we were about to have a test. I was staring out of the window because I was stuck on a question. Suddenly I saw a small furry creature on my arm, it was very cute and cuddly. I had no idea what it was, I could not believe my ears when it said, 'Hello, my name's Jenny and I am here to help you with your test.'

How? I wondered. I didn't say anything for a while and I rubbed my eyes to make sure I was not daydreaming, but I was not.

'I can help you with your test,' she whispered.

I knew it was wrong but I did it anyway. She didn't take much time to answer all the questions.

That night I dreamt I was the cleverest girl in the whole world and that I had lots of money and a big house and a lovely new car. I woke up and I was so excited. I got into school and all the teachers were looking at me, like I had done something wrong. I thought about it and I knew I hadn't done anything wrong. Then I realised that they must have found out about my little furry friend Jenny. I was very worried, all day long I tried to avoid the teachers.

That night I had a nightmare of being the thickest person in the world. I got to school and found out that my results were not good - they were zero, zero, zero. I was glad that they knew I had cheated, but I don't know what my mum and dad are going to say. I've now learnt to think for myself.

*Lauren Grundy (11)*
*St Mark's School, Harlow, Essex*

## I'M NOT SHELLY

This is a story about a girl and a hospital!

It begins one Hallowe'en night when Liz has to have her tonsils taken out. The hospital had horrible blank walls which could make anyone sick, if they hadn't already been, by the doctor who just ran out of the room screaming. 'Argh, it's blood and guts in there . . . *Save me please!*' He was sick over a tray of new medical equipment and then fainted, as the receptionist called in his last patient!

(Cough . . . back to Liz)

'Mum, do I have to have my tonsils taken out, especially on Halloooweee'een night?' whined Liz.
'I imagine you won't get any more horrible coughs and colds, and Hallowe'en isn't safe. *I've seen things Liz, terrible things,*' joked Dad.
Mum looked annoyed at the interruption.

(Can we skip to the scary parts?)

Liz was lying in bed. Her neighbour . . .
(Boring . . .)
*Shut up!*

Liz spotted a card which read 'Dear Shelly,' Liz asked, 'why are you in hospital Shelly?'
'*I'm not Shelly!*' she screamed. 'I'm Jodie.'
'Cool! Why are you in?'
'Shelly's gotta 'ave 'er leg amputated. There's been a mix up with names, but I'm sure it'll all get sorted soon.'

That night Liz had a dream that she saw someone at the end of her bed holding a clipboard and grinning. In the morning she was woken up by her bed being pushed down the corridor, she saw a doctor holding a clipboard reading 'Shelly, leg amputation.'

'*I'm not Shelly!*' screamed Liz.

'No use, *they warned* me,' cooed the doctor.

'*Nnnnnoooooo!*'

**Lelldorin Gaskell**
**St Mark's School, Harlow, Essex**

## POISON

'Do you take this bride?' asked the priest.
'I do!' spoke Alec.
'Do you take the groom?' asked the priest.
'I do!' answered Julie.
'You may kiss the bride,' spoke the priest.
'Yes!' shouted every one.

*Four months later.*

'Hi Harry!' said Julie.
'Hi, want to come to my house for a drink?' asked Harry.
'Okay, let's go,' spoke Julie.

*In the house.*

'Let's go upstairs Julie,' said Harry
'Okay, come on,' answered Julie.

*In the science lab.*

'Why would they do this to me?' screamed Dr Alec Drax. 'I must make a plan to kill them both with *poison.* I must make the poison now or never, I will test it on my dog. Rats' pee, bogies and spider's webs, all of these are what I need,'

*Outside Harry's house.*

'Harry may I come in to your house?' asked Alec.
'Yes, why not!' answered Harry.

*In the house.*

'Do you want a cup of tea?' asked Harry.
'Why not!' answered Alec.
'Ha, ha, the poison is in the tea, just wait until he's out of the toilet,' laughed Alec.
Sip. 'Argh!' screamed Harry.

*In the garden.*

'Now he will go in the hole next to the swimming pool, ha!' laughed Alec. 'Now the same goes for Julie, ha, ha!'

*One year later.*

'Argh!' screamed Alec, 'why did I poison myself? Argghh!' Splash! Alec fell into the swimming pool.

Now every full moon, the ghost of Alec walks . . .

**Christopher Lloyd (12)**
**St Mark's School, Harlow, Essex**

# WHEN WISHES COME TRUE

'Where have you been?'

'Out!'

'It's half one, you're fifteen, it's a school night and your curfew's eleven! You know the saying, *Early to bed, early to rise, makes a woman, smart, pretty and wise!'*

'Mum, I'm not a woman yet,' then she muttered 'I wish I was though.'

Krystal stomped upstairs, sat on her bed and picked up her puppy Sally. 'You're the only one who listens. I wish Mum would treat me like an adult, I can make my own decisions. If I lived on my own, I'd be happy. Goodnight!' she hugged her puppy and went to sleep . . .

*Brrriinggg!* 'Uh . . . I'm late for school!' Kristal jumped out of bed and called, 'Mum, where's my uniform?' She looked in the mirror, but someone older looked back. Huh! She looked in her bag, according to this I'm twenty, own a car, a credit card and this flat. Cool!

Krystal dressed and found she needed food. She drove rather dangerously to Tesco's. When she reached the checkout Krystal said, 'Charge it please.'

'Sorry, you've reached your credit limit.'

'What!' Krystal was embarrassed. She left in a hurry.

When she got home she checked her messages. Beep. 'Krystal you've been coming in when you feel like it. If you don't turn up tomorrow, you're sacked.'

Oh, and these bills - rent, credit card, electric. I'm phoning home.

*Beep, beep!* 'This number has not been recognised, please check and dial again!'

Noooo!

Be careful what you wish for . . .

. . . it may come true.

*Elaina Crehan (12)*
*St Mark's School, Harlow, Essex*

# WORLD CUP 2006

It was the 12th June 2006 and the World Cup was well under way. It was the final match.

*England v France*

It was the 35th minute, Beckham was running down the wing when suddenly Vieira came sliding towards Beckham, but he jumped out of the way. He got to the right corner of the 18-yard box and Henry stuck his foot in front of Beckham. He flipped over the ball and landed on the side of his ankle. The physiotherapist came out with his sponge, but he didn't need treatment. He got up, but by this time it was the 45th minute, the pressure was on. If Beckham scored from this free kick, we would be one up. He stepped up . . . he ran . . . he kicked it over the goalkeeper's head into the back of the goal, then there was the whistle for half-time.

*Second half.*

*England 1-0 France*
*Beckham, 45*

England kicked-off and already Owen was on a run, straight through the middle of the pitch but Wiltord tackled him and hit it to Henry. Up the other end, he knocked it through Ferdinand's legs and put it neatly in the top corner which meant it was 1-1.

When the French were celebrating, Seaman booted it to Vassell who then crossed the ball to Owen who was in the box. Owen turned and gave an overhead kick, it then hit the crossbar and bounced in. The goal was timed at 90 minutes. The whistle went and the result was -

*England 2-1 France*
*Beckham, 45   Henry, 67*
*Owen 90.*

**Matthew Bowden-Scott  (12)**
**St Mark's School, Harlow, Essex**

## SANTENEE AND THE DREAM

Once upon a time in a faraway land there lived the most beautiful girl you have ever seen, called Santenee. She had long golden hair and bright blue eyes. She lived in a castle surrounded by trees. She was put there as a baby by an evil witch who wanted her for herself. She was really happy living in the castle, but did not miss her parents because she had never seen them. She couldn't escape from the castle because the evil witch had put a spell on her, so if she went outside the castle, she would die.

There was something puzzling her though, ever since she moved into the castle, she had the same dream every night. She dreamt that she went up to her window and just flew out of it. She then arrived at a cave. A green goblin with yellow hair sat at the front of the cave. Santenee went and knelt down in front of him and he cut off a lock of her hair. Then she flew back to her castle. That night she decided to see if she really did fly to the green goblin - and she did. But instead of the goblin, there was an old lady.

'I am your mum and I have come to rid you of the spell which the evil witch put on you. I've collected your hair for 16 years to make the spell complete.' So Santenee and her mum made the potion and now Santenee is free.

*Lindsey Colley (12)*
*St Mark's School, Harlow, Essex*

# WELL DONE BRAZIL

The World Cup has been full of surprises, France and Argentina knocked out in the first stages, and Sweden winning their group. But nobody ever thought that the team who struggled to qualify, would go on to win.

The Germany-Brazil game kept people on the edge of their seats. Everyone in England hoping Germany would lose.

But the key player in the whole game was Ronaldo. Within nineteen minutes into the game, Ronaldinho who was back in the team after a one match suspension, slipped the ball to Ronaldo who slammed it into the back of the net. We wish! Everyone waiting to see a goal! Instead, he pushed it wide, everyone was astonished. By now everyone was thinking Brazil wouldn't score when the 68th minute arrived. Ronaldo kicked it past Kahn. The crowd went wild, except for the German side. Kahn looked embarrassed and couldn't believe. what had just happened. David Seaman felt his pain I should think. Brazil, knowing they would win, stayed calm as the German defence came towards them, but Thomas Linke tried to challenge Ronaldo but couldn't stop what was about to happen. The Brazilian player scored a goal on the 79th minute. Then it was a race against time for Germany, but the final whistle blew. Kahn broke down on the ground as the Brazilians celebrated. Brazil had won the World Cup for the fifth time.

*Kayleigh Henderson (12)*
*St Mark's School, Harlow, Essex*

## DEATH DAY DISCO

'Great party mate,' I shouted to Phil.
'Cheers, the DJ's wicked, isn't he?'
'Yeah!' I replied.

The music thumped in the background as I scanned the club for my brother Joe. He was no doubt trying to pull a girl, then I spotted him up at the bar with a tall, slim blonde. They both had drinks on the bar side, Joe had a bottle of Becks and the blonde had a bottle of Hooch. My eyes then suddenly wandered towards the barman. He was quite tubby and he was wearing a black suit and a big gold medallion hanging around his neck. His hand was hovering around the rim of the bottle of Hooch. Then I saw it drop. A pill! He was spiking her drink! I saw the blonde putting the bottle to her lips. I sprinted over to her, 'Stop!' she put down the bottle.
'What do you think you're doing bro?'
'That barman spiked her drink,' I told him.
'What!' she screeched.

The barman started to run, Joe and I both started after him. He went out the back way, then there was a gunshot. We ducked behind the bar and a glass bottle above my head smashed. I dived through some double doors into what looked like a warehouse, shortly followed by Joe.

Joe stood up and I heard another gunshot and then a heavy thud on the ground. I looked up and saw Joe on the ground, badly bleeding. I stood up and charged at the shooter. Then there was another shot. The world around me went dark and silent - *I was dead!*

*Jordan Weir (12)*
*St Mark's School, Harlow, Essex*

# STONE AGE DISCOVERY

A museum in London have recently told the press that whilst renovating the history section of the museum, they have discovered a preserved ice structure which they claim has a figure inside! No one has yet seen this figure, but they say that their scientists believe it's from the Stone Age!

Whether or not this is true, no one can be sure. We spoke to the head of the department and this is what he had to say, 'The figure was unknown, and the ice has not made it very easy to see, but we are taking samples'.

The history part of the museum has got a Stone Age section, and whether it is for publicity we cannot say, but we sent in a reporter who reported that they are not showing the findings to anyone, but have pictures of the discovery in the 'discovery cave'. they do look realistic but you'll have to wait and see if they release it. There will be specialists going in later this week from 'Canterbury Finds' they'll report later. Until then, no one can say whether the finding is an actual caveman or even from the Stone Age. But we will keep you posted on the story.

If you'd like to look yourself, it's in the London Museum in Trafalgar Square. Decide for yourself, real or fake!

*Holly Bailey (12)*
*St Mark's School, Harlow, Essex*

## MOON DANCER

*(Based on the Half Moon Ranch series by Jenny Oldfield)*

Once upon a time there was a girl called Crystal, she lived on a ranch - Half Moon Ranch and she loved horses. She had two of her own, she lived in London until her nan became ill, then moved there to help them.

On one summer morning, Crystal got up and went to see her horses, she had to take them for a walk, after which, she left them in a field until she had finished her dinner. When she had put her horses away, she sat outside for a little while, then she looked up and saw something white pass by the bushes. Crystal got up to take a closer look, but as she did so, it started to move away. She got to the bush and pushed aside some branches, and there standing on the hill was a beautiful white horse. The horse was standing in the moonlight.

'Crystal!' shouted Kerry her sister.
'Coming!' answered Crystal.
When she got in, she ran and told her mum, but she didn't believe her. Crystal had noticed that the white horse only came out at night.

One night she went to see the horse and its leg was bleeding, so it was back! She saw some wolves with blood on their faces, so she ran and got her dad's shotgun. She shot it in the air to scare away the wolves. Then Crystal called a vet and when the horse was better, Crystal could keep it. She called it Moon Dancer, because it dances in the moonlight.

*Natasha Christmas (12)*
*St Mark's School, Harlow, Essex*

## STRANGE, STRANGE, STRANGE

Jeremy, Peter and John were all brothers, they were triplets. John had a nice sense of humour, Peter was always grumpy and Jeremy was a goody-goody. They went to school at St Mark's, it was only a two minute walk away.

Their teacher was named Mrs Buckly and she's very weird. She has bites on her neck and green fingernails and different coloured hair every morning.

The children decided to follow her to her vehicle, it was a big, humungous flying saucer and eerrgghh! she was transforming, eating all the nearby trees, picking mud up off the floor to her disgusting tongue-less mouth.

The three went back to tell their best friends.
'She was gross, green, slimy and freaky.'
'Who?'
'Mrs Buckley,' they shouted, 'meet us here tomorrow.'

It was Thursday at 6.58 and we were all in the bushes when bingo, there she was. She walked out of the gates, down the alley and into the forest. There were now two aliens and they were talking.
'I can smell children nearby.'
'Get them!'
'Aaarrrggghh!' he had them all by the neck, except for Simon, the friend, and the children were kidnapped.

This story was told several times, but no one knows the truth . . .

*Daniel Hockley (12)*
*St Mark's School, Harlow, Essex*

## A DAY IN THE LIFE OF ME

In the mornings, I wake up at about half-past seven. I get dressed in my school uniform and do my hair. Now my hair has to be perfect, no lumps or bumps. If there are, I have to start from the beginning again and when I've done that I do my school bag which takes me about five seconds, probably that's why I forget most of it.

I run downstairs to grab a quick snack before I walk to the bus. On the way I stop to meet my friend Faye to catch the five past eight bus. We get on and have a good chat, which makes the time go quicker. We finally get to school, good old school. Then I walk through the gate and walk up to the year area to meet all my best mates, Danielle, Sophie and Suzy and we go to the shops before school starts. We just get back as the bell rings and I make my way to my form, where we do the register and talk about our charity week which is coming up. Then it's off to our first lesson of the day.

The bell's about to go for the end of school. *Yes!* And then the whole school runs to the ice cream van to get to the front of the queue and I'm always pushed out. I finally get to the front and my bus goes past. Oh no! Now I have to wait for another five minutes to catch the bus.

*Jaye Hacker (12)*
*St Mark's School, Harlow, Essex*

## THE SNAKE

Hundred and hundreds of years ago, there was a tough scary snake about 30 feet long, with gigantic teeth. It lived in Africa and had been crawling around the African village for years. It had killed thousands of children, cows and pigs.

The Africans had been building up their own little army to kill this monster for quite a while now, and were planning to kill the snake very soon. The only weapons they had were poisoned spears. They had tried killing it loads of times and now they had found its weakest point - its eyes.

The next week the Africans had about 50 people in their army and all were armed. The snake was called Vandell. Vandell would always roam around the village in the evenings, preying on the cattle.

The army had tied a cow to the ground and they hid behind a bush waiting for Vandell. They didn't have to wait long for him, he looked at the cow for a while then he slithered closer. The snake was about six feet away and the cow was making a horrendous noise. Suddenly the snake jumped up and went through the bushes, eating about 20 men in one mouthful.

The leader of the army was called Simone and was one of the survivors. He got up and jumped on top of the snake. The snake had already got about ten spears in him, but Simone's spear went into his eye. This was the end of Vandell. Everyone in Africa remembers his name.

*Ross Ashcroft  (12)*
*St Mark's School, Harlow, Essex*

## DEVILS STRIKE TWICE

Greg was an old man, a scary old man. His eyes were pitch-black and his face wrinkled and sour. He lived on a housing estate, it was a small estate and not many people lived there. His house was falling apart, the windows were boarded up and the door made a loud shriek every time it was opened. In his garden there was a large hole, it was meant to be a pond, but when it happened, it was forgotten and used for another purpose.

Greg had been watching a certain person, she lived alone, all of her family had move out as the suspicion of Greg's murderous nature grew. She was called Lori, she couldn't afford another house, so she stayed put.

One afternoon, she set off to see her mother, she had to go down a long road in the middle of a field. It passed just by Greg's garden, and Greg often waited there for unsuspecting victims. As Lori passed Greg's house, he was already in his van waiting for her, and when she passed, he turned the key and his van charged towards Lori's small car. As he got closer he started to bump the back of her car. She started to panic, but her car was already at maximum speed.

He knocked her car flying forwards and it crashed and burst into flames. Greg took her singed corpse to the pond hole in his back garden and laid her there. In the night, a devil came and did exactly what it did to Greg.

*Sam McFarlane (12)*
*St Mark's School, Harlow, Essex*

# A Day In The Life Of A Soap Star

'Sarah it's time to get up.'
She turned to look at the clock, it said in red numbers 6.30am. It was time to get up and start another busy day in EastEnders. Today we are recording the scene where Dr Truman and Zoe tell her family she is getting married. It was going to be hard because Kat was such a nutter anyway!

I play Sam Mitchell, I am Peggy's daughter. I work in the Queen Vic with Phil and Sharon (I wish she'd make up her mind who she wants, first it was Phil, now it's Tom).

Right! Back to today, we have just finished doing that scene.
Zoe's just stormed out crying, into the square.
Ant says, 'Do you love me?'
'Of course,' she says.
'Well then, if you love me and I love you, why can't we get married?'
'I don't know!'
Then they kiss. It was kind of sweet.

Now we are all going to the TV Awards 2002. After the Awards, EastEnders has 36 Awards, I've won two of them (sexiest female and best actress). Well that's just about a rap. Bye!

*Sarah Cholerton (12)*
*St Mark's School, Harlow, Essex*

# A Day In The Life Of A Pop Star

'Come on Amy, get up. Your singing tutor will be here in ten minutes.'
When she looked at her clock, it was only ten to six in the morning.
'Good morning Miss, would you like anything? Can I get you a drink or
even something to eat?'
*'No thank you!'* I interrupted.

After her singing tutor had left, she could hardly speak, let alone sing.
'Miss you have just got time for a quick shower, then you have to pick
some clothes for your TV interview,' the maid said, rushing around.

It is now 9.00am and she is on her way to the Disney Studio, to sing and
be interviewed. At about 11.00am when she is finished, crowds of
people were screaming and shouting for her outside the studio. Amy
finally got home at 12.20am and was about to take a bite out of her
doughnut when - 'Oh Miss, you can't have that, it will make you
chubby like me, here have this.' The maid handed her a salad sandwich.
'Thanks,' Amy said trying to hold her temper.

'Hi dear!' her mum said, 'you have time for a little sit down before you
have to fill in all of these forms.' She put about a 100 pages in front of
her. By the time Amy had finished them it was 6.00pm.

'Miss, I think you'd better go to sleep now, you have a busy day
tomorrow.'
At last, I'm glad it's all over.

*Amy Pemberton  (11)*
*St Mark's School, Harlow, Essex*

## SO DO YOU LIKE THE DENTISTS?

The door opened with a short squeak. Elenor walked past it, shaking, her knees like plates of jelly. Her stomach churning. She peered round the sharp corner into the dreaded room.

'I'm not going. I'm not going!' screamed Elenor.
'Yes you are!' her mum said, pushing her into the room. A nice lady with a mask hanging from her chin said 'Not to worry, the dentist, Dr Tooth, will be with you any minute!'

Elenor sat in the big chair, she felt so small, and waited. After a few minutes the dentist Dr Tooth came through the door, he said, 'Let's get cracking!'

'Actually, my tooth feels 100 times better now thanks. We will be on our way!' Elenor announced.
'Not so fast!' Dr Tooth poked her tooth, she screamed!
His assistant put her to sleep with anaesthetic and Dr Tooth pulled out the tooth and cackled!

After a few seconds she should have woken up, but he had killed her, her mum and his assistant.

*Catherine Fisher (12)*
*St Mark's School, Harlow, Essex*

# THE MAGIC BOX

Hi my name is Chloe and I am here to tell you a story about a box. It's not any old box, it's magic.

'Chloe!' shouted my mum up the stairs.
'Yes!' I shouted.
'Don't forget to tidy your room,' Mum shouted again.

I stopped playing and began to tidy my room. I went to the cupboard and noticed a plank of wood on the floor. I moved a box of toys off of the wood and I picked up the plank to find a secret place to hide things. In the hole I found only a box, I picked it up. 'Mum, I'm popping round to see Rosie,' I shouted.

When I got there no one was in, so I went down the park and as I sat on the swing, I opened the box to find nothing in it. I gave it a rub to get the dust off and at the same time wished for something to eat. I opened the box again and found a bag of sweets.

Now I couldn't wish for anything more than once. I made at least one hundred wishes and I was the only one to know about it. After a while the box and its magic got boring, so I decided to make one last wish. 'I wish I'd never found the box,' I said. I opened the lid and *poof!* I was back in my bedroom. That's my story!

*Elizabeth Woodland (12)*
*St Mark's School, Harlow, Essex*

# THE EVIL OF THE LOCH NESS

Deep in Loch Ness lives the Loch Ness monster. How he got there is left untold.

It was a cold, dark, rainy night, when a father and his son were out fishing on the loch when suddenly it appeared from nowhere. Yes, the Loch Ness Monster.

His life could be over. What could he do? There in front of him was the monster; sharp, shiny teeth and very long claws. There was nothing they could do. They thought they were going to die. Would they live to tell this tale or not?

Would you like to know what happened? Will the father live and his son die?

People have believed this for years,  now it's time to find out the truth about the Loch Ness. It's time to go into the loch. What will we find? What if the tale is true? Will we die?

It's a cold rainy day but it has to be done. We plunged into the water. *Splash!* There was no going back, when we were in the water, we wondered what the Loch Ness monster looked like?

There in front of us was the nest of the monster with lots of white soft eggs. Our friends were in the boat on the surface. Wished they were here with us, it is an amazing sight, only to be seen once. *Bang! Splash!* Oil tanks are being launched into the water, coming towards us was the monster. That's all that is being told for now.

*Donna Murphy  (11)*
*St Mark's School, Harlow, Essex*

## ALL ALONE!

The old car slowly came to a halt. The engine stopped moaning and the dim headlights went out. The driver looked around in despair. 'I need to find a telephone, I might be gone for a while, but whatever you do, don't leave the car!' He gave his wife a kiss and the children a cheeky wink. He left the car and walked into the dark distance of the woods. His figure disappeared into the darkness after only 30 seconds and the defenceless family were left alone, alone in the uninhabited woods.

Ten minutes passed, then 20, then an hour. No one had returned. The family were stiff and apprehensive, clueless of the whereabouts of their parent and husband. The mother spoke quietly to her worried children, 'I'm going to look for Dad, I'll be back soon.' The children gasped and nervously clutched each other's hands. Their mum kissed them on the foreheads, exited the car and locked the doors. The children rested their heads on the cold glass windows and looked out into the fierce woodland.

The bushes roared and the trees moved and fought. The rain splashed against the mud floor and the lightning struck down large oaks. Time passed and the children reluctantly fell asleep.

*Crack! Crack! Crack!* On the window. The children suddenly awoke. Nervously the children peered out of the window. A large figure stood outside. The silhouette was hunched and had long hair.
'Children, I know where your mummy and daddy are,' in a sarcastic way, 'come out, they want to see you.'

The puzzled children looked at one another. Both confused and frightened. They daren't say anything, sweat dripped from their heads and rested on their brows. Their grips got tighter.

Slowly the eldest child opened the door, he looked out into the woods, the man was gone. The rain soaked his hair and clothes, from the corner of his eye he saw something. It looked like two lollipops, he cautiously walked closer in the pitch-black of the stormy night. He was about one metre away when he froze . . . they weren't lollipops . . . they were heads!

*Joseph Calvino  (13)*
*St Mark's School, Harlow, Essex*

## TOKYO NIGHTS

Track after track of loud rock music blared out of the giant screens which were blindingly bright against a jet-black night sky. No stars, no moon. An endless vacuum of technology and more lights than the Blackpool Illuminations. Every so often, a police car passed. A typical night in 24/7 Tokyo.

In the middle of this, one man calmly walked along the pavement. He looked around and sighed. This man was Matt Williams, ex-commander of a special operations group in England, the Dark Night Shadows.

The DNS completed countless missions. On relaxed nights, they usually helped the police with intelligence gathering. On stressful nights, all hell broke loose. Explosions, screaming and the deafening sirens of police cars were all in a day's work. After a few years, Matt's dreams of Japan came true when he was called up for service in the Tokyo Police.

At first, life in Tokyo was sweet. A luxury apartment in the heart of the city, all the gadgets in the world and missions that were actually challenging.

Matt was a hero - he brought down the Japanese Mafia alone, one by one, the crime group Damare and finally the separatist group Bou. The latest group to feel Matt 'Warrior' Williams wrath was a private army.

Recently, no work had come through. Matt was an inch away from losing his job and the police were one cutback away from collapsing. It was dog eat dog and Matt was a small poodle. He hated life.

*To be continued . . .*

**Tom Mortimer  (12)**
**St Mark's School, Harlow, Essex**

# THE SPECIAL OBJECT

Jodie was looking at all of her things that were saved from the fire in her old house. As she was looking through her burnt possessions she came across an object which she had never seen before, it was small, round and had pretty pictures of people dancing on it. She was trying to get it open, but then realised that it needed a key to open this special object and reveal the mystery inside.

'Jodie the bus is here,' shouted her mum.
'Alright,' Jodie replied, gathering her books and the object and then running out of the door.

'Natalie, look at this,' Jodie said getting off the bus and then getting the object out of her pocket.
Natalie looked at it and replied, 'I don't know, but it needs a key to open it, have you got one?'
'The only one I have is the one on my necklace,' Jodie explained showing her the necklace.

As Jodie was about to put the key in the lock, the bell rang for school, Natalie asked Jodie to meet her at the gate and they would try the key, so Jodie agreed.

When it came to the end of school Jodie and Natalie met, Jodie got her necklace out and placed the key in the lock, she turned it, and then by surprise it opened and inside it was a tiny little ballerina. She decided to turn the key a little more and then suddenly the ballerina started turning round and the object started playing a song!

*Kayleigh Hart (12)*
*St Mark's School, Harlow, Essex*

## KLONOA EMPIRE OF DREAM

Where did I come from?
Where the blue wind blow . . .
Where am I going?
Where the white clouds flow . . .
So if I dream, I'm sure to wake . . .

Klonoa was asleep in his bed till there was a loud knock at the door and suddenly the door opened . . . 'Huh?' said Klonoa. Two men came in and grabbed him, 'Hey, what the . . . stop!'

Klonoa was in a castle he had never seen before. As he walked in he saw an emperor. 'So you're the stranger who dares to dream in my empire! I am Jillius emperor of this empire,' he said, 'if you have time to spare, you should fall in love. Dreams are of no use.'
'No! That's not true! Why is it so wrong to dream?' Klonoa shouted.
'Wait,' a voice roared, it was the Princess of Julius 'Uni', 'let's test his metal,' she said.

Klonoa left the castle but he was thinking about what the Princess had said. There is a monster terrorising the land. Her father would pardon him, if he got rid of it and when he and the Princess were alone they got to know each other and hugged. Uni kissed him on the cheek when he got outside of the castle. 'Huh, what's that sound?'

The monster came and grabbed Klonoa. He thought, if I take a feather and tickle the monster it might stop. He quickly got a feather and tickled him. It worked. Klonoa went back to the castle.

'Klonoa, you're alright?' Uni said. She went up to Klonoa and they hugged.

*Emma Lingard (13)*
*St Mark's School, Harlow, Essex*

# NASA Astronauts Dead

On the 22nd of June 2002, three of the bravest men that walked the Earth set off to travel to Mars for the first time ever. They were due to arrive on Mars on the 27th but unfortunately failed to do so.

On the morning of the 25th a fuel leak began at the rear of the rocket causing a huge amount of panic for NASA and the astronauts. The astronauts themselves didn't notice until the smell of smoke drifted into the cockpit. At first they didn't know what to think until Jimmy Bredel saw the reflection of fire in one of the several windows onboard the rocket. He then alerted the other crew members but was just too late. They all knew that that was the end of the line for them which is why they gave their final messages to their loved ones. After all this had been completed all they could do was wait.

Eventually the time had come, fifty-four minutes later the rocket turned into one big fireball and slowly burned away into pure essence. The crew stayed right at the front hoping for some sort of a miracle but their prayers weren't answered. They soon were taken, without a care in the world.

*Rick Coghlan  (13)*
*St Mark's School, Harlow, Essex*

## THE ALIEN DRAGON RIDER

The year is 2075 and man is about to cross a border, make history . . .
because Professor A Lewis has invented warp technology and now we
can explore all the other galaxies in the universe . . .
'But Dad!'
'No buts,' cut in Dad, 'I'm going if you like it or not.'
'What if the field around the shuttle breaks up and you lose all the
oxygen?' said Marie.
'I'm going,' he yelled as he climbed into the space craft.
But Marie wasn't having that so she climbed in after him.

An hour later . . .
'Why is there so little oxygen left?' Dad asked himself.
'Because of me!' giggled Marie.
'Now I'm going to have to stop and put in a new oxygen canister!'

As the craft slowed to a stop, a strange shape appeared in the distance.
'You are in my space territory!' yelled the alien rider of a dragon-like
creature, which had just appeared.

I don't know why the alien bothered saying anything because it
immediately blasted them all into a pile of dust which would one day
form a planet.
'That was uncalled for!' said the dragon nobly. So he dumped his rider
and used his left paw to make a giant flash which managed to spread
into all of space.

Back on Earth . . . 'What happened, I've got an awful headache. Marie,
have I been out at the pub again?' groaned Marie's father.
'I don't know Dad, I can't remember a thing!' she replied.

*Katherine Saville (13)*
*St Mark's School, Harlow, Essex*

*Countdown to release of great film.*

Thousands of fans worldwide await the day when 'The Fellowship Of The Ring' will be released on video and DVD. J R R Tolkien's masterpiece The Lord Of The Rings has encouraged generations of readers and continues to influence new fans worldwide. New Line Cinema brought to life the adventure of good against evil last December. The Fellowship Of The Ring, a heroic journey set in a time of uneasiness in Middle Earth. It all depends on the 'one ring' which has placed itself into the hands of Frodo Baggins, a young hobbit.

A terrifying task lies ahead of Frodo knowing that the ring must be destroyed in the fires of Mount Doom where it was forged. A fellowship bands together to lend Frodo (Elijah Wood) the wisdom of Gandalf (Ian McKellen), the loyalty of Sam (Sean Astin), Pippin (Billy Boyd), Merry (Dominic Monaghan), the courage of Aragorn (Viggo Mortensen), who loves an immortal elf named Arwen (Liv Tyler), and Boromir (Sean Bean), the accuracy of Legolas (Orlando Bloom) and the strength of Gimli (John Rhys-Davis). Elrond (Hugo Weaving) and Galadriel's (Cate Blanchett) knowledge of the ring brings light to the true danger and the importance of their journey.

Now in less than six weeks fans all over the world will be able to live the terror and excitement of this endless adventure.

*History became legend . . . Legend became myth . . .*

*Alice Holdstock (12)*
*St Mark's School, Harlow, Essex*

## THE DISASTER!

As soon as I stepped foot on that ship I thought it would be the best trip of my life. The captain and the crew welcomed us onto the boat. The captain was a very nice person, he was in his late thirties and quite tall, about six foot nine, with ginger hair and brown eyes.

The room just topped it off even more a king-sized bed, gigantic wardrobe and even a personal mini bar, in the bedroom alone.

At about eight o'clock I went to one of the eight restaurants. I had salmon with Thousand Island dressing and salad on the side containing rich lettuce, tender cucumber and scarlet tomatoes. Then they brought out the biggest wine menu I've seen. I just went for something simple but gorgeous.

After eating such a filling dinner I though I'd go and have a nap before the midnight samba. It seemed like the journey to my room would not end. Finally I found if after ten agonising minutes.

The sight of my bed just lured me into a daydream about beds (how odd). I just ripped my clothes off and dived in. Zzzzzz, sssshhh, zzzzzzz.

Then I suddenly woke to see thick black clouds of smoke, at first I thought it was a dream so I tried to wake myself up, then I realised it was reality. I sat and just prayed. After a while I realised that there is no one coming for me so I just ran for my life up to the emergency deck. I just ran, closed my eyes and dived over the deck. The second I pierced the surface of the ocean the boat burst into flames. *Bang!*

*Keiron McGlone (11)*
*St Mark's School, Harlow, Essex*

# WORLD CUP FEVER

Every day I walk to school, the same way with my same friends. I passed the same houses, the same buses go by, the same things day after day, week after week, month after month. Then suddenly things changed, lots of houses had Union Jacks or the flag of St George hanging from the windows, what's going on, then I remembered it's June. Lots was going to happen in June, the Queen's Golden Jubilee and the World Cup.

People were talking to each other, not only Great Britain but all over the world. The whole world had something in common, football. Everyone you met seemed to be buzzing, schools and places of work were letting the people come in after each match, each time England won there seemed a great sense of joy and friendship. Then that fateful day came with England lost to Brazil. Everyone was upset but people were still pulling together, there was still a chance Tim Henman could win Wimbledon and we did win the test match against Sri Lanka. So I said to myself, I wonder what it would be like if people came together like this all the time? Wouldn't it be nice if the whole world was united in friendship and silly wars were no more?

Do you think the world will ever be as one? I wonder will it ever happen?

*Erin Walters  (13)*
*St Mark's School, Harlow, Essex*

## GERBILS VS HAMSTERS

No one thought or even dreamed of killing Mr Fuz, until the night he became president. He had a dream of hamsters and gerbils uniting together and becoming fellow citizens. When the gerbils had found this out they immediately took action against them. The gerbils had elected a new leader called Mr Flaire. He was not a nice man to deal with, for instance a rumour has gone around saying he had killed seven hamsters with his bare paws.

The year of 1945 was a shock to the whole nation of animals. The gerbils had taken over the rat and chicken nation, and were coming for the hamsters. The hamsters luckily had allies who were the frog and toad society. They also had another card up their sleeve, they had created a citrus bomb.

'Sir, Sir, they've come over the mountain,' said Malcolm tearing from his seven metre run.
'Man, the citrus bomb!' said Mr Fuz.
'Bit Sir, it is not finished, it could wipe us all out.'

Meanwhile the toads and frogs were firing their reed launchers and the hamsters were firing their pea bazookas and carrot grenades. It was a horrendous bloody field of dead rats and hamsters and gerbils and chickens and toads and frogs. All of a sudden the sun was blocked out by a flying lemon which was heading their way.
'Retreat!'
'Croak!'
'Pluck!'
Everyone was running but it was all too late, they all were squashed and burnt to citrus. But one man or should I say hamster survived, his name was Malcolm. Sadly Mr Fuz was killed but not by the bomb!

*10 years later.* Malcolm was talking to his 23-year-old son with Mr Fuz's wife in a room still not known to the rest of animal kind. Malcolm was proudly showing off his war scars when he stopped, grinned and said aloud four painful words, 'I killed Mr Fuz!'

*Thomas Jewell (13)*
*St Mark's School, Harlow, Essex*

## FAIRY TALES IN TIME!

Once upon a time, there lived a young fairy. She was the most beautiful fairy alive. But there also lived an evil fairy, who hated the young princess fairy.

When she was born, it gave her parents a song of joy. Her parents were so happy, that they threw a party in her name. The evil fairy did not like the idea and wanted to stop it.

Meanwhile, the family was thinking up a name for their new child.

The family had a close friend named Goodness. Goodness was a fairy that liked to do what was right.

The celebration was about to start when the evil fairy arrived. 'What, a party, why didn't you invite me?' said the evil fairy, and before anyone could reply, she ran over to the child and snatched her up.
'Put her down,' said the King and the Queen.
'No! I am the next queen,' then she vanished.

Twenty years later it was a dark night with a full moon and clouds. One of the nights that don't come around a lot. As the princess lay asleep in her bed, the evil fairy came and killed her family and friends.

Five years later the princess fairy with no name, made a time machine, went back in time to fix it, she killed the evil fairy, then returned to the present time, got married and lived happily ever after with her friends and family.

*Michelle Tomlin  (13)*
*St Mark's School, Harlow, Essex*

# GAME

A young boy was playing a computer game, he was playing the final boss. 'Easy peasey,' he said.

Then to his shock the lizard-man-beast said, 'Easy peasy eh?' and a white blinding light flashed.

The boy found himself standing in front of the massive lizard. The boy was now carrying a sword and shield and was also carrying an extraordinary heavy pack.

A fairy was tinkling by his ear, 'You have to kill Sera the dragon Lord to get out of here,' it said.

'Arrgh!' he screamed as he charged at the monster with his sword. Sera flicked the sword out of his hands.

'Puny mortal!' it roared.

'Pause!' the boy screamed, the monster stopped dead.

The boy dived into his pack and pulled out a bow. Unluckily the pause ran out and the monster spanked him across the arena.

He jumped up all battered and bruised, said a spell and launched a glowing white arrow at the monster's eyes.

'Nooo!' the monster screamed as a sword zipped past his eyes and into the boy's hand.

'Now!' tinkled the fairy.

The boy slashed with the sword and a blinding white light shone . . .

*Daniel Spiller  (13)*
*St Mark's School, Harlow, Essex*

## THE MISSING PLAYROOM

Sarah was slowly walking down the corridor of her nan's old, creepy mansion. Sarah was exploring, she had never been there before.

As she walked down the long, windy corridors, she was looking at all the family photos on the walls. When she'd reached the end of the corridor there were two doors facing each other. On the wall at the end, was a picture of a little girl sitting on a swing. She looked closer, she saw that the little girl was her. Then she heard footsteps, she looked around, she didn't see anything so she ignored it. She'd left the picture and went to one of the doors. She tried to open it, it was locked so she tried the other door, that was locked as well.

Then she heard another noise behind her, she turned quickly. On the floor was a little antique box. Sarah picked it up and opened it. Inside, was a big brass key. Sarah took the key and tried it in one of the doors. It didn't open, then she tried the other door. It opened straight away.

When she went in she saw some glass doors and then through the windows she saw a little white swing, the same swing she was sitting on in the picture. Sarah went out there to the swing. She sat on it, it brought back loads of memories of her there. When she went back in she found the door locked. No one had seen Sarah since then.

*Jade Rencontre (13)*
*St Mark's School, Harlow, Essex*

## DEATH MANSION

*Bang! Crash!* Went the thunder. Flash went the lightning. It was Hallowe'en, deep in the forest. I was with Ben and Lucy, my best friends. Lucy was scared but Ben wasn't.

We were about to go home when I realised Ben had disappeared. I looked around then saw him, standing by a huge, old house, I'd never seen before. It was deserted and looked like It was from a scary movie. As Ben was opening the door we ran over. Written above the door was Death Mansion. I was frightened and wanted to go but Ben was already inside, we had to go in and get him.

As soon as we were inside, the door slammed shut. Lucy screamed. We tried opening it but it was locked. My heart was racing. Strange noises were everywhere, doors opened and shut.
'Can you hear that?' whispered Lucy.
'Hear what?' Ben asked.
'Footsteps!' she answered.

We all went silent and stood still, she was right, there were footsteps, and they were getting closer, even Ben was scared now. We opened the first door we found and hid inside, it was very dark, I couldn't see properly.

Lucy tripped over something - a trapdoor. We opened it and found stairs. The door handle turned. We ran down them, then up another staircase. The footsteps kept getting closer. Another trapdoor was above us, we pushed it open and crawled out into the forest and all ran as fast as we could run.

*Laura Fleming (13)*
*St Mark's School, Harlow, Essex*

## BOMB

*Bang!* There was an almighty explosion that rocked the small village. The three emergency services came immediately from other nearby towns and villages. The bomb was detonated in the village hall; this was extremely bad though because there was a meeting going on in the hall. There were twenty police cars, five fire engines and another five ambulances. The police cordoned off the whole area. In the hall there was an estimated twenty-five to thirty people. The firemen were working frantically to put out the flames even some of the onlooking villagers and some policemen were also helping.

Half an hour later finally the flames looked like they were going out. However they were very doubtful whether anyone would survive. John, one of the firemen, was optimistic though he'd served in the fire force for fifteen years there had been a few cases like this in his career. He said to one of the paramedics, 'Do you think there's any chance?'
He replied, 'It's hard to tell really but I don't think there isn't much of a chance.'
After the paramedic said that John put on his mask and entered the smouldering building.

John emerged a couple of minutes later carrying two people, one on each shoulder, the paramedics rushed over to see if there was anything they could do but there was nothing they hadn't tried. John and some more colleagues went in again.

*Bang!* There was another explosion, the hall and surrounding buildings collapsed. Did John survive?

*Joe Earll (12)*
*St Mark's School, Harlow, Essex*

126

## THE SOLDIER

Rain thundered onto the deck of the aircraft carrier, making a noise like a drum beating in our cabin; I lay awake, dreading the next day, when we would arrive in Argentina.

It was two o'clock in the morning, the waves of the ocean below us, getting colder and harder to pass through; we were forced to slow down to a slow four knots . . .

A mist was falling around our ship, the only sight we had was by radar. A shiver of fear shot down my spine, as a loud bang sounded through the metal walls of the ship. We had been hit! An Argentinean torpedo with an explosive nose cap had pierced the side of our vessel, and now it was only a matter of time before we either sunk, or were blown out of the ocean.

Chaos everywhere, the upper deck was swarming with armies of men charging to lifeboats, trying to save their lives. Realising the damage to the ship, I dived out of bed, grabbed my rifle, ran to the upper deck and jumped in a lifeboat. Using the knife in my boot, I cut the ropes and rowed to the mainland.

Looking back, all fifty lifeboats had been used to carry three armies; the other seven sadly lost . . .

We arrived off course, in the south of Chile. Though it was a mountainous area, we managed to set up camp and survive in a trench for a couple of days, preparing for the approaching battle.

*Lee McDonnell (13)*
*St Mark's School, Harlow, Essex*

## THE SAPPHIRE RING

It's October 19th, 1945 in London. It's raining, wet and cold, my curly blonde hair has not turned blonde but brown. The war has just ended, I am coming home on the train from the countryside. It was my birthday on the 17th and my nan bought me a sapphire ring, that cost £25.

Nearly home now, we pull up at the station and I see my mum and da . . . where was he? My dad is nowhere to be seen. I run to my mum who is crying. 'Mum, what's wrong? What's wrong?'
'Your father was wounded, and on the way to hospital he passed away.'
'He can't have,' I cried a lot.

My ring started glowing. What's going on? I fall to the floor and fall asleep. The next thing I know, my dad's waking me up, he is alive.
'Dad, you're back.'
'No sweetie, I'm off to war, go to sleep.'
'But Daddy, I feel faint, don't go.' So he stayed and lived. It worked. But, there were consequences. My mother got ill. We had another child, but when she had Sarah, she died.

I went to the past again. This is what happened, we didn't have Sarah, it was Ben, he was healthy, just like everyone else.

*Brooke Fryer (13)*
*St Mark's School, Harlow, Essex*

# THE ENCHANTED FOREST

One cold, misty morning in December, the light shined through the fog. The fresh water dashed through the pebbled stream. The sky was dark and grey and for what Sam and Rachel knew, the sky held a mysterious adventure.

Sam and Rachel Banks lived in Green Park. They were friendly people and were always willing to help others. They decided to go for a walk in the chilly air. They were going to the forest, but little did they know that the forest was a place of magical, mysterious, fascinating events.

They set off to their unknown adventure. They entered the woods and from a far distance a bright light was shining distinctly through the mist. They decided to go and see what it was.

As they travelled through the woods, bark breaking under their feet, leaves rustling and crunching, the light became clearer.

As they approached the light, a hobbit was sitting on a rough edged stone. Sam and Rachel approached the hobbit and in his view were other hobbits having a party. They were dressed in smart clothing, suits and evening gowns. They looked like they were enjoying themselves, all apart from that one little hobbit.

They watched from a distance under a bush. He looked distressed and started to cry. A lady came over and started to talk to him.

After a while, they looked cheerful and went off to dance. The forest had certainly held an enchantment.

*Tara Arnold  (12)*
*St Mark's School, Harlow, Essex*

## THE ROCKING CHAIR

It all started on a normal Thursday morning. I woke up, got dressed and went downstairs for my breakfast.

I put my bread in the toaster and went and collected the paper. I glanced through the front page and something caught my eye. It was an article on some 'weird happenings' around the town.

*Pop,* my toast had popped up and it was just how I liked it - burnt. I buttered my toast and ran out of the door on the way to school.

School flew by on this particular day and I was soon back at home having dinner and preparing to go to bed. I went to bed around 10pm and fell asleep shortly after.

I awoke and looked at my clock, it read 1.45am, I turned over and tried to go back to sleep but was disturbed by a sort of humming noise coming from outside. I got up and checked it out, it was coming from the old derelict house across the street, at closer inspection I saw an old man in a rocking chair . . .

*James Kennard (14)*
*St Mark's School, Harlow, Essex*

## A DAY IN THE LIFE OF A SOLDIER

It started off like a usual morning at the old war hospital. Some people came into see loved ones and others just lying there on their own.

The hospital ward was a dull grey colour with doctors and nurses tending to patients who had just had an operation or who had just come for a check-up. All of a sudden all these people came rushing in with burnt faces and then a bomb fell down and the earth shook around us. Next there was a humungous blaze of fire and all the people came rushing in through the wooden doors with horrified looks on their faces.

That day the hospital was jam-packed and as soon as the people had been treated, they had to go straight home because there weren't enough beds to go round all the people. Also the noise was so loud that the really sick people wouldn't be able to get much rest.

After the war the birds started singing and the noise seemed strange and the smell wasn't of fire but of sweet flowers and I could see trees blooming again.

*Danielle Warwick  (12)*
*St Mark's School, Harlow, Essex*

# WORLD WAR III

'Keep moving! Hold your ground.'
It was muddy, and we were crawling through a vast area of artillery fire.
'Snipers, in the trees!'

Just then our heavy artillery burst through the trees behind us, and was in full fire against the barricades. I made my run through the defences and cleaned out the area. I sat down behind a wall and ate some rations.

My name is Nigel Tramber, code 8 1469, private, English army.

Just then a newly designed photon cannon sent a rapid wave of electricity into our artillery, it burst into flames and blew to the ground.

I picked up my A62 solar chain gun, I couldn't run with my backpack and giant gun, but there light infantry were no match for me. I could see the main control centre guarded by two awesomely, fierce obelisks of light.

Our tanks and hovercrafts were getting slaughtered, the only way we were going to get past was to get in there and destroy the main control terminal.

Our main weapons were planes with our new technology in A6900 steel jet mounted with homing photon cannons, and built in laser chain gun, was taking out their turrets and sam sites but taking heavy damage by their Goliath, a giant robot with two automatic rocket launchers and chain guns for inventory.

Our tiberium rifle inventory men made a run for the obelisks along with our ion cannon beacon, if they placed this their main defence would be down. Yeah! Get down . . .

*Alex Keene (12)*
*St Mark's School, Harlow, Essex*

# THE LOCH NESS MONSTER

It was early morning and the sun had just risen over the jungle in Africa. Everywhere was silent, not even the sound of the screaming monkeys or the roar of the lions could be heard. Suddenly the peace was broken by the sound of engines and the dazzle of headlamps. The engines stopped and men jumped out of these huge lorries.

'Hey Pete, look at this!' A beefy man pointed at a small lizard clinging to a tree.

'Look Mike, it's a lizard, big deal! We're going to cut down this tree in a minute anyway!'

Soon there were more sounds - of chainsaws and of trees falling with a crash. Then of trees being pushed into the lorries and the vehicles driving away. Nobody noticed the small green lizard still clinging to the tree . . .

The next morning was completely different to the last. The lorry had now stopped and was on a boat to England. Nobody even noticed the lizard when they were driving to Scotland. They only noticed it when the lorry was unloaded.

'Hey Pete, it's that lizard!'

'Blimey, it must be thirsty or hungry, get it some water.'

'What if it's dangerous, and the water's off!'

'Get some out of the Ness!'

No one saw what happened next but the lizard ran away. It plunged itself into Loch Ness and was never seen again.

However ten years later a diver reported seeing a huge green lizard swimming in the depths of Loch Ness.

*Emma Bell (11)*
*St Mark's School, Harlow, Essex*

## TIME TRAVELLERS

Hi, I'm Alex and this is how I travelled through time.

I was just walking around minding my own business, when I saw this beautiful diamond ring. I could just afford it, so I bought it for my fiancée.

The next day I gave her the ring, she was so happy. I made her a gift, it was a time machine. I made it so that we could live a better life in the future.

We were walking back to my house when a man pulled us into his carriage and said, 'Give me all your money and jewellery, now!' We both did as he said, but Sophie wouldn't give him the ring. He started to pull at her finger, but he shot her instead. The carriage started to fall and it hit the floor. I got out but I couldn't get Sophie out. The carriage started to catch fire. I was screaming, trying to get Sophie out but I just couldn't, so I ran away.

I jumped into my machine and went into the future. First it went to 2010, 6400, 7999 and finally 31472.

Whilst I was there we were all being attacked. I meet lots of people. Mel was captured by the mongoras. I went into their den and tried to save her. I succeeded in saving her, but my time machine broke whilst I had to save her, but I didn't mind. See you soon for another adventure. Bye!

*Vincent Cuming (13)*
*St Mark's School, Harlow, Essex*

## ITO'S STORY

It was a warm and sunny morning when Ito woke up. This was the last day of Ito's life.

He had been picked to be a Kamikazi pilot in the war. It was an honour to die for the Emperor.

Ito felt sad, he was only 21. He got up and dressed, then he went to the temple to pray for an honourable death and hoped he would go to Heaven.

He went back to his room. On the side was a letter to his family saying how much he loved them and hoped that they would be proud of what he was to do. He gave his possessions to his family and friends.

All he had to do was wait. He was nervous and scared of what was to come.

The captain came and called all the pilots to the airfield. They marched proudly past their friends. By the side of the planes was a table with the Emperor's picture and a bottle of drink. The captain poured out each pilot a drink and saluted them.

Ito and the other pilots put on their bandannas with the picture of the rising sun on it. They got into their planes and flew towards their enemy (a battleship.) When Ito reached the ship he lined up his plane at the ship. He could see and zoomed in towards it. This was the end.

*Luke Bowering (12)*
*St Mark's School, Harlow, Essex*

# D-DAY

*30 seconds!*

Nothing I knew could tell me these were going to be the shortest 30 seconds I would ever experience.

I thought of my childhood, my parents, my first hospital stay. Everything I remember or have today passed through my mind, my wife, my daughter, my mother.

I had never been much of a churchgoer as a kid, or as an adult, but today I did my fair share of praying. I clutched my Thompson close and cursed the captain's stripes on my arm that had bought me my place on this suicide.

*10 seconds!*

We were the last to land, the battle had already begun. We stopped, there was a whirring sound and the ramp fell. A sea of golden sand met my eyes, but on this sea there was death. Arms, rifles and helmets littered the beach amongst the writhing green uniforms.

I stepped out onto the blooded sand, a thousand flashes, a dozen screams, my men were dying. I stared up at the colossal concrete bunker. It was dark and climbed all the way up to the cliff. A shower of yellow and red bursts greeted my already blooded face. A sharp pain in my side, my leg, my chest. I sank slowly to the ground.

I remembered one soldier in my outfit's words:

*And when he goes to Heaven,*
*to Saint Peter he will tell;*
*'Another soldier reporting sir!*
*I've served my time in Hell.'*

**Dan Stack (12)**
**St Mark's School, Harlow, Essex**

# A Day In The Life Of A Poor Victorian Child

Edward felt the cold hit his bare feet as he stumbled out of his little mattress onto the damp, mouldy floor. The only good piece of winter clothing he had was a frail wool scarf.

It was snowing heavily outside, it looked beautiful from the inside of the shack, but Edward knew it would be bitterly cold. The sharp icy winds felt like knives on his pale cheeks. Edward Johnson was ten years old and had to juggle school and work. This morning it was school.

Edward hated school because he had trouble writing and the teacher beats him because of it. He sat down at a rough wooden desk, the chair hurt his weak back.

Edward began to write on his little board with a tiny piece of chalk, but it was extremely difficult to write on slate, especially with his writing problem. The teacher was a tall, balding man with a long hooked nose. His name was Mr Thompson. He stalked up behind Edward with his long birch cane firmly in his long, bony hands. Mr Thompson peered over Edward's small shoulder. Edward felt a butterfly flutter across his stomach, he knew what was coming. Mr Thompson whacked the birch cane onto the table, just centimetres away from Edward's hands. 'How am I supposed to read that mess?' shouted the teacher as his face was beginning to redden. 'Come here boy and do not move!'

Edward's eyes closed as the hard birch cane came down upon his knuckles.

*Jazmine Marsh (13)*
*St Mark's School, Harlow, Essex*

# IMAGE

Hi! My name is Joe. My home town has just been attacked by German bombers and the whole town has been turned upside down.

For some reason I'm still alive, but I still got to find a way to escape this tragic and horror. I was separated from my friends and family two years ago when the horror started. I have nothing to stand for - no food, drink, but a magnum.

As it is getting darker, it seemed to be chillier and chillier. I am hungry so I am going to seek for foods where the shops are, or shall I say were.

I still do not see any survivors to be seen. Wait a minute, I hear slow, moving footsteps. I turned around just to see a friend of mine, in a different form.

He looked as if his spirit has gone and his body decaying. He seemed to be attacking me. He tried to take a bite out of me, I had no choice but to pump the mindless corpse with lead until it dropped to the ground.

Why? Why is this happening to the town? I managed to get to the food store, still in one piece, but not for long for I am in flames from the bomb. I just opened the shop door only to find an old man who seemed to know a lot about the situation. I drew my magnum and shot the old man in the leg, because I thought he was a rotting, mindless corpse as well.

'I am not one of them, why did you shoot me in the leg?'
'Sorry, I did not know which side you are on,' I replied.
'The town has been infested by a mixture in the bomb which caused the victim's who got bombed to turn into zombies.'
'What's a zombie?'
'A zombie is a half minded, rotting corpse who can spread the virus if the victim falls into a hand of a zombie bite.'
'Yes, I encountered one a minute ago and killed it with my magnum.'
'Beware not all of them are dead after they fall to the ground,' the old man replied.
'Will you be all right on your own?'
'Yes.'

I walked through the back door thinking about what the old man said about the zombie things. The door was nailed shut so I had to barge my way in and find two zombies staggering towards me.

Once again I drew my magnum and found a quicker solution to kill the zombies and save my ammo. One by one I pulled the trigger of the weapon making mincemeat from the head. I finally got to the food storage room where I found a couple of dozen packets of crisp choc bars and some cans of soda. I took some spares in case I got hungry and left in a hurry.

When I got outside I saw dozens of zombies on the left so I had to run to the right, climbed up the stairs off a half-destroyed building and slid through the window like a snake. On the left of the crumbling room I saw a professor-looking like guy. 'Are you a zombie?' I asked.
*Nothing.*
'I said, are you a zombie?' I shouted.
'No, actually I created the zombie,' the man said.
'Why?' I said.
'The Germans made me do it, they put the g-virus in the bombs.'
'What's a *g-virus?'* I replied.
'Never mind about that, you must destroy the town now before the trouble gets worse by setting the self-destruct mechanism at the biscuit factory. After that there should be a sports car near that area to make your quick escape and leave me here. I deserve to die.'

I headed to my next destination and found the switch. All of a sudden thousands of zombies were everywhere and I turned the switch and ran for the sports car. I turned the car on and ran over a few zombies. I had five minutes left. That was plenty of time.

As it got to the end of the route, I put the car in full blast and then it was my home town destroyed.

'Goodbye,' I said looking at the scene.
'Goodbye.'

*Kenneth Kwok (14)*
*St Mark's School, Harlow, Essex*

## THE BEGINNING

There she was, stuck inside her dark cocoon, her home for the last nine months and now she was ready to leave and become the person she had been working on all the time she was in there. Like the caterpillar turning into a butterfly, something so small but yet so beautiful and powerful.

It was happening. Her warm pool of water which had been her home, safety and comfort had gone. She knew it wouldn't be long, soon she would meet the world. But something happened, something she did not expect and it wouldn't stop. She was being pushed, forced and shoved. An invisible force made her every move a struggle and there was no way to stop it.

She was sure this had never happened before. She needed to think. What could she do? How could something so small stop a force that was almost crushing her? But it wasn't. Was her cocoon bigger than she thought? Did it have an opening? She wiggled her way down, the wall that had seemed to stop her, was not a wall at all, but a never-ending tunnel.

The force which she was running from became more often and more powerful. She had to get out. Suddenly there was a blinding light a light at the end of the tunnel. She had made it, she was out. She was blinded, blinded by the light. She knew she was free and her world had just begun.

*Lauren Cunningham  (14)*
*St Mark's School, Harlow, Essex*

# 1 HOUR SUPERMAN

Is it a bird? Is it a plane? No, it's Superman!

'What's he doing?'
'Looks like he's falling.'

*Crash!* He landed in a pile of boxes. This is Superman, 1 hour Superman! He can only use his powers whenever he eats a chocolate bar (at least 70% cocoa.) After that, he gets these special powers for 1 hour!

'A tidal wave's about to hit Japan!' he shouted. He broke a piece off a bar, ate it and flew off. He arrived in Japan half a second later. He flew to the wave and pushed against it. It seemed to take hours then he suddenly fell down and down and down, his 1 hour was up.

He woke up, he was washed up on shore and was very wet. He looked around and realised he was still in a Superman costume. He quickly changed into a formal suit and walked to the city. He had no money and his chocolate bar had melted. He couldn't get back.

He looked around and decided to sell something, his tie. He had just enough money to buy a cheap bar. He quickly gobbled it up, hovered a few seconds and fell on the floor. He looked at the ingredients, 25% cocoa! He sold more things that he had on him and just had enough money to buy a 69% cocoa chocolate bar.

He started to fly home. He had flew  along way and suddenly fell down and landed in Paris!

*Fu-Wah Kwong  (12)*
*St Mark's School, Harlow, Essex*

## A Day In The Life Of A WW2 Soldier

I had got in the boat and sailed to Normandy. There was no turning back now. I could see the beach being pulverised by heavy artillery and machine guns.

I heard someone shout, '5 seconds to landing.' Then the whistle blew and the front fell down to a rainfall of machine gun shells. I heard screams as the Nazi's bombarded my friends with them. Someone then shouted, 'Get to the bunker.' I ran to it as I could and dived in. On my fall I broke my right leg, so I used my morphine injections to ease the pain. I moved along the bunker to find my brigade when I discovered my best friend laying on his back motionless.

I limped over being very cautious about any Germans that may have infiltrated the bunker. As I got closer he moved his hand and put it over his right arm. I saw a gunshot wound and he had a piece of barbed wire stuck in his leg. All of a sudden a tidal wave of machine gun shells came over the bunker wall and got me in the right hand, then from nowhere a hand grenade was thrown over. I tried making a run for it but my friend was lying on his back, helpless. Then it exploded taking my best friend with it. Now I ask myself was it worth losing all that?

*James Cox  (13)*
*St Mark's School, Harlow, Essex*

# HELP!

'Lucy, Lucy, come on out,' I shouted as I knocked on her old wooden door. I thought carefully for a moment, something wasn't right. I pushed open the door carefully. It creaked loudly, someone must have heard that, but still no one answered. I gingerly tiptoed in, in case her father was asleep upstairs, he worked very hard on the farm all day, and he gets very angry if he's disturbed. I carried on walking through the hall, a sudden chill ran down my back and the door slammed shut. From that moment I knew something was wrong.

I peered through the crack in the door and I heard the radio on upstairs. I smartened myself up and walked confidently into the room. There was Lucy, her beautiful soft, pale face was covered in bruises and she was bleeding. She lay nervously on the floor in an awkward position so not to hurt her bruises.

'Lucy, what happened?' I asked puzzled.
'He hit me,' she whispered.
'Hit you! More like tried to kill you.'
She began to cry. 'Mum left and now he's blaming it all on me. She left because she got fed up of his moaning and shouting, and now he's saying it's all my fault.'
'Who's down there?' an angry voice shouted out from upstairs.

My head began to spin. I then took Lucy carefully by the hand and began to run towards the door, 'Don't worry Lucy, we're going to make it.'

*Natalie Walsh (13)*
*St Mark's School, Harlow, Essex*

# A DAY IN THE LIFE OF LUCY WASHINGTON

*7.00am*

As I get out of my bed, Jessie comes up and licks me to death.
'Lucy!' shouts up my mum.
'What?'
'Get up!'
'I am up! Mum, did you leave the hot water on last night?' I ask.
'Yeah.'
'I'm going to have a shower.'

*7.45am*

I get out my white skirt and blue halterneck, as I'm dying my hair.
James comes. 'Mum says you have to come down now.'
'OK, one minute.'

As soon as I walk down the stairs, Mum says to James, 'Oh look, Lucy's going through that tarty phase.'
'Mum, shut up!'

*8.30am*

Time to set off for school. As we're driving past the shops I see Willis (my crush.) My heart stops. 'Mum, stop the car!' I say.
'Why?'
'Um, um, because I need a drink.'
'Oh for goodness sake Lucy, we've only just left the house.'
'Sorry,' I say.

Mum gives me the money and I go and get a bottle of Coke.

'Hey Lucy!' says Willis.
'Hi,' I says, I had butterflies in my stomach.
'Lucy!' shouts out my mum.

My face goes bright red. When I get back in the car I scream at my mum.

*9.16pm*

Willis comes and knocks for me. 'Hi, is Lucy in?' I hear him say. 'Oh my goodness,' I scream. (I think he heard me.)

As I walked down the stairs I see him. He looks so nice.

All night we talk and talk. I find out we have a lot in common. This could be the start of something new.

*Natalie Strong  (13)*
*St Mark's School, Harlow, Essex*

## ALIEN

Alan and his mum were indoors watching television. It was a warm atmosphere with a fire lit and a mug of hot tea each. They were watching Jerry Springer at the time. The show was about a couple that had split up. They were arguing about who should have the kids.

Alan's dad walked through the door with a miserable look on his face. He came in and sat down next to Alan.

'How was work dear?' asked Alan's mum.
'Fine, apart from the fact that I got made redundant.'
'You're joking! Why on earth would they do that?'
'I didn't hand in a report on time, OK?'
'Sorry, I was only asking.'

Soon an argument broke out. The warm and cosy atmosphere turned to a miserable, cold atmosphere. Alan got up and shouted, 'Shut up! Both of you, you're behaving like kids. I'm fed up with this.' Then he walked out of the house and slammed the door behind him.

He went off over to the park and sat on the swings alone, for half an hour expecting his mum or dad to come looking for him. They didn't.

Just then he heard a sound, a rumbling sound. It was getting louder, then it stopped. He looked round and he saw an alien spaceship. It was circular with flashing lights. It was no more than six metres wide and three metres high. It hovered for a bit then dropped to the ground. It didn't fall apart - surprisingly.

The small dome on top opened and a creature about five foot tall walked out. It was a human-like figure with huge oval black eyes. It had a naked silver body and human length arms and legs.

Alan was so surprised to see this creature, especially the fact that it could speak English. The alien said his name was Baranio Stuffalone. They were talking about various issues. They ended up talking about culture. Baranio wanted to learn more about English culture.

In the end Baranio learnt all about Earth. Alan's mum and dad got back together. Baranio kept in touch with Alan and nothing ever went wrong again.

*Jack Dench  (13)*
*St Mark's School, Harlow, Essex*

# A Day In The Life Of . . .

Waking up this morning was actually quite good, knowing I have training today. As I'm a footballer I need to be on a healthy diet so for breakfast I will have my Sporties which taste like I'm in Heaven. I need to keep light as I'm moving all the time.

Now I'm going in the shower. I'll be out in about fifteen minutes. I'm dressed and ready to go to football. The thing I need to do is my hair, I love my hair. I'm just getting into my brand new car ready to go training.

I'm at training now, ready to train with the boys. Jamie Carragher is a proper scouser. He is the joker, he will take the mickey out of anything you do. In training we do jumping over hurdles then we do some shooting practise against our goalkeeper. I'm going to David Beckham's house for dinner after.

Driving in my car everybody notices me, which is good. At David Beckham's house we have a roast dinner made by Victoria, then we have ice cream which is assorted flavours with marshmallows. David Beckham's house is fantastic and big. I need to leave early for football tomorrow.

*Patrick O'Sullivan  (12)*
*St Mark's School, Harlow, Essex*

# FURY OF THE SKY

Fire erupted from the green scaly mouth of a dragon. It slammed into the Empire State building making it crumble at the foundations. The dragon had achieved his goal, not a building was in sight, he had destroyed New York. He could now rest.

Later in the night the green dragon was awoken by a loud roar. He opened one of his big, slitted, yellow eyes and looked around, then a huge ball of fire burnt into his skin. Almost immediately he flew into action.

The two dragons circled each other shooting fireballs at one another. Darting towards the pink dragon, the green dragon turned it into a chase. Every so often the pink dragon would swiftly turn his head and shoot flames at the green dragon behind him and the green dragon firing flames at the pink dragon's behind.

The pink dragon dived and pulled up, grabbed the green dragon and threw him down. The dragon's face cracked under the force. His weak body collapsed and he lay down. The impossible had happened, the mighty fortress had crumbled. The other dragon circled in victory, shooting flames as a sign of power.

The green dragon lay there, knowing of its defeat, knowing it would die. Silently he closed his eyes.

The triumphant pink dragon flew steadily into the glowing sunset until he became just a mere dot on the horizon.

The fury of the sky had been unleashed unto the world.

*Sam Cunningham (12)*
*St Mark's School, Harlow, Essex*

# A GREAT METROPOLIS, A GREAT ARMY

The colossal Metropolis of Shehara, Tiyauh, has revealed today that they have created an immense army.

Tiyauh is the only civilised area of the watery planet of Shehara. The ancient metropolis is known throughout the galaxy as a peaceful place.

The inhabitants of Tiyauh told us the Army has been under construction for years.

The Republic has claimed that they have known nothing about this army and are disgraced with Tiyauh's actions and also very disappointed.

'The planet of Shehara has always been very diplomatic and honest to the Republic and have reported all of its actions to the Senate', says Senator Allgelgar of Torá.

The Senate has agreed to disable the army until they can reach a decision.

The army is made up of millions of machines designed for battle.

The King of Tiyauh, Geo Gallatorné, spoke - 'The Army is simply for defence, we had no intentions of going to war with anyone.' He continued, 'I have agreed with the

Senate that the army can be disabled until they reach a verdict on this annoying and stressful time'.

Whether Geo Gallatorné's idea was to create an army of sheer size and scale just for defence or not is what we really need to find out.

Is the planet of Shehara suspecting an attack, or are they planning an attack themselves? This is the question.

This newspaper is also available in Toranée, Tiyauhee, Metrogaté, Hermian and Gratteex.

*Matthew Mouncey (13)*
*St Mark's School, Harlow, Essex*

# THE STORY OF MY LIFE

Waking up was the worst. An old piece of carpet for a duvet on an old floorboard. It was my great auntie's house, left to me in an inheritance deal with my lawyer. It is huge but an empty house. The dust, that showed that this house hadn't been lived in for years, swam up my nose. The dust, I'll always remember that dust, for out of it came a transfigured shadow, straight from Hell. These mere particles changed my life, these turned me into a man, yet this pulled me lower than itself. This is the story of my life . . .

My head had sores on it where nails had pricked it in the night. Coldness swept through me. It was silly of me really to ask if anyone had opened the door. I felt a fool afterwards as I was by myself. My auntie had keeled over suddenly. Her death was mysterious. Nobody knew what had killed her. That scared me.

All night noises were being made upstairs, scraping noises of knives being sharpened but it couldn't be. I made it all up. I scared myself half to death over it. As I stepped up to wash, a shadow towered over me. A shadow of evil, a shadow with glaring eyes. Stupid as it sounds an axe towered over me. I closed my eyes in prayer as its foul breath hung over me and as I heard a swipe, I felt nothing - then nothing.

*Callum Healy (13)*
*St Mark's School, Harlow, Essex*

## The Gangster Experience

I am Jack, head of security here at the Piranha Nightclub and now it is my turn to tell you my gangster experience.

*Boom!* 'What was that?' Straight away I leapt out of my seat to check it out. The smoke was coming from the boss' room. Without thinking I sprinted to the boss' room. There was a club member lying there dead, blood dripping out from the carcass. It had been blown across the room from the point of explosion.

I made my way through the dark grey cloud of smoke with my hands stretched out in front. When I got through the smoke I couldn't see anyone there. 'Boss!' I shouted. 'Boss! Where are you?' I ran over to his desk, opened a drawer and took out a pistol. I walked back through the smoke and thought this seemed like a perfect distraction. People were running around like headless chickens, screaming. No one could get out, all the fire exits were shut.

The fire was beginning to spread, but I couldn't find the boss. Someone must have kidnapped him. I couldn't tell the police, he must be in debt or something.

The TV was still on in the bar. I noticed there was a bank robbery on. The club was falling apart, I had to get everyone out so I went to the middle of the dance floor and fired the gun in the air. 'Right everyone follow me in single file.' I ran to the fire exit and with my pistol, I shot at the lock. The lock then flew open and I barged through the doors and at that point, the fire engines arrived. I ran to the bank robbery scene which was only over the road, to see what was happening. The police were going mental.

I decided to go to the boss place. I had a spare key so I jumped in my car and made my way there. I got to the door and heard the voices of a big gathering. I turned the key slowly and then pushed the door open quickly, pointing the gun into the centre of the room. Everyone looked at me and pointed guns at me. The boss shouted, 'Don't worry, it's Jack.'

I saw loads of money being counted. 'What's going on boss?' I asked. 'Have you done a bank job?'

'Jack, Jack, sit down.'

So I sat down and he explained that the club was just to cover for other activities and wanted me to be part of that. I quickly thought of an excuse to leave without raising suspicion. 'I had better get back to the club now I know you're safe and sort things out there. I'll see you later boss, OK?'

I quickly left, jumping in my car and I never went back to that city again. That was my *gangster experience!*

*Jack Wieland (13)*
*St Mark's School, Harlow, Essex*

# THE SUMMONER

One day in Masad, a boy named Joseph was born, with a mark on his hand which was the mark of the Summoner.

In the prophecy of the Jade temple it proclaims that the evil king Murod would be destroyed by the Summoner. He found out that the Summoner lived in Masad and he sent his troops to get the Summoner but not to kill him or a new Summoner would be born. He launched an attack on Masad.

Joseph was given the ring of darkness, which only he could use. He summoned a creature to save his village but it destroyed his village. After that dreadful day he threw the ring down a well and promised never to summon again.

Yago came with his daughter Roslind and they trained until Roslind and Joseph were 19. Joseph learned to summon and Roslind learned to use her magic. Soon they found out that there was war against Medeever and Orenia. The gods were to be involved in this battle.

With Roslind and Joseph they were unstoppable. Meedever had the advantage in battle and Joseph, Yago and Roslind put their magic together and formed the biggest and most powerful creature to ever be in existence. It took out all the gods that battled with Orenia. Finally, the beast eliminated the Orenian army. A huge fireball hovered above its head then it vanished.

Medeever soon got back to normal and Joseph ruled the whole of Medeever and was married with Queen Roslind.

*James Hammond (12)*
*St Mark's School, Harlow, Essex*

## HORRIFIC MOMENT

Jake is a perfectly normal boy thank you very much; up for a laugh and gets on with his work. It was a few days ago when his laughs came to an abrupt end:

He and his five best friends were sitting in the attic telling ghost stories then it was Jake's turn.

'In this very house at 12:15am, on the night of his death he will arise from his coffin in Hell and haunt for a week everyone in the house . . .'

His friends sat and stared straight into each other's eyes. The clock struck exactly 12:15am and silence wrapped its arms among the boys.

A fire broke out and the boys were petrified, the flames turned as blue as the sea when a man strolled out.

All of the gang *except* Jake ran home but no, Jake stood up and confronted the ghost.

Jake's dog, Spike, walked in and the ghost seemed to have a most bizarre reaction to it. Dan Smith began to fly at great speed round the room before flying through Jake and back through the fire.

Ever since that peculiar disturbance, Jake has been able to see any danger that is about to happen.

That night, when Jake came face to face with Dan Smith, was his horrific moment.

*Matthew Wood (12)*
*St Mark's School, Harlow, Essex*

## THE BATTLE OF THE TRENCHES

Dear Anna,
The bombs are constant now. It's hard to hear myself think. I'm fine.
Two men were killed yesterday that were in our band. We've been told
to attack the Nazi front line. We're succeeding at the moment . . . we're
under attack I'll write soon.
Jack.

'Keep your heads down,' repeated Colonel Harrison. Jack appeared
across the line and then a Nazi soldier. He took his aim, firing two shots
and killed him. The clouds darkened as the battle raged on. He dragged
himself over the trenches and advanced towards the Nazis. Jack fired
shots at random.

Catching Jack unaware, a shout from 40 yards back; 'Charge!' a loud
cry broke the sound of machine-guns. *'Charge!'* 60 men stood up and
ran as fast as they could. They jumped it to the trench of the Nazis
killing every enemy there.

40 men took their position and fired at the second line. A day and night
passed; with continuous battles. British and American planes controlled
the skies and the ground, then a swing of fortune. Nazi tanks arrived
and the British were forced seven miles back.

Jack's colonel decided on a different mission. The band was to split into
two. 15 men apiece to attack the sides of the Nazis. Band two (Jack's
band) took out the right flank. It was a grave move. Jack and ten others
jumped into the enemy's trench. As he looked to his right he was
staring down the barrel of a rifle and the soldier wasn't British . . .

*Kane Read  (13)*
*St Mark's School, Harlow, Essex*

## I HATE MY SISTER

I hate my sister. Everything was fine before she came along. Mum was still alive, Dad wasn't bankrupt and hiding out elsewhere. Everything was fine, everyone was happy, everyone was alive.

I wouldn't be here today if I had trusted my sister. She's evil. The nurses don't believe me, they think that she's just some sweet five-year-old kid. Well they're wrong. If anyone else had to spend just one week living with my sister, then it is unlikely that they would come out of it sane.

I remember when I was little and I'd be taken to the park by Mum and Dad. We had a dog then. He was a chocolate Labrador, Sam I think his name was. My sister later saw to it that he had a grisly death of pellet poisoning. We were never allowed to keep any pets after that.

We first visited the orphanage about a year ago. Mum died giving birth to my sister, that's why I can't help but blame Mum's death on her. It's like, as soon as she stuck her head out she decided it would be hilariously funny to kill her own mother.

My sister is short and chubby with blonde hair and baby-blue eyes. I'm tall and skinny with brown hair, brown eyes and freckles. I'm twelve.

Still, not long now. Shut up Carol. You know you're getting what you deserve! Now look, you've gone and got your blood all over the carpet.

*Catherine Donovan (13)*
*St Mark's School, Harlow, Essex*

## THE DOOR THAT CREAKED

As Jill fell asleep her door creaked. There were howls and barks.

Jill woke up dazzled by the blinding light. She got out of bed and went to see her parents. She screamed and shouted. Her door was locked. She didn't know what to do.

The vibration of drums dragged her in. When she was in, it was silent and dark! She was wearing a coat and found herself in mountains covered with snow. She turned around; there was no door, just snow. She walked on further and further. The land changed to reveal a desert. She walked some more. 'I wish I had some water,' said Jill. On the ground was a bottle of water. Jill walked on and on till she fell asleep.

When she woke up her brother Sam was beside her. 'What happened? Say it was a dream!'
'No can do!' replied Sam.

They clambered along the rocky, sandy desert. They came to a field and when they went through that they found the mountains again. *'I wish we were home, home, home,'* replied the echoes. There was a bolt of thunder! A bridge appeared and on the other side there was a door surrounded by smoke breathing flames. They ran across the bridge as fast as they could. *Bang! Bang!* The exit was locked . . .

*Christina Gargan (13)*
*St Mark's School, Harlow, Essex*

## THE WRONG IDEA

Luke and Ben had been best friends for seven years, until something horrible happened to Luke that Ben would never forget.

One boring day at school for Luke and Ben, second lesson was French and they didn't want to go, so during registration they planned something they thought they would never do . . .

'I know, we could stay in the toilets for the lesson,' explained Luke.
'No, that's way too boring! Let's sneak out of school.'
'Well, okay, but we have to be careful.'

So just after first lesson they ran around the back of the school and went through the old gate. 'We are free!' shouted Ben at the top of his deep voice.
'Keep quiet! Do you want to get caught?'
Ben shut up, eventually.

They ran to the park and sat on the tacky swings. 'Come on, let's do something more fun.' Ben requested.
'Maybe, just watch out for any police in case we get caught being out of school.'
'Sure, I know, let's play *chicken*.'
The game where you stand in the middle of the road and move out of the way just as a car is coming.

They played and played until their luck ran out. A small car with big impact knocked Luke down. There was silence as Ben looked on with fear in his eyes, worried and anxious of what might happen. The man ran out of the car to Luke's side, while Ben ran to the nearest phone and dialled 999. Passers-by stood in suspense and watched.

*Amy Hartgrove (13)*
*St Mark's School, Harlow, Essex*

## THE NEW KID

She had actually slapped me. I could not believe it, I didn't understand what had happened, it was so fast.

I ran from the scene hiding the tears, running and not looking back. I ran to the toilets and hid. I waited but no one came. I unlocked the door of my cubicle and faced the mirror. My face was red, my eyes were sore and my left cheek had a red hand print on it.

The school bell rang. I walked, hiding my head but you couldn't hide anything with my head teacher. As I got closer to my form room I could hear voices.

'Yes, she called me a stupid tart.'
'Okay, I'll talk to her.'
As I came round the corner Cordell said, 'There she is!'
I stood still, not knowing what to do.
'You, to my office.'
Those words rang in my head!

Ben, who was also involved, was there. He was the cause of the fight.
'Go through what happened please, Mary.'
'Yes Sir. Cordell and I were talking about who we fancied the most and she had said Ben, but she didn't know that I was going out with him.'
'Then I came over and hugged Mary,' said Ben.
'Cordell stood up and gave Ben a really big kiss so I called her a tart and explained that we were going out. Then she slapped me.'
'This is the fifth time Cordell has slapped someone. My only suggestion is to move her.' So he did.

It was a few weeks later before the new kid arrived. She went by the name of Roglan. She was about my age with short black hair. On her first week she had about a thousand people ask her out and she had a mobile. '*C U l8er,* do you have any idea what it means?' she said. 'See you later, everyone was so impressed.'

I was really jealous. My week was really bad, like a curse had been put on me. The worst thing was Ben dumped me and guess who he went out with, yep, Roglan.

*Nicole Kelly (13)*
*St Mark's School, Harlow, Essex*

## THREE WISHES

Everyone at Sunnydale School knew that Melanie Hunter was a bully. She was a teacher's pet, but only because they never really knew her! She had lots of friends, but she didn't know they were just scared of her! She was best at everything and she knew it!

One morning she was walking to school, when she noticed a snail on the ground. 'Stupid snail,' she muttered and was just about to squash it when a voice cried out, 'No! Don't please!'
Melanie looked around her but no one was there. 'Excuse me?' she answered.
'If you don't squash me I'll give you three wishes!'
She looked down to see the snail peering up at her. 'Don't be stupid, you're just a snail!'
'Try me then,' the snail answered.
'OK, I wish for a pair of rollerblades!'
'They'll be in your cupboard when you get home.'
Melanie looked at her watch. 'I wish for pierced ears!' she cried and a pair of gold studs suddenly appeared! At that moment the bell rang. 'Meet me here at 3.30pm for my third wish!' she cried, as she ran up the street to school.

As she got to her class the teacher said, 'You're late Melanie!'
It was the first time she'd ever been late. 'Oh no, I wish I was dead!'

*Kristle Kilburn (12)*
*St Mark's School, Harlow, Essex*

# FLYING BACON

Flying pigs have been flying up and down the country in the past week. These pigs are not dangerous and will not harm you.

These bizarre animals are said to have come from a farm in Wantage, near Oxford. Wantage is just a small town in the countryside.

Molberry Farm is where it is said to have all started. I had a talk with the owner of the farm, Mr Day.

He said, 'I have no idea why the pigs have started flying, but I know they were from this farm'.

The pigs are pink but they have large wings which are hidden under their fat. The pigs are sweeping the country in the night, some have ended up as far north as Newcastle upon Tyne and as south as Portsmouth. When these animals fly through the air, they glide without resting.

Scientists have said that the farm site used to be a dumping site for radioactive waste. They think this may have something to do with these creatures. Other scientists say it could be a cross between a pig and a big bird but that's very unlikely.

These pigs do look like they will make good pets, but if you capture one please phone the Animal Trust on 01279 101055.

*Andrew Swanton (13)*
*St Mark's School, Harlow, Essex*

## STRAWBERRY SUNSET WEDDING

Once upon a time in a beautiful forest called Elmwood, there was a family of strawberry fairies. The two parents, Edward and Della, were two fine fairy folk. They were about 200 years old but have never aged. Tammy and Faye were both twenty-one, they both had long strawberry blonde hair and baby-blue eyes.

Faye was engaged to Timmy, Timmy was an oak fairy who came from a very rich family. Faye and Timmy were going to get married on a Sunday by the strawberry bushes at sunset.

Sunday came and Faye's dress was nearly ready. Her mother, Della, had been making it and now Tammy was finishing it. The dress was cream with white beads on it, it was like a dress for a princess.

As sunset grew nearer, everyone was getting really excited. Faye looked great in her dress and she was standing by the altar with Edward. They said their vows and gave each other their rings.

After the wedding they had a meal that was better than the queen ever has. It was full of different fruits and lots of lovely flowers that could make the saddest person happy. By this time the sunset was a lovely strawberry pink.

As the moon came up, the fairies danced to the magical fairy music and sprinkled fairy dust over the strawberry bushes. Everyone had a lovely time and Timmy and Faye lived lovingly ever after.

*Aimee Bloomfield (11)*
*St Mark's School, Harlow, Essex*

# A Day In The Life Of Dylan

Dylan wakes up in front of the fire, stretches his muscly paws and prowls around the living room.

After tearing up the curtains, he decides to come up and wake my family. Usually he sits on your head and starts dribbling for attention. He finally wins the battle and we give him all the attention in the world.

After a while my mum takes him downstairs and feeds him chicken and turkey chops. He loves it!

Dylan goes out and plays with his *friends* who are: Buster, Thomas, Marmalade and Biscuit. They all have games to play such as *who can catch the most flies!*

Dylan comes back in at around 5.00pm for more attention.

*Elisabeth Charge (12)*
*St Mark's School, Harlow, Essex*

# A DAY IN THE LIFE OF A COLONEL

I get up at 6.00am, make my bedspread ready for inspection, then go to the dining hall for a quick breakfast of either cereal, porridge or toast. Next I have morning fitness training with the privates for about two hours, then stay in until something comes up. If it does I would be in the front line. I shall be using either a M16 or an AK47. I would also use grenades, petrol bombs, maybe a M79 and maybe a bazooka. Covering my back would be a major or captain and behind would be the privates. The general would have no part in the actual fighting.

If there was no war or feud I would have a nice, quiet day, unless the president has special orders. At 11.00pm most go to bed but I stay up for night watch till 3.00am then lights out.

The next day would be different. Tomorrow I shall get up at 9.00am and get the captains and train them by going through the assault course. Then check data files of new privates and inspect privates' quarters. Then go to the infirmary for a quick check-up, then go to bed at 6.00pm because I have to get up at 6.00am.

*Jack Pavitt (12)*
*St Mark's School, Harlow, Essex*

## DAYS IN THE LIFE OF KATIE SANN

Hi, I'm Katie Sann and this is my story. It all started on a Monday morning . . .

We were sitting at the table, me, Mum and Dad, when Mum started shuffling about and looking at Dad. When I realised that she didn't need to go to the toilet, I asked her what was wrong.

'I think we should tell her,' Mum said. I had an image in my head about Mum saying, 'Oh darling as we love you sooo much, we decided to buy you a present,' and then Dad majestically revealing a beautiful white horse. But oh no, I was quite wrong.

'I'm pregnant,' Mum said smiling. My mouth hung open but I quickly regained my balance before falling off my chair. This was just the start of my so-called adventures.

When the baby was born, sure she was sweet and cuddly, but I knew she would be trouble. First she threw up on me, then she was sick on my lunch. But this was just the beginning! Soon she started to grow and also became more mischievous. When she was three, Mum asked me to take her out for a walk. Sure, no trouble I thought.

Little did I know the baby knew how to work the brakes, so off she sped down the hill towards the pond. In I dived, catching her in my arms. Home I went, covered in pondweed. Many more mishaps happened and before I knew it Mum was pregnant again!

*Danielle Lamb (12)*
*St Mark's School, Harlow, Essex*

# LOTTERY TICKET

A family of four sat gazing at the telly, waiting for the six numbers of the lottery to appear on the screen. The first number appeared, that was one of theirs, so was the next and the next and the next and so were the last two numbers. They had won.

A little while later - after they had all calmed down, they rushed over to the newsagents to buy an envelope and stamp to send the lottery ticket off. On their way, Paul and Trudy, the parents, were in front of their two children, Kirsty and Miles. Trudy had the ticket in her back pocket . . . she stumbled and the ticket fell out. Miles saw it and picked it up.

Miles was mischievous. This time Miles didn't tell his parents, he just slipped it into his pocket and carried on. When Miles went down to pick it up, Kirsty questioned, 'What are you doing down there? We're in a rush, Mum and Dad will wonder where we are.'
Miles replied, 'Oh, I'm . . . tying my shoelace.'
'Hurry up then.'

Half an hour later they arrived home with the envelope and stamp. Paul shouted, 'Where's the ticket, where's the ticket?'
Trudy replied, 'It's in my . . . oh no, where's it gone?'
Miles laughed inside.

Five months passed and they were still looking for the ticket. A case was delivered to them the next day with the lottery winnings. Miles had sent the lottery ticket off without telling his parents a thing.

*Dominic Steingold (12)*
*St Mark's School, Harlow, Essex*

## A Day In The Life Of My Mum

This is a story about my mum and what it is like to be her.

She is always working, my mum. She never stops even if she is ill, she still continues to work hard. But sometimes I think she works too hard. Just like the beginning of last week . . .

. . . She was walking my younger brother to school and after making sure he was OK, she started making her way home, she was crossing the main road when this car full of teenage boys came rushing around the corner.

My mum tried to run out of the way, but wasn't quick enough and got hit. The car didn't stop, it just kept going. Some people came out to see what was going on, then they saw my mum. She got rushed to hospital and it turned out that she had only broken her leg and had a couple of bruises. But this meant she couldn't go to work; couldn't take my brother to school.

So, to help her out, me and my brother were trying to behave and get along. My stepdad had to start work later and take my brother to school. Then once I had finished school, I had to walk him home.

My mum was very grateful and finally felt like someone was helping her for once, unlike when she never stops. We all realised how much she has to do and now have tried to help her out as much as possible.

I hope this can help you all to realise how much work mums have to do and how much help they need.

*Stevie Hamill  (13)*
*St Mark's School, Harlow, Essex*

## THE SUDDEN SCREAM

One dark night in a very old house, there lived a horrible old lady. The people in her road thought something was very strange about her, something so terrible they would have to run past her house every morning. This very old lady was very strange, but something scared her one night that drove her away from the house and she was never seen again. Nobody dared to go near the place, until one day.

About ten years after, somebody wanted to buy the house. Everybody warned this girl, but she wouldn't listen.

One long, warm day, she was standing in her window, just looking at the horrific garden. She walked out of the house and she shivered and heard the wind blowing behind her. She said to herself, 'Nothing to worry about.'

After doing the gardening, she went back inside the house. She sat on the floor and started to write.

Later that evening, everybody in the neighbourhood got an invitation to go to a house-warming party. They were all worried, but they decided they would go.

She started to decorate her house before the party.

The party started, and everything was going fine. The food was fine, and so was the music. Then the room was chilly, even though the heaters had been on for nearly an hour. The lights started to flicker, then the room went black, the music stopped, and then the loudest scream ever; the girl was now gone - never to be seen again.

*Graziella Castronovo (12)*
*St Mark's School, Harlow, Essex*

## TIGGER'S FLOWERS

'Look Tigger,' bellowed Roo, 'dandelions.'
Roo picked up the white flower, thought for a bit, and blew, the white seeds floating along on the breeze.
'This is my flower,' whispered the tiny kangaroo as he tugged at his blue T-shirt.

Tigger bounced over on his springy tail. 'Flower? I haven't got a flower,' moaned the unhappy Tigger, 'Tigger's don't have flowers.'
'Don't worry, I'll help you find yours, it must be somewhere,' announced Roo. Then, without a word, Tigger bounced off to find his flower.

As they bounced, they saw a lonely donkey desperately trying to re-build his house of sticks. *Smash! Bang!*
'Hello Eeyore,' said Tigger as he climbed off Eeyore.
'Hello Tigger, hello Roo,' said Eeyore desperately, as he looked around at the pile of sticks that was once his house.
'Eeyore, what's your flower?' asked Roo.
'Mine?' said Eeyore, with a small smile, 'mine are thistles, they're so tasty to eat. Why do you ask?'
'I'm looking for my flower,' answered Tigger, 'it's the most biggest, bestest, springiest flower in the world!'
'I'll help you look if you want,' whispered Eeyore.

So they strode off, looking for Tigger's flower.

'I'll never find a flower for me,' said Tigger, 'It's hopeless.' He bounced off gloomily.

He bounced and he bounced until he passed Christopher Robin's house, and until he saw in the distance, the most biggest, bestest, springiest flower in the world - a sunflower.

Tigger was so happy he invited his friends around for a party to celebrate him finding his flower.

*Jodie Davey  (12)*
*St Mark's School, Harlow, Essex*

## THE BOX

There was once a girl called Amy who was an only child. She was so lonely at nights and the weekends. She had lots of friends but they had their own little brothers and sisters to play with.

Amy sat down every day by the oak tree in her back garden and read a book. Her mother would occasionally join her and have a chat with her. One day Amy was bored of reading, she decided to ask her mum if she could buy some seeds so she could grow some flowers down by the oak tree. Her mum said yes straight away. She wanted Amy to try new things.

The next day her mum had bought her two packets of sunflower seeds. She went down to the oak tree, with her seeds and shovel, and started to dig the soil. After she had planted the first couple of seeds, she stuck her shovel in, so she could go and get a drink, when it hit something hard. She got excited by this and started to dig it up, faster and faster.

When she reached the object, she found it was a box. She lifted it out and tried to open it. It was jammed shut. She got up and went to get a knife. She came back and tried picking the lock. After an hour of trying, it finally clicked open. She opened the lid and a bright light shone. She gasped 'Oh my gosh . . .'

*Sarah Packer (14)*
*St Mark's School, Harlow, Essex*

# THE SECRET DOOR

It was so cold and deserted, that it made me shiver. I walked down the never-ending stairs. It all went dark and it was then that I realised I was all alone.

I opened the door that lead to my science class, switched on the lights and started walking towards the stock cupboard. I opened the stockroom door and there before my eyes, was something I thought I would never see! I got a bit closer and reached out my hand to touch it. It was only the class skeleton. I pushed it out of the way and started to look for the black door that everyone had been speaking about, but no one dared to go into it. There it was, the door. It was well hidden and it looked like no one had entered it for ages as it was covered in cobwebs. I pulled my jumper over my hand, and began to wipe the cobwebs away. Suddenly, from behind me, I heard voices. They seemed to be getting louder. I had to do something and quickly, as I wasn't meant to be there.

There was only one thing I could do, and that was go through the door. As I reached for the handle, my hand was shaking with fear and the voices were getting louder and louder every second. I closed the stockroom door, so no one knew I was there. I took one breath, opened the door and was gone.

*Amber Selway (14)*
*St Mark's School, Harlow, Essex*

# THE DAY THEY TOOK ME AWAY

It was a warm summer's day. I was walking home from football training, at a steady pace, not paying attention to what was around me. I was about two blocks away from my house, when in the distance I saw Sam Marshall. Sam Marshall was one of my best friends, so I was glad to see him. I called out to him, but he ignored me and walked past. I called out to him again, this time he stopped and turned around. His face was completely pale and he had a scar running all the way down the right side of his face. He was staring straight at me. I knew something was wrong straight away, because of the way he was giving me that cold stare. I asked him if he's, but he didn't reply. He stood and stared at me with the same cold stare. He began to smile at me, this scared me more than the cold stare. I felt a chill running through my body, somehow I knew I was in danger. He started walking towards me, I tried to run but I was paralysed by fear. He grabbed me, he felt cold, I tried to yell but nothing came out. He was wrapping his arms around me. At first I thought he was going to swallow me up, but I figured out he was just trying to keep me there for someone or something. All I knew was that I was in trouble . . .

*Kwasi Debrah-Nkanah (14)*
*St Mark's School, Harlow, Essex*

# NIGHT AND DAY

It was a cold, clear night, the half crescent moon was shining high up in the sky, watching a lonely girl sitting on the park bench, staring into the depths of the town pond. It was silent. She felt sure she was the only one alive in the entire world and that person was Louise Taylor. As the pond rippled gently and the trees swished and swayed in perfect harmony as if everything was moving to a beat, the beat of the wind.

Suddenly, she heard a rustling in the trees. She abruptly turned her head to see what or who was making the noise. No one was there. She had a strange sensation of being watched. Louise quickly got up and walked as fast as she could, with sweat pouring off her. The thing raced through the trees, as it came after her. '*Argh*' She screamed as the earth rushed at her. She had tripped on an old pipe. She could feel blood dripping down her face. Quickly, she got to her feet and ran for her life. She heard it running after her too. It was too dark to see who or what it was.

'*Argh!*' She screamed as she woke up, what a scary dream, she thought to herself, as she headed to the bathroom. As she walked in and looked into the mirror, she saw something which was all too familiar, the same bloodied cut on her forehead. She collapsed as the realisation that last night wasn't a dream . . . it was reality.

*Joanna Bergh  (14)*
*St Mark's School, Harlow, Essex*

## THE MYSTERY TEDDY

Sophie was slowly unpacking her toys from the big cardboard box in the middle of her new room. She had just moved into the old house at the end of Creepers Lane. She was so excited about her new home that she didn't notice the old brown stool with a scraggy looking teddy bear sitting on it, in the corner of the room.

As she was arranging her toys, she stumbled across the old bear. She picked it up and examined it carefully before putting it back where it came from.

'Sophie, time for bed,' called up her mum from the bottom of the stairs, 'I'll be up to tuck you in.'

Sophie got undressed and climbed into bed. Her mum soon came up to say goodnight. Sophie turned to her mum and said, 'You see that bear over there?'
'What, this one?' questioned her mum.
'Yes, is that yours?' she asked.
'No, I've never seen it before,' she replied, 'well, goodnight.' Her mum placed the bear on her bedside table and turned off the light.
'Goodnight Mum,' said Sophie.

When Sophie woke, she turned to look at the bear, but to her astonishment, it was gone. She sat up and looked around the room, and saw that the bear had back on the stool.

Whilst making her bed, she took the bear and placed it between the blankets. She went downstairs to eat her breakfast, thinking her mum must have moved it. She later returned to her room, to find the bear had once again moved. She stared at it and the bear suddenly turned it's head and winked at her, then turned back.

She snatched the bear from the stool and ran downstairs and put it in the bin at the end of the driveway. She then ran back to her room and watched it get carted away in the dustman's lorry. 'Go haunt someone else,' said Sophie, turning away from the window.

*Lisa Adnitt (14)*
*St Mark's School, Harlow, Essex*

## A New Beginning

I start a new beginning in England. I am 14 years old. I am a Malaysian. I used to live in the city of Selangor. I have been studying in Malaysia for ten years already. The studying systems in Malaysia and in London are quite similar. The only difference is that we start a new term in January and end it in November. There is also a mid-term break in May. It might be different because of the time difference and the weather too. We also wear uniforms to school. It is similar because the British once ruled Malaysia.

School begins at 7.30 in the morning where the whole school gathers for a short assembly. Here, we start school at 9am. Then we return to our classes for our lessons. The students are sorted according to their ability. After four periods, we have a break, which is our only break for the whole day because we do not have lunch in school, so we usually eat or we could play games in the field. After break, we have five periods, then that's the end of the day. Nine periods seems long, but there is only a maximum of five subjects a day. We spend six hours at school, in Malaysia.

It is compulsory for every student to join a game, a club and a society of their interest. It is held every week in school. I was a member of the netball team, art club and the Red Cross society. I have been here for only three months and these are the differences I have noticed.

*Mun Loi  (14)*
*St Mark's School, Harlow, Essex*

## In The Night

The girls had a great time. Played games, phoned boys and ate chocolate! They told ghost stories and talked. Half of the night had gone and it was almost three in the morning but they were still awake. The listened to music and dared each other. Kristy had dared Claire to dance with Stacie's brother, if she didn't she had to kiss her dog! So Claire did the dare, quite unwillingly. She sat down and then it was her turn to dare someone.

'I dare Sarah, to . . .' Claire began. There was a very loud bang at the door. The girls scrambled around giggling but scared. They turned out the lights and stayed still. It was Stacie's house, she got up out of her seat and walked down the hallway to the dining room to peep out of the curtains. There was nobody there. After a while they forgot and fell asleep unaware of what could happen.

It was 8.30 in the morning and all of the girls were awake, Stacie began to tell them of a weird dream that she had. 'That knock was in it, but it kept on going on and on. Knock, knock, knock. It was scary 'cause then the door was open and . . .' Stacie was interrupted.
The girls were laughing telling her what a stupid dream to have. Although it couldn't have been stupid, could it? Erin ran to the stairs to answer her mobile, when the door . . . it was open!

*Stacey Barbet  (14)*
*St Mark's School, Harlow, Essex*

## NIGHTMARE

It was a dark and dismal night. The raging clouds swirled above the house rumbling and roaring.

I walked up the grand staircase and I saw an old wooden door at the top. The stairs creaked as I stepped carefully onto them. I looked down at the large eerie ballroom below. Everywhere smelt musty and the tiny sounds echoed around me, filling my ears. My heart pounded.

I placed my trembling hand onto the latch and gradually I opened the door. Screeching as it moved, the door opened to show a sinister deserted attic. Every inch of the space was covered with cobwebs. I gasped. The candle glowed and flickered in the coldness as a breeze gusted through the room. Cloth swayed over a broken window. I felt myself shiver. I stopped. There was something about this place that made me feel hesitant and apprehensive.

In the corner of the attic I saw a large mirror. I wiped my finger across the glass clearing away the dust and dirt. As I looked up a bright glowing light gleamed from the mirror lighting up the whole attic. A young girl stood in the image. I paused. Her pale face looked distressed. She was dressed in Victorian style clothes. Suddenly moaning and crying raged throughout the room. It was like everywhere had turned evil. The image of the girl started to fade away. 'Save me please,' screamed the girl as she vanished into the mirror. Wind hurled past. The candle crashed against the floor, pouring the attic into darkness.

*Gemma Buck  (14)*
*St Mark's School, Harlow, Essex*

# THE CARE OF KATIE

After the double tragedy that Katie Johns (7) suffered, everyone thought she would be put into a loving and caring home, but now Social Services have reported that 'loving' parent Mrs Martin has been abusing her. Will little Katie ever find the happiness she used to know?

On 28th January 2000, Mrs Johns was diagnosed with cancer and on the 8th July she sadly died.

Four months later, on 12th November, Katie Johns, five at the time, was taken from her father, Mr Johns, due to a mental breakdown, and put into a foster home under the care of Mrs Martin.

For two years Katie lived quite happily in her new home, but on 25th March 2002, Katie came to school with a small bruise on her face. When questioned about it by a teacher at her school, Katie's reply was 'I made Mummy mad!'

The week after Katie came into school again, this time with a large cut on her forehead. This time when asked what happened, Katie replied, 'I was a bad girl'.

This time the teacher reported these marks to the headmaster.

Katie was checked up on every day and in the space of two weeks, Katie received several cuts and many bruises.

When the police were informed of the abuse, Katie was immediately taken from the care of Mrs Martin and placed into The Whitebridge Children's Home, where she has been staying for the past three weeks.

As the days pass by and Katie is staying in the home, an inquiry is taking place to find out why such a tragic thing could happen to such a vulnerable girl.

*Stephanie Difrancesco (13)*
*St Mark's School, Harlow, Essex*

## SOMEONE'S IN TROUBLE!

Chris came panting frantically up the street and by the expression on his face, he looked as though he was about to faint. I looked at him, expecting him to stop and talk to me but instead, he just ran past. Why didn't he stop, I thought to myself. Maybe he didn't see me. I could just make out where he was so I yelled as loud as I could, 'Chris.' It was no good, he couldn't hear me. The strange thing was, he kept looking back in my direction, but didn't acknowledge me. I felt as if something was wrong and I was right. About half a minute later, whilst slowly making my way down the street, a gang of boys approached me.

'Oi, you!' one of them yelled. 'Did you see some stupid midget run past here?' he said in a deep voice.

'Why?' I asked. I now realise that was a stupid thing to say but I wanted to know what he had done.

'Did you see him?' he reiterated in an angry manner.

I didn't know what they were going to do to him and I didn't want to find out. 'Umm, I think he went that way,' I told them whilst pointing to my right.

'If you see him, tell him we're gonna beat him so badly, he won't be able to sit down on his backside ever again.'

I pointed in the wrong direction, which seemed like the right thing to do after what I'd just been told, and the boys believed me. Surely, whatever Chris had done, couldn't have been that bad, could it?

*Prashant Thakrar (14)*
*St Mark's School, Harlow, Essex*

# THE NOISE HEARD ALL AROUND THE WORLD

On a cold winter's day the 19th of February, the noise that was heard around the world arose. The CT tower in Montreal, Canada, was severely damaged due to the promise of the Britains to blow up a major Canadian building. The Canadians provoked the British by bombing Westminster Abbey. In retaliation the British blew up the CT tower. Many lives were taken including the prime minister of Canada. The American government has stated that they will take this very seriously as many innocent American civilians were killed. The President of the USA has promised to take action on the British citizens. This may be the beginning of World War III. This could invite many other nations to fight for the British. These include Russia, China, Australia and India.

The Americans flew over to Britain and saw over two million war-fit soldiers fighting for Britain. (Most of them were not Britains.) The war lasted only for two years. There were no victors and losers from this war, but America and Britain realised that they were both good friends before this war was started.

Two months after war had ended the president of the USA was shot and died. The assailant was found to be a Canadian general. He was questioned 'Why?'
He said, 'Because he stopped the war with Britain.' He was killed two months later by electric chair. He was named as Francais Marcos, born in Canada, died in the USA.

*Lewis Quinlin  (13)*
*St Mark's School, Harlow, Essex*

## THE BUTTON

There was a girl called Stacey and she was very polite and well mannered, it ran in the family. Her neighbour was a mysterious and friendly old man.

Stacey was playing in the garden when her neighbour called her over and handed her a skateboard. She smiled and said, 'I can't ride skateboards.'
'Ahh my dear girl,' he answered, 'this is no ordinary skateboard. It gives you wishes,' he said.
She looked at him rather pathetically!
'No, seriously, try it. Put you finger on the left back screw and make any wish you want and it will happen.'
'OK! Erm Orios,' she chanted and *poof* it appeared. She shouted 'Wow!' and stood there quite amazed. Her cousin Jim walked in showing off his new skateboard, 'Look what I have.'
'Yeah so, I have one too.'
'Ha, is that home-made?' he smirked.
'*No!*' she shouted. She showed him the powers and he was also amazed. He walked in with Stacey, she stopped in front of her mum and said, 'Wanna swap?'
Stacey's mum was nodding at her and she had to say yes. 'OK,' she sighed.

When they went home Stacey ran into the garden and told Alfie about it and he went in the shed with her skateboard and kept her waiting. He finally came out and it is exactly the same as the other one, but newer.

Meanwhile, back in the car Jim tried for the sixth time and ended up with a very sore finger!

*Yasmin Uddin (12)*
*St Mark's School, Harlow, Essex*

## THE ABANDONED BOY

Deep in the forest lived a boy who was abandoned when he was six years old. He had black hair, brown eyes and a nice smile. He ate dinner with the elephants, swung with the monkeys and stole at night.

His name was Jan. He was not an ordinary boy, for when he was sitting against a wall he fell through and found a lamp. He rubbed it and out came a genie. 'You have three wishes,' said the genie.
'I want my mum and dad and I want to go home,' said Jan.

So he went home and live happily ever after.

*Laurence Ashoori  (12)*
*St Mark's School, Harlow, Essex*

## EDISON LIGHTS UP - THOMAS EDISON INVENTS THE LIGHT BULB

On Tuesday 15th April 1879 Mr Thomas Edison invented the light bulb, a revolutionary new instrument that will replace the candle. As some houses, mainly the richer ones, have electricity installed, the light bulb will hang from a special socket in the ceiling or wall. They can be obtained in different strengths. The main ones for households will be 40 watt, 60 watt and 80 watt.

The light bulb is made out of glass and metal. The screw in bit screws into the socket in the wall or the ceiling to hold it in place. The glass shell keeps the oxygen out so it can heat up without catching fire. The metal coil heats up immediately and glows, it is this that produces the light. Eventually the metal coil burns out and then snaps, so you have to buy a new light bulb every so often. When you remove or touch a light bulb be careful because it will be red-hot after it has been used. The light bulb will be turned on by a switch on the wall that will connect and disconnect the circuit.

Light bulbs are obtainable through these nationwide stores, Liam's Electrics, Tesco, Spar, Wickes, Do It All and Halfords. Standard bulbs will cost around three and tuppence.

*Jamie Reilly (12)*
*St Mark's School, Harlow, Essex*

## SUNSET PARADISE

One day a family decided to buy a boat and go out to sea. The family were called the Luckys. Their names were Marni, who was the mum, Barney, who was the dad and Emily and Danielle, who were sisters and were both 12.

They set sail from the coast of Spain in their brand new shiny white boat called Sunset Paradise, because it had a tiny picture of a sunset on it. The family didn't realise that they were going to hit a storm.
'Mum, is the storm going to get much rougher than this?' said Emily, shouting.
'We don't know love, that's why we're trying to find Minorca's docks so we can rest there, but we're not sure if we will be allowed to yet!' said Marni, sounding very worried.
'Oh no,' said Barney, 'the boat is tipping.'
'It's going over!' screamed Danielle.
Before they knew it the boat was tipped over and then the Sunset Paradise sank to the bottom of the Mediterranean Sea.

The family was washed ashore to a beautiful island. Barney woke up on warm yellow sand and started calling his family. 'Marni! Emily! Danielle! Where are you?'
'I'm over here!' called Emily.
'I'm over here!' yelled Marni.
'I'm over here!' yelled Danielle.
They all ran to each other. Barney said happily, 'Thank goodness we're all right.' Then they turned around and saw the most beautiful island in the world. They named the island Sunset Paradise after the sunken boat.

*Isobelle Ancient*
*St Mark's School, Harlow, Essex*

## A DAY IN THE LIFE OF DAVID BECKHAM

I woke up one morning. It was a Saturday. First of all I had breakfast in bed, which my wife made while I was watching TV. After I ate my breakfast I got ready for football training. I went football training. The coach said I was doing really well since I had a broken foot.

After football training I went out to watch Victoria sing. After that I went out with Victoria and we took Brooklyn with us to get some clothes and we went for a meal in a restaurant.

*Rees Foxwell (12)*
*St Mark's School, Harlow, Essex*

## BEST FRIENDS ARE ALWAYS THERE!

'Hi Stephanie, do you want to come up the town with me, Laura and Adel?'

'Yeah, sure Stacey, what time are you going?'

'One o'clock, come to mine, see ya.'

'Bye.'

Everyone was at mine by one o'clock. We walked to the town, looking in all the shops, trying on clothes. We went in the arcade and had loads of fun. We decided that everyone could sleep at mine, so we started walking back to my house. When Laura stepped into the road, suddenly a car came speeding round the corner. Nobody saw this, except Stephanie, who stepped into the road and pushed Laura as hard as she could, when suddenly the car hit her. Adel and I started screaming. We didn't know whether she was alive or dead. Then I saw Laura get up. She was on the other side of the road. Laura looked down and burst into tears, screaming. The driver got out and rang an ambulance. Adel and I looked down and saw Stephanie under the car pouring with blood. She was alive, but didn't look like she was going to last long.

The ambulance arrived, they got Stephanie out from under the car and drove her with Adel, Laura and I to the hospital. They asked for her details so they could get in touch with her parents. The police asked how it happened and they questioned the driver, to see if he was over the limit.

The girls and I brought Stephanie a dog because she had always wanted one and it was a thank you gift from Laura, for saving her life. The man got a fine as he was over the limit. Stephanie got better. Now we are best friends more than ever.

Never drink and drive!

*Kylie Airey  (13)*
*St Mark's School, Harlow, Essex*

# A Day In The Life Of A Teenager!

'Daisy, are you ready for school yet?'

'No Mum!'

'Hurry up otherwise you'll be late for school!'

Every day had the same routine, Mum shouting, going to school, having lunch, being bored to death by the teachers, then came home time and by 7.30pm I was asleep in bed. What a life eh! Well, that was before I had got a boyfriend. We're perfect together and it all started at my best friend's 14th birthday. We were playing truth or dare and his truth was, who would he love to go out with? Yes, you guessed it, it was me!

When we got back to school he kept bugging me and asking if I wanted to go to the cinema with him. I don't know how many times I'd said no but he just wouldn't leave me alone. It felt like an annoying bluebottle just asking to be swatted round the head! Any time now he was going to get a punch in the mouth, until, well until I realised he wasn't that bad after all. I finally said yes and we went to the cinema together.

Things went well for those first couple of months, but that was all before we had a massive argument. He thought that I said to him that he played football like a girl! Doesn't matter now, he dumped me, all over that stupid argument. I'd only said he plays football really well, see, well a girl rhymes. He obviously misheard me!

Now all I hear from school is the teachers giving me homework every second of the day. The same old routine is back again!

*Louise Spicer  (13)*
*St Mark's School, Harlow, Essex*

# DEAR DIARY

Today was one of the silliest days ever because I broke up with one of my (supposed) friends. Next thing I know she's run off complaining to our head of year. Now we've been told (my best friend and I) that we have to go and see him at lunchtime, because of the stupidest incident. To me that just shows that she isn't woman enough to stand up for herself and sort out her own problems. I reckon that I will get the blame, as I always do.

I didn't want to go, but I don't think I have a choice because I would probably end up with a detention or something.

We are always breaking up (my friends and I) and I think it's getting a bit out of hand. This problem is meant to be getting sorted out, but it never gets sorted. The teacher always goes on and on about it, but no one takes much notice because by the time we leave we're still not friends.

I'm not sure how I'm feeling at the moment because I feel that I have all the emotions coming to me at once. I don't know what to do about it, but all I know is that I'm not going to say anything to her, I'm just going to walk away from her. We might make up, but then again we might not, although I hope we do.

*Amy Tovell (13)*
*St Mark's School, Harlow, Essex*

## THEY TELL THE TEACHER

'Another dull morning!' exclaimed Amy. It was Monday morning and the sky was grey. All the clouds looked as if they were going to fall down. Amy turned over to look at her clock. She never looked her best in the mornings. 'Golly! It's eight o'clock!' she screamed. Amy jumped out of bed and leapt in the shower, sung her everyday song 'Wild Thing' and got dressed. Amy was a very shy girl. She had big brown teddy bear eyes and brown bushy hair. Her socks were always pulled up to her knee caps and she dressed smartly for school!

When the first bell rang for lesson, she ran into the school's rebel Jamie Clarke. Jamie is two foot tall, with spiked up blond hair, who always wears a cheeky grin and never does as he's told! He is a teacher's worst nightmare, he is very pale and scrawny. He hardly ever comes to school. 'Watch it bushy! There is precious stuff in this bag!' screamed Jamie.
Amy was shaking, she ran all the way to English.

Jamie walked into the classroom and placed something under her chair. It was small and transparent. He then announced a plan of what was going to happen when Miss Foster walked in. She was a small thin lady who wears droopy earrings, with a very stern face.

Miss Foster opened the door and gave us a five minute lecture, like she always does and then it happened. She slowly pulled out her chair and we all heard a crack and a loud ripping noise. Miss Foster went all red and everyone kept shouting 'You smelly thing!'
All of a sudden a deep voice boomed 'Everyone *outside now!'* Everyone jumped up and scrambled outside.
Two girls immediately said 'Jamie is responsible for that!'

Nobody forgot that day and since then the two girls have gone through nothing but hassle, even at the age of 22.

*Toni Beard  (13)*
*St Mark's School, Harlow, Essex*

# THE WORLD CUP 2010, AFRICA

I couldn't believe it! I'd worked hard all season to make the team and I did it. I had a feeling I would be in the squad. With eleven Premiership goals, and thirty assists to my name, I had a reason to be confident. Not bad for a midfielder.

The tournament flew by. We scraped through a hard group 'D' (also named group of death), by managing a draw against one of the hosts, Senegal beating Portugal 2-1 and drawing 1-1 with Chile. I scored a free kick to bring us a draw against Chile, so that secured my place in the starting eleven.

And now we're here. In the semi-finals of the World Cup, we drew 2-2 with Italy after extra time, so it meant penalties. I didn't bother listening to the brief team talk. I just stood at the halfway line, knowing I had to take a penalty. Flashbacks of penalties missed as a kid came flooding back to me. I blocked them with thoughts of a World Cup final.

After two penalties it was my turn. It seemed like a mile to the penalty spot, but it still wasn't long enough! As I placed the ball, I didn't know where I was going to put it. My fingers were numb and tension was running wild in my body. I took a short run up and before I knew it I'd hit it. The sound of a ball hitting the net was sweet music to my ears.

My closest friend on the team missed the last penalty, which sent us out. I held a brave face and comforted him, 'Only another four years,' I said, 'only another four years!'

*Harry Doyle  (13)*
*St Mark's School, Harlow, Essex*

## SWIMMING THE TUNNELS

He saw a murky light. It gave him hope. Only a bit of hope, but it was enough to power him a bit more. Yet his arms and legs refused to move, just dithering around helplessly. He couldn't stretch them far but they were starting to get into motion. The air started climbing back up his throat. He pulled himself along with pure exasperation. His legs started to work faster and stretch. Slowly flailing them about then faster, but it didn't help.

He was getting disorientated. His brain needed fresh oxygen. It started to spin. It went all bubbly in his vision. The tips of his body were tingling, but this feeling its way deeper into his body. It felt nice, but it wasn't the thing to do. He would not get KO'd. His stomach started screaming filling with air. The water foaming up his nose.

He slowly pushed his head out of the water. He got some air. It didn't help. He had forgotten how to breathe, his lungs were new to the concept of air. He struggled out, pulling himself out depleting his energy supply completely. He felt heavier. The pressure was higher here, so he felt weaker.

He sat facing the water appreciating how beautiful it looked, the water twinkling off the surface and some of the rocks. It felt good looking down because his neck had been craned by all the time he was in the water. He felt like he was gonna puke but he had nothing to puke up. Completely exhausted he laid back looking at the blue sky with a few clouds he closed his eyes laughing. He had proved himself.

*Qasim Ali (14)*
*St Mark's School, Harlow, Essex*

## BEWARE

As the corpse-like hand crawled creepily up Brooklyn's bed, Brooklyn had no idea that it was anything inhuman. Thinking it was Tilly the dog, she called sleepily, 'Here, Tilly.' But as the hand got nearer her neck, she realized it wasn't the dog and as the hand wrapped itself around her throat, she started to scream with all her might.

As here voice grew hoarse from all the screaming, her mum and dad came running into the room.

'What's wrong? What's wrong?' her mum asked, extremely worried.

'The hand . . . it tried to strangle me,' Brooklyn said, trying not to cry but the shock was too much for her.

'What hand?' her dad asked, concerned.

'It was at my throat,' she replied weakly.

But as quickly as it came, the hand seemed to have vanished.

An hour later Brooklyn was finally asleep, but her mum and dad were downstairs discussing her.

'I think she should see a psychiatrist,' Arthur said.

'But why, honey? It seems to have started since we've moved here,' Jane replied, her brow furrowed in anxiety.

Suddenly, the lights went out and they were plunged into darkness. As a cold draft wrapped itself around them, time seemed to stop and go backwards. A murderous scream, an image of hacked up bodies . . . Arthur and Jane were sitting there rigid with terror watching this horror.

The next day came bright and cheerful, but in the Derby's household, all was deathly still. In the living room were Arthur and Jane, frozen dead with terror. Upstairs Brooklyn was hanging by her neck with the telephone wire, her body swinging lifelessly to and fro. The sound of evil laughter broke the silence and as the bodies were stored under the floorboards. Fear waits for his new victims to move in . . .

*Holly Grady  (14)*
*St Paul's Catholic School, Milton Keynes, Buckinghamshire*

## MIND TRAP

The hum of the laser got louder and louder as it inched its way closer and closer to my body. Cold sweat covered my brow, my heartbeat was thumping at the speed of a hummingbird's wing. Still the laser moved closer and closer, getting louder and louder.

My leg was torn open. Hot blood was pouring freely onto the shiny, steel table. The cut was so deep that the bone began to crack and split. *Snap!* I screamed in agonising pain as the laser slowly moved up my leg, eating and burning the tissue as it went.

The laser decreased its speed. It crept up my thigh bone and up the side of my body. It came level to about my stomach and it sped right across to the centre, just above my belly button. It had soon passed my stomach, slowly sucking the life out of me. It approached my heart and began to slowly slice part of it off. The pain was like thousands of knives and blades stabbing into me.

The laser moved up my neck up through my jaw. My lower jaw fell off and bounced on the unseen floor. The hum of the laser was deafening. A final thought crossed my mind, I am going to *die!* Until . . .

*Luke Atkins  (14)*
*St Paul's Catholic School, Milton Keynes, Buckinghamshire*

## THE LAST GLIMPSE

I heard a quiet *ting*, like a small bell ringing as the lift came to a halt. I felt a judder as it stopped. I waited patiently for the silver doors to slide open. Five minutes went by and the doors still hadn't opened. I began to feel the uneasy pangs of worry, starting in my stomach and chilling up my spine, as I heard screams of panic-stricken people flying to the exits for their lives in horror.

Now I was completely enveloped in a veil of terror as I heard a rumbling grumble and at first I thought it was thunder, but then I heard a crackle of something burning. More screams. I looked to my right and saw the silver buttons flashing like small stars blazing, with clouds of black, putrid smoke, fizzing and squeezing out between the buttons. Frantically, I searched for a way out. Scrabbling, I began trying to claw my way out of the corner with my fingers, as gallons of decayed gas replaced fresh air. Fresh air - I wish! I tried to breathe, but my lungs inhaled the decomposing poison and I tried to cough out, only failing and inhaling more.

I listened intently. The only sound I heard was the desperate people outside. But there was another sound - a creaking sound, like a wire under immense pressure. It was the wire holding the lift up. It was snapping! Desperately, I thumped at the door, then turned to the buttons. I began pounding them as though trying to find an emergency exit. The gas still billowing out, I put a tissue over my mouth, coughing. I heard a loud *snap* and felt a jolt as the lift plummeted towards the ground.

I was forced to the floor and I grabbed onto whatever I could. My ears popped and I swallowed hard. I looked up. Maybe I could get out that way? It's no use, I'll never reach it!

I closed my eyes. Ready. *Whoosh!* I felt a great smack on my side and I flew into the air. I landed in a crumpled heap with pieces of silver-sprayed metal around me and a great fire behind me. Slowly, everything started to go black. My eyes closed and I lay there, pulverised, wallowing in blood . . . my blood.

*Chloe Brown  (13)*
*St Peter's School, Huntingdon, Cambridgeshire*

## AWAY WITH THE FAIRIES

'Look Mum, it's a fairy thing,' claimed an innocent, small boy, pointing at a sculpture as he was marched past.

'Well, at least someone knows what that thing is, eh Helen?' chuckled the curator.

'Yeah,' she thought, giving a mild smile, 'at least somebody did.'

Helen's workbooks, journals, any piece of paper were covered in doodles, etches and sketches of pixies, fairies and other endless pages of magical creatures. Life for her revolved around magic. There had hardly been a day in her youth that she hadn't produced some fantastical creation. But it didn't stop. Life's responsibilities were taken on board, but within her there was also the little child, always ready to run back to the fairies. This child had lain dormant, but had woken every now and again.

As an artist, Helen was free to express what the child thought with no obligation to anyone else. No one could question the things that didn't exist. But they did.

Fame was a long time coming, if criticism counted as fame. As it persisted, every time a new piece was presented, she asked herself *why?* The young boy made the answer clear. Her perception of art meant everything to her. Obviously, not everyone could see it. Her obsession was the problem, it was the failure.

She left the museum. It must stop. No more fairies, not one.

*Tanya Rowland (15)*
*The Cedars Upper School, Bedfordshire*

# UGLY AND ANNOYING

'I hate her.'
We watched as she walked a little further ahead of us, her shoes scraping against the dry mud, sending little clouds of dust into the air.
'You do, huh?' Rachel kicked at a stone.

Rachel was a new girl. I was the one who got to show her around, introduce her to people. I liked her. She was pretty and funny, and everyone had labelled her 'nice'. Tricky thing to live up to, I always thought.

It was a dry, humid day. We were walking back from school and Emily was wandering ahead of us. Emily is this girl whom everyone hates. She's ugly and she's annoying.
'No one likes her.'
We'd reached the end of the field, standing in front of the road. Emily looked at us nervously.
'No one at all?' Rachel enquired.
I shrugged. '*I* heard, even her *parents* don't like her!'
Emily had obviously overheard. She stepped out on the curb, a car shot past, and she started to cross. But she'd misjudged the distance of the nearest car. She was running and it was going fast, and we all realized too late.
'No! Emily!' Rachel shrieked, even though she'd said earlier that she didn't like her either. She ran out to them.
'Emily! Oh my goodness!'
The driver got out of the car and bent down next to her. Other cars were stopping to see what was happening, even though it was as plain as day.
I was just staring in horror . . .
The people who'd hit her were Emily's parents.

*Sarah Barrett (14)*
*The Cedars Upper School, Bedfordshire*

# A FIELD OF POPPIES

I was under the rule of Captain Justin Matthews. He ruled our platoon with a strong iron fist. There would be no slackers when he was in charge. We were in the middle of the war, Jerries on one side, us on the other.

The guns thundered on, shelling our opponents. We had heard rumours that both sides were meeting to discuss the ending of the war. It was very hopeful that this long, perilous war would end soon. We would have clean, fresh air again, rather than the foul stench of rotting corpses.
'I hope this war ends soon,' said Lieutenant Bradshaw.
'Yeah, I agree. I want to go home and see my baby daughter,' replied Private Salter.
'Oh, come on, pull yourselves together. Are we men, or a bunch of pansies?' said Captain Matthews. 'We are not going to let this war get to us. If the Jerries can stand it, surely we can?'
'Yeah!' shouted everyone.
'We will not be the ones to give in first, understand?'
'Yeah!' they all cheered.
'Now come on, it's almost our turn to shoot some Jerries,' said the Captain. 'The one to shoot the most wins.'
They all went running behind the Captain.
'Come on Walker,' said Salter.
'Okay!' I replied.
He ran on and I followed. We grabbed our guns, leapt up onto the platform, assumed position and fired. I think I got about three or so. The Lieutenant got at least seven and was boasting about it all through the break we had after cleaning and loading the guns.

I couldn't stop thinking about my wife Sophie and my little daughter Emily. How sad they looked because I had gone off. She's probably thinking about when I will come home, or even *whether* I will come home. I can't even bear to think about how sad they would be or the look on their faces, or even how Sophie would tell Emily that the father she'd known for only four years was dead. The thought sickened me.

It was now lunchtime. We went to our dugouts, got our sacks and opened them. I fished around through the mouldy and mushy rations. I found a tin of bully beef. With great difficulty I opened it and feasted on the cold, mushy meat.

'I heard that only half a mile down the trench from here, there was an attack. It was shelled and several dugouts caved in, with no survivors,' said one of the fellow soldiers.

'Some of us are trying to eat here. It's bad enough with the corpses, let alone you trying to tell us another one of your stories where there are no survivors and blood everywhere,' said another.

'Just ignore them,' said Salter.

Salter was one of my only friends down in the trenches. He was a kind, caring and generous person and not only that, but my friend.

Three days later, we heard it. The end of the war would be in two days at 11 o'clock. The platoon had arranged to have a big celebration tonight where we would listen to the radio and play games - generally have fun.

It all went well. I won a few noughts and crosses games. The Lieutenant boasted some more about killing another fifteen Jerries today, but nothing could have prepared us for what came next!

Captain Matthews came in white with fear. We stopped our games and celebrating. The Captain gulped and said, 'T-t-tomorrow is the b-b-big *(gulp)* push!'

Everyone was dead. I was hanging on to what life I had left. The Captain had said, 'On the whistle, company will advance.' He then blew his whistle. Shaking with fear we leapt over the top and like many others who had stood in our place, faced the enemy's blazing weapons.

We vanished! The platoon was gone. The Captain was gone. All my friends gone. I was gone.

*Glyn Spencer  (14)*
*The Highfield School, Hertfordshire*

## SHORT STORY

It was a cold, dark and scary night. Along the winding and weaving paths it was silent, like it is in church on Sundays. The air was vile, the wind was heavy. Bushes and trees rustled in the wind. I heard scary footsteps and noises echoing in the background. I came up to the cemetery gates. I felt a shiver run down my spine. A leaf rubbed slowly against my face with an evil feeling something would happen.

I moaned and groaned like a whining dog. I went through the cemetery trying not to step where anyone had been buried. I went slowly and quietly through the gate to the other side, when I heard a voice and felt an icy hand on my shoulder.
I wanted to run, I wanted to hide, but I couldn't because the hand was gripping onto me so tightly.
'Who is it?' I asked, shaking.
'It is the ghost of Ebenezer Howard,' replied the croaky voice.
'What do you want with me?' I cried.
'I am going to take you to my grave so I can put you in it, and so I can get my spirit back and be alive,' laughed Howard.
'But I am only 12 years old, so you had more life than me,' I muttered.
'Well not anymore,' he announced.
I felt like a mouse compared to him. We walked slowly back through the cemetery gates an we finally came to his grave. He slowly took his hand off my shoulder, so he obviously thought that I was going to stay put. But he was wrong. I ran back the way I had come, looking behind me just to check if he was coming. I jumped over the cemetery gates and kept on running.

At long last, I thought I had lost him, but instead of him being behind me, he was in front of me. How could that have happened?
'I've got you now, little girl, haven't I?'
'Oh my, how did you do that?' I asked nervously.
'Well, I am a ghost silly,' he answered.

I didn't know what to do now. He grabbed my hand and he also grabbed me behind my neck which hurt very much and his hands were cold. I was doomed wasn't I? He walked me back slowly through the woods, down the roads and back into the cemetery. I was going to be buried alive. How was I going to escape? I felt sick. I was shaking in my boots. We walked slowly past all the graves, benches and trees. So many people were buried here and one of them was going to be me! We went past my mother's grave.

'Can I quickly say goodbye to my mum? She died a long time ago,' I muttered shyly.

'Well go on then, but be very quick,' he replied angrily.

I took a few minutes to say goodbye to her and I heard her voice in my head saying 'Be careful Claire, be careful.' It faded away after a while and I got up an turned around slowly. He took my wrist and grabbed my neck again. We walked for a while, but he couldn't find his grave. Suddenly, we were in the air and I was flying. Well, he was lifting me. This was so cool! Although I was still very scared. We finally saw his grave and with a crash to the floor, we were sitting right beside his grave.

He shouted at me saying, 'Dig girl, dig.'

I was exhausted by the time I got to the bottom.

'Well girl, this is where you are supposed to get in the grave,' he informed me.

My heart was beating hard. I felt like a horse being captured by evil men. I thought I was going to faint. I got into the grave and he covered me with all of the mud and soil. Now that I was buried, he had turned back to life and I had been buried alive!

*Kirstie Robson (12)*
*The Highfield School, Hertfordshire*

## OUT OF THIS WORLD

I looked at Emma. She winked. I looked at Gary, who was on my right. He was staring out of the window. I just rolled my eyes, then kept them fixed on the door as our first victim walked in.

She was an old woman who seemed to be as gentle as a lamb. Perfect.

You see, our teacher was away on a fabulous tropical holiday in Hawaii, as her new husband's surprise honeymoon. So, supply teachers would be taking our lessons. Poor defenceless supplies - *all* week!

My motto for supplies is - *They come in smiling, they come out crying!* With the help of my two best friends, I've managed to uphold that motto for three years now! Admittedly, there have been times when we've been caught, but usually we are quite sly and successful.

So, this kind, old woman, Mrs Deerhant her name was, was probably one of the easiest victims we had ever had.

Emma went up to her and started asking her questions about her family, as she wrote on the chalky blackboard. Mrs Deerhant answered politely to every one. Then Emma 'accidentally' knocked the glass of water onto her lap.

'Look everybody! Miss has wet herself!' Emma bellowed, laughing.

Mrs Deerhant then rushed out quickly with a beetroot-red face.

Altogether she lasted approximately ten minutes! Our best score yet!

The next day a man stepped into our territory and we were prepared for it. Totally prepared.

That day it was Gary's turn to trouble the teacher. We stared at Mr Rogers. Firstly, we had used the oldest trick in the book - the whoopee cushion. Everything seemed to be in slow motion as he plonked himself down straight on top of the chair, in which we had placed our weapon.

'Ha, ha!' The class laughed and laughed.

'Very funny children. Now can we please start the lesson?'

The class calmed down and we started maths.

'Right then,' Mr Rogers began, 'who knows the answer?'

I stuck my hand up high and with the other, gave Emma the thumbs up sign.

'OK then . . .'

'Emma, Sir,' I told him, and nobody disputed it, even though they knew perfectly well it was Sarah.

'Fine, Emma,' he said.

'Yes Sir?' answered the real Emma.

'Ah! Are there two Emmas in this class?'

'No Sir, just me,' I replied.

'But - but you just said that you were Emma!'

'I am,' Emma bluntly stated.

'So which of you is the real Emma?'

'I am!' we chorused.

'I *cannot* teach under these conditions.' And he picked up his briefcase and left.

I smirked. The type of smirk you see the bad guys in films have, just as the bomb's about to go off, or the hero's about to be chopped into tiny pieces.

The next day, I and the rest of the class were chatting away excitedly, waiting for our next teacher. I suddenly whipped my head round as the door handle rattled and a young, blonde woman stepped in with a flourish.

'Good morning children. My name is Miss Dewberry and I will be teaching you today.'

She seemed so nice, that it was a shame to embarrass her. But she was smarter than I thought. She picked up her coffee cup and removed the fake fly, then went to the sink and carefully wiped one finger smoothly - as though it was glass - over the soap. Then she examined the ink left on her finger. The class looked dumbstruck as she went about the classroom removing and examining the tricks we had so carefully placed.

'Right. Now that's done, on to science.'

I just slumped in my chair, pouting. It seemed so unfair.

When I looked up later on, there she was looking straight back at me with an evil, lopsided smile and her eyes seemed so unreal. I quickly looked around to see if anyone else had seen her, but no one had.

A couple of hours later, it was raining heavily and there was a huge clap of thunder. Miss Dewberry went very pale. I watched as she was telling Henry Horn off, but keeping an eye on the window nervously. When she had finished, Henry looked frightened by the scolding he had just received. Emma and I looked at each other and raised our eyebrows. Then suddenly, as quick as the queen gets a new hat, a lightning bolt struck through the sky, leaving Miss Dewberry a quivering jelly, quite literally.

A pink blob of ooze sat there on the floor lifelessly, where she had been standing and it wobbled furiously as I picked it up. It felt as unreal as her eyes had been. At that very same moment, a second lightning bolt lit up the playground, taking with it Miss Dewberry, and I stood there with nothing but air touching my fingers.

None of the other classes believed us, of course. They thought it was some wild excuse we'd concocted. Although saying that our teacher turned into a pink blob of jelly and disappeared *isn't* the most believable excuse ever.

Since then, I haven't messed about with teachers. I've found that some are kind and down-to-earth, but some are just totally out of this world!

*Rebecca Barnes (12)*
*The Highfield School, Hertfordshire*

## DENNIS STRIKES

*Dennis strikes again at a psychologist.*

Today at 1pm, Dennis was taken to a psychologist to find out why he is so naughty:
'He started off fine. I thought I was going to find out why he is so naughty, but he lashed out at me', said the scared psychologist to the press.

We asked Dennis, but all he said was, 'I can't help the way I am. I was born to be a menace and forever will be a menace'.
We will continue to be on the lookout for anymore menacings, but for now guard yourselves against peashooters and slingshots. Goodbye!

*Steven Smith (12)*
*The John Bramston School, Essex*

# A Day In The Life Of A Dog

Doggy Diary:

8am Saturday morning
Yawn! I just had the most wonderful sleep. I was dreaming of giant, chewy bones. Sigh!

8.51am
Yum, yum! Forget dreaming of bones, Mummy Wilma just gave me one. I finished it in a couple of chews. I begged for another but Mummy said no. Life's so unfair!

9am
Daddy Jeffrey said that since I had been so good at breakfast, he would take me for my walkies early.

10.22am
Walkies was tremendous fun. Daddy took me to the park. Guess how many cats I saw? Go on, guess. I saw three! I chased them all, they then yowled at me and ran away. Tee hee. But I think all that chasing has worn me out. I'm going to have an afternoon nap.

12.07pm
Mummy just gave me some Pedigree Chum dog food, but while I was eating she told me the most horrible news. My auntie Sally is coming to visit this afternoon! I don't know what to do. Maybe I could hide upstairs, but knowing aunt Sally, she would just come and find me.
I mean, I like having people fuss over me and give me lots of attention, but aunt Sally gives me too much! She is always stroking my face, tweaking my ears and holding me tight, giving me big hugs. To top it off, she gives me stupid names like *Cuddlekins* and *Mr Whiskers*, when she knows very well what my name is.

1.33pm
After over an hour of panic, aunt Sally finally called and said that she couldn't make it due to roadworks. I tried hard to mope and look upset, but it didn't really work.
All this worry has made me tired again. I'm going to have a nice long sleep.

5.47pm

I've just woken up to the sound of Daddy shouting, 'Walkie time!' at the top of his voice, and I don't need asking twice!

7.05pm

Daddy and I are back from our walk, and are both tired out. Mummy just gave me my tea and I gobbled it down quickly. I have no more to say, so I think I'll go to bed. Night, night.

PS: I wonder what I'll dream of tonight? Yesterday was bones, so maybe today will be cats. I sure hope so.

*Charlotte Deighton (12)*
*The John Bramston School, Essex*

## DRAGON SLAYERS

There was a very greedy dragon who would destroy villages and take all the money and food. Gradually he destroyed kingdoms. He lived in a cave in the mountains. Brave knights went to fight him, but never returned. If they did return, shortly after they would die of injuries. Sometimes people sent a man out with cows, so he did not attack their villages.

There was one man, however, who came back from the dragon's lair with loads of gold. When the dragon returned he was furious. He followed the man's footsteps, but the villagers were waiting for him. They fired arrows and threw spears, but they just bounced off his thick, scaly hide. The dragon flew into a rage and slaughtered all the men, apart from the king and he took the king's daughter prisoner.

The king was desperate to get his precious daughter back safely. He decided to offer a quarter of his kingdom to anyone who would slay the dragon and rescue the beautiful princess.
'Hear ye, hear ye, we have an important announcement to make!' shouted the town crier. 'I, the king, will offer one quarter of my kingdom to anyone who will slay the dragon and rescue my beautiful daughter.'
Everyone just walked off muttering, 'That's not enough.'
The king didn't hear what they said.

He waited but no one came, so he asked the town crier to offer half the kingdom. He sent messengers to carry the message far and wide. There were many people who set off to fight the dragon, but none returned. They needed to chop off the dragon's gruesome head and bring back the princess, but no one succeeded.

The king gave up hope and became extremely ill, until one day five brave knights came and declared, 'We will slay the dragon!'

The five brave knights journeyed to the dragon's lair. Three of the knights distracted the dragon and two tried to kill him. One knight stabbed him and he fell to the ground. The other knight chopped off the dragon's head. With the dragon's last breath flames rushed out, killing one of the knights. The other four knights brought the beautiful princess, the dragon's gruesome head and their friend back to the king. They shared half the kingdom between them and their friend got a hero's funeral. The king got better and the five brave knights became known as 'The Dragon Slayers'.

*Dominic Burton (12)*
*The John Bramston School, Essex*

# PITTER-PATTER

Pitter-patter, pitter-patter, the rain is thumping down hard on the shop canopy. *Bang, bang, bang,* is the noise that I hear, sounding like deep drums. I looked behind and saw the man changing from a walking pace to a run. He is chasing me! I start speeding up and run down the street as fast as I can, trying to get away from him. My hair is getting very wet and my face is dripping. I stop to get my breath back and look behind to see where he is. He's very close. I try to merge in with the crowd to lose him. Yes, I think I've lost him.

I start walking down the street. I put my hand on my heart. *Thump, thump, thump,* is all I can hear. My mouth is dry. I run into the street, open my mouth and try to collect some of the rain. I stand still and look around to see what is going on. I see him. He's spotted me. He's running. I look around and see something in his hand. It looks like a knife. I am getting very scared and don't know where to run. I start to run, but trip on a hole in the road. I fall down in the wet and murky puddle. My new white top is ruined. I get up and look in a shop window. I can see my reflection and on my face I can see that I've got a cut which is bleeding. My top has dirty water splashed all over it. I am so scared that I stop to give myself up. I close my eyes and wake up to find it was a dream.

*Justin Hook (14)*
*The John Bramston School, Essex*

## POP STARS 2

Yes, that's right, another couple of nail-biting months every Saturday evening on ITV and ITV2 for digital viewers, only because Pop Stars is back! But this time they are choosing a girl group and a boy band. Auditions have already started, but if you feel like taking part, here are the dates: 24th June - Manchester 30th June - Newcastle 4th July - Leeds 8th July - Wembley 10th July - Wembley

Winner of Pop Idol 2002, Will Young, says, 'You have to hope and pray you are what the judges want'.

Winners of Pop Stars 2000, Hear'Say, said, 'It's really good fun on Pop Stars and a good experience. We hope Pop Stars 2 will bring lots of pop stars in to British music'.

*Emily Brown (12)*
*The John Bramston School, Essex*

# HELL HOUND OF GRISMOOR

It was late one night. My friend and I had been to a party. My friend left me at 12.35am and I walked the half mile across the moor alone.

I should imagine I was at least halfway home when I felt something brush past me. I froze. It was dark and the only sound was the rustling of branches on trees. It must have been the wind, I thought to myself. I carried on walking (faster this time).

Suddenly, there they were! In front of me were the glowing eyes of the hell hound. I tried to scream, but nothing came out. Suddenly it leapt onto me, its yellow fangs in my face. It drooled everywhere. At the last moment, when I thought I was done for, there was a shot from a gun. The beast ran away faster than a train. Mr Smith, who owned the turkey farm, ran over to me. His torch shone brightly in my eyes. He helped me up and took me home!

*Hayley McGarry (12)*
*The John Bramston School, Essex*

## OLD AGE IN BRITAIN TODAY

*How many?*
There are lots of old-age pensioners in Britain today; most of them are women as men seem to die quicker than them.
Most men die by the age of 65, only some of them live longer. Most women between the age of 85 and 89 are either divorced or single.

*How much money do they have?*
Elderly people do not have very much money as most of them don't have jobs. If they do have a job they would only get about £55, or even less, per week.

*How is it spent?*
Most elderly people spend their money on basic necessities, such as fuel, housing and food.

So now you see how old-age pensioners live their lives.

*Suzanne Curl & Emma Brett (11)*
*The John Bramston School, Essex*

# A DAY IN THE LIE OF JAMIROQUAI

I woke up in my four-poster bed, then went downstairs for breakfast, which was a delicious bacon roll. Today was a very special day because I had to pick my new car up - a brand new Subaru Impretza. I was so excited. But before all that, another important job was to pick a hat to wear on my special day.

I eventually decided to wear my purple one, then got into my car and drove off. On the way I was listening to the radio and my number one hit song came on - 'Canned Heat' - and before I knew it I was there in London in a place called 'The Taylor Street'.

A man called Marcus was in a big warehouse and he showed me to my car. It was really nice. It was black and had leather seats. I was really pleased. I left my Mercedes at the warehouse and drove my new car home.

When I arrived at my mansion, I parked my car on the drive and went in and phoned my mum and dad to ask them if they wanted to come over for dinner. They said that they would come over, so I started getting dinner prepared. I was going to make pasta with a cheese and herb sauce, with salad and garlic bread.

When Mum and Dad arrived, I had dinner ready and the table had been laid out by my maid. We tucked in. After, I invited the rest of my band over and we performed a few numbers for my parents. Time was getting on and Mum and Dad had to go. After they had gone I had a coffee with the band, they then went and I retired to my lovely bed.

*Jazmin Harrington (12)*
*The John Bramston School, Essex*

# A DAY IN THE LIFE OF DAVID BECKHAM

I woke up at 7am and had breakfast in bed. I was very nervous about the big game. I phoned Victoria to see if she was alright. I walked downstairs and was speaking to the rest of the team.

The coach pulled up and we got on. There were loads of fans waiting to see us. We arrived at the training ground. We had to wait for a bit because the fans were in the way. We got off the coach. I signed some books and then we went to do some training. My foot started to hurt, so I stopped. I think I had a bit of cramp.

We got back on the coach and went back to the football ground. We had a bit of a rest. It was an hour before the match and our manager started to read the team out. A policeman came running through the door and told us to get out as someone had planted a bomb.

We were all outside and the bomb squad went in. We went to a café for one and a half hours. The game should have started half an hour ago. The bomb was not real, so we went back to the ground. We started to get changed quickly. The match started and the winners were England. We went to a party after the game. Everyone was happy. David Seaman cut his hair off and we had great fun.

The next day we went home. I was looking forward to seeing Victoria.

*Jamie Long (12)*
*The John Bramston School, Essex*

# A DAY IN THE LIFE OF MELISSA CARTA

Melissa Carta is the most popular girl in school and I wish I was like her. She has everything - nice clothes, loads of friends and all the cute boys like her.

It was lunchtime at West Side School and all the popular girls were sitting with the cute footballers. All the geeks were sitting together and there was me and a few of my mates.
I was eating my lunch and I noticed Melissa looking at me. I thought to myself, please stop looking at me, it's making me nervous. After a while she came over to me and asked to talk to me in private.

Whilst Jade and Melissa were talking, Carrie, Alex and PJ were wondering what their little chat could be about, but inside PJ knew, it had happened to her before. She told the others her opinion and they all thought she was being silly.

Jade came back with a huge grin on her face and said, 'Melissa thinks I'm cool, semi-popular and she said that I have good fashion sense. She even said I could hang around with her tomorrow. Of course, I said yes - an opportunity like this happens once in a blue moon.'

Jade went home feeling very pleased with herself. She was really excited and couldn't sleep or eat anything, but she totally forgot about all her other friends.

Jade went to school really early and met up with Melissa in the girls' loos. At the start of school Melissa saw someone fall over and she instantly made fun of them. She told me that if I wanted to fit in, I would have to follow the crowd. I know what she meant by that.

Period one was science and Melissa mixed the chemicals up so that we would be the only ones to do it right. Period two was sociology. Melissa told PJ (my best friend) that this lesson would help her get a social life and PJ ran off crying. I told Melissa she was a snob and ran after PJ. I said to myself, I never want to be like that.

*Danielle Elton*
*The John Bramston School, Essex*

# BULLIES NEARLY KILLED ME

When Laura* got to school one morning, she had no idea that she'd be ending the day in hospital. For most of her life she'd been picked on, but one fatal day, the tormenting almost cost her her life. There was this girl in her class, Hannah*, she never used to pick on anyone else, just her.

One day, they had a man come in and talk about the danger of fire and matches. At lunch the same day, Hannah got out a box of matches. 'Oi, Laura, what do you think I should do with these?' she said. Laura just shrugged. Then she lit one, she put it in front of Laura's face and dropped it. Laura couldn't remember anything after that. She woke up in bed with her mum peering over her. The doctors and nurses were relieved when they found Laura awake. Soon after, her mum explained that she'd been in a coma for six months. She said they were going to turn off the life-support machine if she hadn't woken up. Her mum also said that when the police went to investigate at her school, they found out that Hannah had put small amounts of petrol on her coat when it was in the cloakroom. Laura had skingrafts and the doctors said that there was a chance of brain damage, but fortunately, the only signs of the event are scalds and a lot of emotional scars. Everyone at the hospital said it was a miracle she survived.

Hannah has gone to juvenile prison and only has two more years to complete. It has been three years since it happened and Laura's not going to let the bullies ruin her life.

We spoke to Laura's mother, she said, 'Hannah's punishment was a slap on the wrist. She deserved more'.

*Names have been changed to protect identities.*

*Emma Sands (13)*
*The John Bramston School, Essex*

# REVENGE

Somebody murdered me. I know who it was but it doesn't matter because I'm dead. I'm going to get my revenge. I'm going to torture him forever.

I'm going to go to his house and scare him a little. 'Argh!' I said. He jumped out of his skin. That's good for starters.

Next I'm going to torture his child. It'll be worse than torturing him. I'm going to kidnap her and take her hostage till he admits he killed me.

I spent the next few days looking after the girl, I didn't want her to die as well. I got her everything she wanted, she had a widescreen TV, a PlayStation, a fridge full of food and anything else she wanted.

I went out and looked to see how the family were. They were in despair. I was going to get the girl to phone them and tell him to admit to killing me, but not just yet. I was going to toy with him a little bit more.

I was looking after her well, probably better than she'd been looked after before. She was actually quite happy, she knew I was a ghost and that her dad had killed me.

I went to see how her family were. They weren't actually that bothered. They obviously thought she was dead. This is the time to make the phone call. She said she would do this for me because I had looked after her so well. She rang them, he answered. She pleaded with him and he actually said yes. He was going down!

I told her mother to come and live with me because she would have everything she wanted and her daughter loved it here.

Her husband got imprisoned for life but she didn't care and came to live with me. I still haunt her husband in prison and he is always scared. I got (at last) my revenge.

*Alex Rudd  (13)*
*The John Bramston School, Essex*

# TOYS TO LIFE

Every day Luke and Ian go to the Games Workshop to play with their Warhammer. On Friday they decided to have their own battle. Luke had set up the board and scenery, he was waiting for Ian. He was reading a comic when he thought he saw something move on the board. When he took a closer look there was a Spacemarine's headless body laying there with a Ork axe next to it with blood on it.

When Ian got there they set up his pieces and Luke went to get some drinks when he suddenly heard Ian cry out. He went to see what was up. When he reached the table the Warhammer pieces were fighting for real. The tanks started firing at the landspeeders. The Orks started screaming out war cries while the Spacemarine leaders started shouting out commands to the troops.

Luke and Ian ran outside. When they got outside they could hear the fight coming down the stairs. After a while the Orks came running out of the house making shields out of pieces of wood and bunkers out of the stones from the drive. Ian could see the Spacemarine tanks lining up along the window sill, aiming at the Ork army. The tanks turned back into models, but then the Spacemarine troops came pouring out of the front door and the Ork leader ordered the troops to fire.

Ian and Luke started feeling sorry for the ugly looking Orks and started throwing stones at the Spacemarines. This crushed them easily but they then sent their landspeeders and bandaging up Ian's leg. Eventually the Orks won, thanks to Ian and Luke's help. The Orks took their injured or dead to be repaired and went on their way. So Luke took all the Spacemarines and buried them forever, or did he?

*Mark Brown  (12)*
*The John Bramston School, Essex*

# IT'LL NEVER BE THE SAME AGAIN

It was alright at first, well that was until she came along. Me and my best mate Tally used to do everything together. We didn't need boyfriends, we had each other. That was until Sophie came along. Sophie Porkland, that was her name, she had taken over the school, but worst of all she had taken my best mate, Tally!

It was Tuesday afternoon, the smell of cafeteria chips was in the air, and me and Tally were doing our normal walk around, so we didn't get bored, maybe talk to some boys but mainly it was just us.
*Bring! Bring!* the bell rang.
'What lesson ya got next?' I asked Tally as if it was the worst thing in the world.
'Science, you?'
'Geography, I'll meet you in the café.'
'Alright, bye.'
'See ya later.'
'Bye.'

Geography, that was boring as usual, no changes, the only thing I look forward to during second lesson is lunch and having a girlie chat with Tally. But today we had double geography so I had to wait twice as long.

The bell finally rang and a boring two hours of geography was over.
'Hey what's that?' I asked puzzled, with a girl standing next to me.
'Oh, it's Sophie, she's great, she's so popular, everyone likes her.' Tally went on for ages without even taking a break. 'So can she sit with us?' Tally asked.
'I suppose.'
How could Tally do this? It's just us, it's never been anyone else, just us, it was great, but now oh look, Tally made a popular good-looking girl her friend and she isn't interested in me any more.

*Angela Baker*
*The John Bramston School, Essex*

# A DAY IN THE LIFE OF A HAMBURGER

Hi, my name is Hulk, Hulk The Hamburger - original hey? That's just my parents for you, everything has to rhyme. Well, I've got this English assignment, to explain a day in my life, so here goes. No jokes please!

I wake up every morning at about 7.30 from my state of the class flame grill bed (Ah lovely), then I go and grease myself up in the shower and put on my expensive brand new Nike tracksuit and Ellesse trainers. I go downstairs for Mum's killer breakfast; a bowl of salad, pure meat and a glass of salad and burger juice.

I leave for my school, The John Burger School, at about 8.15 in the morning. I go round for my mate at 14 Lettuce Lane, his name is Harry. We walk together.

At school we learn all sorts of lessons, like how to be the best burger, art, maths, English, avoid humans and GC (opposite to PE). We also have a strange lesson taught by a human, helping us to be the best Whopper meal around. (That's what I want to be).

School is now over, another school day completed. Hoorah! It's a long walk home with Harry but when I get home I'm going to sit, chill our and play my PS2.

*Naomi Williams  (14)*
*The John Bramston School, Essex*

## UNTITLED

It was the end of the summer term and I had just finished school. I was walking along the pier and I could hear the sea crashing on to the rocks and I could feel the sun burn on my back. I walked along thinking to myself and all of a sudden I heard a lady shouting. She said
'Help, help, it's my son, he fell. Help!'
I turned round and I could see a boy struggling in the water.

I flicked off my shoes and dived in. As my body hit the water I froze. The water was so cold compared to the sun. It gave me a shock to the system. I got my bearings and started to look for the boy. After a few seconds my eyes started to sting. They went all blurry and I couldn't see a thing. I started to panic and I flung myself everywhere. I could feel my body getting weaker. I tried to swim to the surface to get more air.

Once I reached the surface I breathed in and then plunged back into the water. I could feel the water getting heavier above me but I knew I had to find this boy.

After going up and down in the water a few times I actually found him. He was unconscious. I dragged him in the water to the pier. Two teenage boys about my age pulled him out of the water. He was motionless. When I was helped up I caught my breath back. I was so weak and worn out.

In the end the boy died. I felt like it was my fault. If I'd jumped in earlier then I might have saved him. I'd tried to do a good deed.

*Leah Batcock (14)*
*The John Bramston School, Essex*

## SLIPKNOT ARTICLE

I think that the press are giving the wrong impression of Slipknot because you cannot blame a band's lyrics on causing someone to go on a killing spree. This is because for one thing the person must have been slightly deranged to do something like that in the first place therefore, you cannot blame the lyrics.

People who think that Slipknot's music is offensive don't have to listen to it. Slipknot's music has been aimed at the crowds of punks, skas, skaters, greebos and goths. They have been aimed at them because society will stereotype these people; the ones wearing baggy jeans and a hoody. This has all happened because *we* are different.

As a greebo, I have had to put up with abuse about being a greebo. I have also had mates who have been attacked because they are greebos, different individuals, most people dislike us because we are different.

*Chris Doe  (14)*
*The John Bramston School, Essex*

# ATTACK OF THE CHUPACABRAS!

This is a story about strange creatures allegedly responsible for hundreds of animal mutilations in the Caribbean island of Puerto Rico. The boy in this story was unfortunately attacked by one. Hopefully he is going to recover but the doctors say that it will take months. This is what happened . . .

It was a bright and starry sky that night. Hector was doing an errand for his father. His father was a shepherd but he became sick so Hector was left with the sheep. Hector was thinking what would happen if a Chupacabra would just leap out of nowhere. As if by coincidence there it was, right in front of the sheep he was herding. The sheep went crazy. The Chupacabra looked like a demon, it was around four to five feet tall, with huge elongated red eyes. It had a long and pointed tongue that moved in and out of its mouth. It was greyish in colour but its back kept on changing colour. Hector was frozen in fear. He tried to run but his legs turned into jelly. The monster circled around him as if it was trying to figure him out.

The Chupacabra looked around. Then when it saw that the sheep were all gone, it turned on Hector. It bared its razor-like teeth at the boy and in a split second it lunged itself towards Hector. It used its teeth to dig into Hector's neck but the boy used his arms to protect himself. The monster bit his arm and sucked all the blood that it could sink its fangs on. Fortunately a hunter heard his screams and came to his aid. The hunter threw a spear at the monster. He hit on its right leg. It howled in pain and ran off into the dark forest.

Hector was brought to the nearest hospital, he needed a blood transfusion. He was considered lucky compared to the other victims of the Chupacabra. Most of them end up looking like a raisin.

Most people believe that the Chupacabra is just a figment of the imagination. Others think that they are products of some kind of *top secret* operation. More and more sightings are being recorded. There are also sightings being recorded in California.

Do you believe in 'super natural' beings? I know I don't!

*Edgar Legaspi  (14)*
*The John Bramston School, Essex*

# A Day In The Life Of A Crime Fighter

Falling off trees, grazing your knee, just the normal things us kids do. Not any more!

We fight crime. We play with the big boys, we are the ultimate champions. I am Special Agent Dustbuster, going over every speck of dust to retrieve my evidence and solve my crimes, that's every crime around. Yeah, yeah! I know it's long, but if it was short and sweet . . . well, I'm not sweet! I am the crime fighter and will not be messed with.

I work for the RSOTBCFE (Royal Society Of The Best Crime Fighters Ever). Remember the sweet bit, yeah!

I have my trusty companions, Mr Toothcombe and Mr Magnifier. Don't worry, I won't bore you with their slogans, trust me, Toothcomb's is long and I mean by a few thousand pages. Come on, it would take me all day to write that for you.

Anyway, as I was saying. I first got into this when I was a small and innocent boy. Yuk! Can we get back to the story?

My uncle had a few contacts in the crime world and right now this story is coming live from Australia. I am in the middle of my fifth mission and believe me, this one beats all. It is the most secret mission of my life . . . well it's so secret I shouldn't even tell you. I shouldn't even tell you that I am a secret agent and I am on a mission to find jewels, stolen . . . whoops! I told you didn't I? Oh, I had to tell someone. Please keep it a secret, promise? Promise with a cherry on top? Promise with cherries and ice cream? Okay you've promised!

My uncle was looking puzzled and worried, (you know, the sweaty palms thing). He was pacing the floor like some mad person but I knew it was for a reason. I quizzed him with every question I know. (Even the one about what colour his socks were? Which I don't think helped the matter.)

Here we are, I am sitting, he's pacing and I'm also trying to get speech from him fast. Then at last he cracked (I think the socks question did it) He blurted everything out at once and I got the picture.

So here we now are. Someone stole jewels worth £900,000,000. You want me to keep going? 00000, no? Well that's fine. I'm trying to help my uncle (he's a crime fighter too) and we are drawing closer, gaining evidence in bucketfuls.

That's about it to sum up the crime. But we really think we are close to a winner.

New news has just come in and I've got to run . . . bye!

*Kristina Fleuty  (12)*
*The John Bramston School, Essex*

## DREAM

I had a dream when I was younger, back then I didn't know that this dream would be the most important thing of my life.

It haunted me, every night it was the same. I didn't tell anyone about the dream, I just kept it to myself. I was eleven years old when I started getting frustrated with it. I wanted it to leave me alone.

It was about a girl, she looked just like me. She wanders around the house screaming the word 'Mum'. It stayed with me always until I moved out of my parents' house when I was sixteen and flew to Australia. My parents died two years later. I needed to go to their funeral, so I went back home. Now I wish I hadn't.

I went to my old house and moved back in. I'd forgotten about the dream until I went to sleep. The girl came back.

This time it was more bright and it looked so real, as if I was awake. I realised the girl was trying to tell me something.

I looked all around my room, looking for something that would tell me about my dream. Then I found it. A one inch brass key underneath a floorboard beneath my bed. I searched the house to find the lock that this key would undo.

I searched for days upon end for it . . . nothing. I thought long and hard. Then I thought of a song my mother used to sing.

'I have a little friend,
his name is Fred,
he lives in the garden,
beneath the flower bed.'

I ran out the back door, along the path until I got to the flower bed. I started grabbing at compost until I came across a medium-sized wooden box. The key fitted perfectly in the lock.

As I lifted the lid and peeped inside I gasped in amazement. Hundreds of photos of a little girl. All with 'Fredrica, my love' written on the back.

This girl is the girl in my dreams I thought. This is the girl that has haunted me for twelve years of my life. But why? Also in the box was a picture of my mother holding Fredrica limply in her arms. I then realised what had happened. My mother had killed my sister.

Then the dreams stopped, never to awaken me again.

*Gemma Davies  (13)*
*The John Bramston School, Essex*

# A Day In The Life Of An Ant

One day Vicky was playing in the garden when she saw an ants' nest. Vicky was a typical child and at the age of five, didn't like ants much and enjoyed stomping on them. On this particular day Vicky had a cup of her mother's tea and she decided to pour it down the ants' nest. As she did so the tea made a sizzling noise and she heard the ants scream in terror.

Vicky looked into the hole in the ground, there was no movement and no noise. Vicky searched in desperation as one ant appeared, then another and another they all climbed onto her and she screamed as she hit them off. They all fell off and landed flat on the floor, none of them moved. She went to pick one of them up, but as she picked one up there was a loud *whoosh* as she shrank and grew antennae. She had changed into an ant!

Vicky was sitting in the middle of the ants that she had hit off of her. One by one the ants got up and shook off all the dust. One looked at her and said, 'That will teach her not to drown us in that rubbish again!' And he walked off with a smug grin on his face. All the other ants followed and as they did she decided she ought to follow them into the hole as well.

Vicky entered the hole. Inside it was nicely decorated with pictures of all the ant kings. There were loads of small useless junk scattered everywhere and a muddy staircase with Vicky's old ribbon as a carpet going into a nice room with a cotton reel and credit card throne. On top of the throne sat a large ant with a Barbie crown on. Vicky followed the ants up to the throne and the ant who had spoken to her before said, 'The deed is complete, we attacked and defeated, she ran away.'
The ant on the throne turned to the ant and handed him a sash. On the sash it said, *Chief of Ant, Look-out Patrol.* All the ants turned to the ant with the sash and clapped. Vicky joined in, wondering what was going on.

After that Vicky followed them back to the colony rooms and she found a spare bed. Vicky sat there thinking what to do when another girl ant came up to her and asked her name. Vicky asked the ant her name. It was Maria. They got chatting and they became friends. Vicky asked her if she could keep a secret? Then she told her about being the girl who drowned the colony.

At first Maria didn't believe her until she told her what happened and what she did over the years. Then Maria finally believed her and felt weird. She got scared and wanted to help Vicky but she didn't know how to. Vicky told her how it happened, how she was sorry for all the pain she had caused not realising what she was doing and that she was going to change. With that Maria took her outside to the top of the ants' nest and they stood there for a while.

Maria asked her where she was when she got changed into an ant. Vicky took her to the spot and they stood there. Maria didn't know what to do and how to get her back to her original form. Then she remembered a film she once saw where someone got stuck in another body. Maria told Vicky about the film and how they had to re-enact what happened. Maria asked Vicky which ant she'd picked up?
Vicky said, 'The one who was given the sash.'
Maria gave her the weirdest look and told her how stubborn that ant was. His name was Chris and he lead the ant patrol. Maria told her she could try and get Chris to come outside so Vicky could knock him out so she could return to the human world.

Maria went down to the look-out colony and found Chris. She asked him to come up to the surface to help her with something. Chris agreed to help and he followed her up. When they got to the surface Vicky ran round and hit him with a cocktail stick. He fell over and she touched his hand. All of a sudden a loud *whoosh* happened and Vicky shot up into her normal state. As she looked down into the hole, she saw an ant that looked familiar and by the right was another lying down with a cocktail stick alongside. Vicky smiled and placed a piece of bread down for the two ants.
She said, 'Goodbye,' and walked indoors and from that day on she never harmed an ant ever again.

*Victoria Matthews (13)*
*The John Bramston School, Essex*

## A Day In The Life Of A Dog!

Hi, my name is Freddie and I'm going to tell you what it's really like for us dogs.

First of all I wake up at about six in the morning and go and wake my mistress up. She is lovely, her name is Sue. She is always cuddling and stroking my fur. I'm a Labrador by the way. I have lovely black fur. I'm not all Labrador though, as my father was an Alsatian, so I have white fur in some places.

Once I wake my mistress up she comes downstairs and gives me my breakfast. I have chicken and gravy, yummy! It might sound disgusting but believe me it's delicious! Whilst I am eating my breakfast my mistress gets dressed. I finish my breakfast in about two minutes but my mistress takes forever to get changed. Finally, she comes down and puts my lead on. This means walk time! I love going on walks, it's the best part of the day. My mistress always takes me down the park where she sits and reads a book. Whilst she is reading I like to play with the ducks in the pond by chasing them. Our walks take about 30 minutes.

When we arrive home again, my mistress has a bath and then it's my turn! I really hate baths. They make me smell even worse. All flowery and girlie. All the other dogs laugh at me after I've had a bath.
'Look, it's little miss flower,' that really gets me because for starters I'm not even a girl!

After my bath I have to go out in the garden to dry off. I'm lucky I don't have to go next door, otherwise I have to face Bruno, that's the dog who thinks I'm a girl! I have to go next door sometimes as my mistress works during the day. She hasn't got a husband as he died before she got me. Once I'm all dried I go and sit in the front room with my mistress. I like to sit next to her on the settee. I end up falling asleep, like I normally do.

When it gets to the evenings I like to sit in the garden for an hour or so. Millie, next-door's cat, just happens to climb over the fence, you know what this means, chase time! I end up chasing her for ages. Every time I've chased her I have never caught her. That's what really bugs me!

Finally my master calls me in for my tea. I have a nice rabbit in gravy meal. It's not as nice as chicken in gravy though, but it's still nice! After my tea I usually watch TV with my mistress but tonight I'm tired already, so I sit in my bed in the kitchen and fall asleep. Zzzzzzzzz!

*Kirsten Frost  (14)*
*The John Bramston School, Essex*

## THE UNDISCOVERED PLANET

Captain's log 30456. We are travelling at warp 4, heading for an unknown distress call. At 1050 hours we come across a strange planet. It was a bit like Earth but a lot more land. Dr George, Lt Roger and I beamed down to this strange and undiscovered planet. To our belief we saw a building but this wasn't any kind of building. It was like a prison, a bit like the one back at home, it was black, dirty and some kind of animal at the foot of prison.

Back on the ship, second-in-command, Chris, spotted two command fighters for the Girtrons. Chris said, 'Red alert, battle stations.'
Back on the ground Dr George, Lt Roger and I were being attack by the Girtrons. I said to Dr George, 'Get your laser out and fire.'
Dr George replied saying, 'For goodness sake Leigh, I'm a doctor not a warrior.'

From the ship Chris beamed us a message about them being attacked. I sent a message back, needing to be beamed up. Dr George and Lt Roger were beamed up but I wasn't. They caught and took me to the High Girtron. The thing that gives them away is that they look like Earth girls.

They put me into a room with a deluxe king-sized bed. A lovely looking Girtron walked through the door with my food and drink. Things between us just got magical that night. Back on the ship Chris had to leave the planet and come back the next day or they would have been vaporised from fighting the two spaceships. The next day the Girtron called Lal, helped me get out of the prison and into the most advanced spacepod that I have ever seen in my life. I asked if she would come with me but she refused.

When I was leaving some more Girtrons shot Lal with a laser and killed her. I landed the spaceship, running towards her.
I shouted, 'Noooooooooo!'

The Girtrons shot me, killing me instantly.
My last words were, 'See you there Lal!'

My friends came back after the Girtrons had left and found me dead on the floor with Lal next to me. This made Chris, the captain of the spaceship decide to name the planet after me, Leigh.

*Leigh Clements  (13)*
*The John Bramston School, Essex*

# A Day In The Life Of Plo-Koon

*Plo-Koon: A Kel Dor from Dorin, Plo-Koon must protect his sensitive eyes and nostrils from the oxygen-rich atmosphere of Coruscant with special devices.*

Greetings, I am Jedi Master Plo-Koon, you are about to experience an action-packed day in the life of me:

'Good morning Master Yoda,' I coughed.
'Something is troubling you Plo-Koon. I can feel a disturbance in the force.'
'Yes, Master. I can feel it too. It is a problem I have suffered since I woke up this morning.'
'We must look into this. Gather the Jedi council, we are going to have a meeting.'

We all took our seats in the Jedi temple and started to meditate. Yoda and everyone else in the room started to get the same vision. It was a lost boy trapped between a group of sand people on Tatooine. Yoda jumped from his seat and chose the three Jedi's he wanted to go and help the boy. This included Mace Windu, Adi Gallia and *me!*

We set off immediately in a large Jedi-Star fighter and were quickly escorted to Tatooine. We all walked out and The Force disturbance grew stronger. The hot weather made me feel sick. I breathed more heavily through my mask and began to sweat. Mace Windu said I should soon get used to the weather and the heat.

We arrived at a small village on the outskirts of Tatooine named Mos Eisley. Suddenly, a group of thugs jumped out from behind some rocks and ran towards us! All three Jedi's removed their light sabres from their belts and killed the thugs in one great slash! Then I spotted two thugs hobbling away holding a small boy between them. Me and Mace Windu started to run after them while Adi Gallia took on some more thugs.

Using The Force, I leapt at least 10 feet up into the air, landed on my targeted thug and cut off his head in one blow! Mace also took on the other thug by landing on him and piercing his sabre right through his spine! We then grabbed the boy and retreated to the ship, meeting Adi Gallia inside.

*Joshua Forman  (13)*
*The Prittlewell School, Essex*

## THE CRAZIEST DAY IN MY LIFE

My craziest day was June 1st. This day started when I was woken up at 6.30am by an extremely bad foot ache. I couldn't get back to sleep, so I decided to get up and take a bath. I thought it would be a good idea to take a bath before anyone else so I had some hot water. Everybody needed a bath because it was my mother and father's wedding day.

I sat downstairs and waited for everyone to get up when I realised my mum and dad had gone out for breakfast. I told my sisters when they got up and we then had to cook breakfast for ourselves.

It was a complete disaster. The eggs fell off the shelf, the bacon wasn't cooked and nothing went right. After that, the flowers arrived and they were dying in the scorching weather. I didn't know what to do because I didn't want them to die, so my sis watered them. My mum and dad then came back to find the kitchen in a state and the flowers being watered.

We all then got ready. Everyone arrived and everyone got ready to leave and go to the registry office.

Next thing I knew my mother and father were getting married and the lady said the word 'impediment'. Then my cousin said to my grandfather, 'What a day! What does impediment mean?'

*Helena Bray  (12)*
*The Prittlewell School, Essex*

## MY NEIGHBOURS FROM HELL

Every night the music would blare out from all the walls. About two years ago, a young couple, the Jacksons, disturbed the quiet neighbourhood of Static Drive.

I thought it would be enough with the Jacksons and their terrible music, until a few weeks ago. My mum had just bought a pet because our pet dog Ripper was getting lonely. We bought a female Alsatian and it had everything you wanted in a dog. The Jacksons were jealous.

Firstly, I caught the neighbours trying to bribe the dog through a hole in the fence with some meat, but I dragged the dog inside. The next day my mum caught the neighbours trying to pick the dog up and carry it over the fence. Was it safe for my dog to go out anymore?

I let my dog out in the morning before I went upstairs to get ready for school. I jumped down the stairs in my boring school uniform. I went into the garden to call my dog in, but I couldn't see her. After two minutes of looking, I saw a stiff Alsatian body in the grass. There was blue stuff dripping from her mouth. I looked over the fence and saw blue slug pellets. The Jacksons had murdered my dog!

It took me ages to get over my dog's death, but I found a way to get my neighbours back. I collected my dog's waste from that week and posted it through my neighbours' door.

*Sasha James (13)*
*The Prittlewell School, Essex*

## A PARTY THAT WENT WRONG

Everyone loves parties, but if just one person does something wrong it can be a disaster and the party is ruined.

It was my friend's 9th birthday party on July 24th in the summer holidays and he invited half of the class, including me, to an ice skating rink. At 6pm, I left my house and my mum was ready to drive me up there. As soon as I got in the car, it was even hotter than outside. It was 90 degrees Celsius and the sun was right in my face.

I was there at last. We parked our car and we were there two minutes early.
'I'll pick you up at 8pm,' my mum said, as the party finished then.
'Alright then. Bye, see you at eight,' I said.

As I walked in, there were loads of presents stacked up. Ben, the birthday boy, must have invited 100 kids.
'Happy birthday, Ben,' I said smiling as I was giving a card and a present to him.
'Thanks,' Ben said.

When everybody was there, we all rushed onto the ice rink as fast as we could. We couldn't wait to get on there. We were all skating round at a fast pace, but a crazy boy called Tim thought it would be funny to do crazy stunts. Tim was sliding across the ice on his belly, falling over on purpose and he just wouldn't stop. I knew he would hurt himself sooner or later.

'Go on Tim, do more,' kids behind me were saying. I couldn't believe they were cheering him on. Tim was on the floor, doing more funny tricks, I suppose. He was there for ages, still as a silent snake ready to attack. A few people started to crowd round, then more. It wasn't long until we had to come off the ice rink. We were watching him, waiting for the ambulance.

After they took him away, we found out he was unconscious at the time. No one else was allowed on the ice rink. The party was still on, but with too many sad faces. Ben didn't even open his presents with a smile.

There was an hour left of eating and talking. We were waiting to get picked up. The party was a disaster.

*Andrew Moore  (14)*
*The Prittlewell School, Essex*

## MY NEIGHBOUR FROM HELL

I had a neighbour from Hell once. It was a young man named John and his wife Jenny. They hated me, but I also felt the same about them. I lived alone in a nice tidy, quiet street. This was the reason I moved to St Pangrong Road. You see I am a very private person. But when this family moved in, I knew my dream was about to wake me up forever.

The night they moved in I heard loud music into the early hours of the night. I had a lot of trouble sleeping that night. The next day I called round to complain and as soon as I opened my mouth, I knew that I shouldn't have. Their faces were nasty and they were going to get me back, I knew it.

That day they collected all the rubbish from the party and chucked it over my garden. I phoned the police and that made it worse. My neighbours were now totally against me and they would do everything in their power to ruin my life.

They used to drive all over my lawn and I knew if I told the police it would make it worse. My nice garden was a dump. I was getting scared to sleep or leave my house in case of what they would do. In the end I told the police. They were put in jail for a year or two, but I knew they would be back.

*Amy Such (12)*
*The Prittlewell School, Essex*

# MY NEIGHBOUR FROM HELL

It was a Friday night when I was sitting in my lounge feeding my baby daughter who was drifting to sleep slowly. Baby Amy was just falling asleep when shouts and screams came from the next house.

I carried Amy to the window and peered out. A big woman stamped out of the house. She was shouting and shrieking at a tall young man who stood at the door raising his arms up and down in a flap. As she screamed, she slammed the door shut in the man's face and picked up some heavy suitcases, trundled to the end of the winding path, opened the creaking gate and left it swinging as she heaved the cases in the back of the car. She then drove off in a flurry.

This had also happened a few weeks ago. The same lady would leave, making a lot of racket and causing the little house to shake and rumble. I phoned the house last week and threatened to call the police if the chaos continued.

They disturbed me every night, crashing around in their little house. They must be a couple who just have rows now and again. She would always turn up in the next couple of days. I saw other people's lights flicker on as they looked out of their windows. If those neighbours from Hell break the peace again, they will be paying a very dear fine.

*Anja Forman  (13)*
*The Prittlewell School, Essex*

## MY NEIGHBOUR FROM HELL

My next-door neighbour is from Hell and I will tell you why.

They are a family of four - the mother, father, son and finally, the cat. Firstly, the problem with the son is he is always playing with his basket ball and never cares whose car he hits with the ball, and his pop music is blaring in the afternoon.

Secondly, the mother's problems. The smell of burnt food in the air, opera singing at 2 o'clock in the morning and bingo every night. Then comes the father. He is always down the pub having a pint or two, or three, and also he walks past our garden and leaves his broken beer bottles.

Finally, and the worst one, the cat. He's always up at night miaowing, ripping the bin bags and pulling rubbish everywhere. He puts dead animals in the garden, picks fights with our cat and gives our cat fleas.

*Matthew Fowler (14)*
*The Prittlewell School, Essex*

# A Day In The Life Of My Mum

My mum is a support worker. As long as you don't get on the bad side of mentally ill people, then they are really nice people. But my mum sees the good and bad side of them.

My mum has a busy day. She gets up and has to take my brother (Sonny) to school. She lies in bed wishing that he could go to school on his own.

When she gets back from taking Sonny to school, she has to get ready for work, which is quite hard for her as she cannot wear whatever she wants. She loves to wear make-up and also likes wearing sandals, but where my mum works they have to wear as little make-up as possible and are not allowed to wear sandals as they can easily get caught on something. So my mum walks around the house moaning that she has nothing decent to wear for work, which is weird as that's something a teenager would say.

On a 'late shift' she has to get to work for 2pm and doesn't get home till 10pm. Another shift she does is the 'night shift', which she finds really hard, but prefers to do them because that way she gets to see my brothers and me more. She loves her job as she loves a challenge.
This day is a normal day for my mum as it happens every day.

*Jade Gilbert (14)*
*The Prittlewell School, Essex*

# A DAY IN THE LIFE OF MICHAEL OWEN

It was the day England played Denmark in the World Cup, to go through to the quarter-finals. I was going to Saitama Stadium in Japan with the team anticipating a win to go through to face Brazil.

The team got into the dressing room, smelling the scent of the Japanese. Everyone started getting changed, laughing and giggling.

I was breathing heavily as I was nervous. Sven Göran Eriksson, our manager, came over to me and started chatting to me and comforting me.

We walked down the tunnel cautiously, waiting for the sight of the Danish. Everyone stopped at the end praying for a win. David Beckham led the team out of the tunnel and onto the pitch, followed by our number one goalkeeper, David Seaman. Every supporter started cheering as the two teams walked onto the pitch. I walked slowly behind Emile Heskey into a line, where we sang our National Anthems and greeted each other by shaking hands and giving the odd smile.

The captains met the referees. I kicked off. We got an early lead by Rio Ferdinand from a corner. With about 20 minutes left of the first half, we were winning 2-0 from a goal by me from a cross by Ashley Cole. A couple of minutes later, Heskey scored!

It was full time. We won 3-0 and everyone started exchanging shirts.

*Simon Burman  (13)*
*The Prittlewell School, Essex*

## MY NEIGHBOUR FROM HELL

One day there was a disgusting stench coming from my neighbour's back garden. I went to the wall that separates the two gardens to observe what was making that pong. I saw the corpse of a rodent. Once I saw the decomposing rat, I sprinted through the back door into the living room. After the shock faded, I phoned the environmental health people. I had a debate about whether they should send an investigator round to my neighbour's garden.

Finally, after a two month wait, the smell hadn't disappeared, so I complained to the environmental health again. The next day they sent an investigator round to see my next-door neighbours. The next thing I knew, one of my neighbours was shouting at the investigator and then there was a silence. I heard a loud *crash!* as the door slammed shut. I ran to my front door and opened it. I saw a disgusted man in a suit walking down the road. I called out to him, 'Excuse me, would you like to come in for a cup of tea?'

The investigator and I had a very long conversation about my neighbours. He was appalled by their behaviour. He had to leave and talk to his superior in the environmental health.

A month had gone by before I found out what was going to happen to my neighbours, but whilst this was happening, I was living in my sister's house and finally I found out I could move back into my house.

*Michael Dowley (13)*
*The Prittlewell School, Essex*

## A Day In The Life Of Alex

I wake up, except on Wednesdays, when I am rudely awakened by the dustman. My name is Michael Caine - nah, only joking. I wish I was that talented . . . I have one skill and one skill only - messing up. I can't even manage a paper round.

My mum is shouting at my sister as I walk out of the house. 'What time were you in last night? I'll tell you shall I? 3am.'

Let's see - what music today? The Verve, that will do. You see, with the Verve you have the soft love songs, like *Sonnet* and you have the deep, dark songs like *Bittersweet Symphony*.

'Alex, we will not stand for these mistakes. I'm sorry, we are going to have to let you go.'
I curse them with every bad word. I know why they sacked me - it's because I cost them £50 in 3 days, just from putting a few papers through the wrong doors.

Lunchtime in a sombre mood due to the masses of homework piled upon by those slaves of the government machine they call teachers. My dad always called me twisted and pessimistic.

'Wake up Maggie I think I got something to say to you'. My Dad's music blares at me as I enter the door. 'Get on with your homework,' he shouts. I put on some Paul Weller. The last thing I remember was the song *Hung Up*.

*Alex Monteith (14)*
*The Prittlewell School, Essex*

# My Neighbour From Hell

June 15th, 2.30pm

It's 2.30 in the morning. I was just dozing off to sleep because I work late, eat dinner late, watch television late and can't get to sleep. Then I heard *bang, bang bang!* As I toppled out of bed, I felt the floor jump. I slowly made my way down the stairs and pushed my hands on the wall to find a light switch, then the light flicked on. It took my eyes a little while to adjust to the light.

I went into the cupboard to find a coat as I was going to knock next door. I banged on the door until my knuckles hurt. The banging was so loud, but they couldn't hear me over their noise. I went back indoors to try and sleep, as I had to work early in the morning.

June 16th, 7.50pm

Today I had to phone work and say I was sick. I was so tired that I couldn't face the hassles of work. I was just about to go back to bed when *bang!* I felt the bed jump. I leapt out of bed in fury. I ran down the stairs and flung the door open. I ran in the gate next door and shouted through the letter box: 'I'm sleeping!'

Down came Mr Hunching saying, 'I'm sorry, did I wake you up? I'll wait until later.' Then he shut the door.

I'm still thinking how to get him back!

*Louise Champion (13)*
*The Prittlewell School, Essex*

## MY NEIGHBOUR FROM HELL

Once, when I came home from the park, I saw my next-door neighbours outside putting rubbish in their garden. I said to my mum, 'Have you seen how much rubbish next door have got in their garden?'
My mum said, 'No.'
I told my mum to look. She screamed and then she fainted. When she came round I said to her, 'What happened?'
My mum said, 'I saw a rat.'
'Was it a big rat?' I said.
'It was massive,' she said.
So I phoned the pest control and told him to come quickly. When I got off the phone, I told my mum that they would be here in about ten minutes. Ten minutes went past and then there was a knock on the door. Me and mum jumped and then I went to get the door.
He said, 'Where are they?'
'In the back garden,' I said. I showed him the way. When he got to the back door I said, 'I am going to close the door so the rats don't get in.'

When he got out, he inspected the garden and put this stuff around the garden. When he came in I said to him, 'What was that stuff you put on the floor?'
He said, 'It is rat poison. The rats will be dead in the morning and then I will be back.'
'I will see you in the morning,' I said.

*Jason Walden (13)*
*The Prittlewell School, Essex*

# MY NEIGHBOUR FROM HELL

*Gareth Gates leaned in towards me and started singing. The rose he had in his teeth he gave to me and he leaned in for the kiss. His lips came close and . . . bang!*

I awoke and wondered what had disturbed my dream. I then realised it had been the neighbours. They had only been here a few weeks and already they had awoken me from *Gareth Land*. Then again, that wasn't the only thing they had done.

There was the father who was into DIY and would keep drills going in the night. Then, of course, there was the wife. You could hear her all night shouting at the three brats. The three children were called Steven, Maggie and the newest member to the family, Ricky. Steven was into loud music, so that kept me awake at night. Maggie had her friends around all the time and they screamed till the morning. Then there was Ricky - he would scream all day and night.

I still remember the day they moved in. Chaos everywhere and enough noise to wake the dead. Things got worse when the whole family turned up on my doorstep to introduce themselves. As soon as they left, I knew they were going to be trouble.

I cannot wait for them to move out. I'm in college and I need to study, but I can't with them next door. The next step for me will be moving out!

*Chelsea Skinner (12)*
*The Prittlewell School, Essex*

## MY NEIGHBOUR FROM HELL

I woke up on Christmas Day and then there was a hard knock on the door. I was the only person awake, because it was 5 o'clock in the morning. I went downstairs to open the door and at first I couldn't see anyone, but as I shut the door, someone knocked again. I ran to the door and opened it, but still there was no one there. I slammed the door shut and ran upstairs to my bedroom window. I looked out and tried to see if I could spot them.

I saw him, but I didn't know who it was. I crept downstairs and as I did so, they knocked again. I opened the door and then went outside. I looked left and when I did, this person threw snow all over me. Then I saw him - it was my neighbour from Hell.

He has always done stupid things like that. He was like a little kid. Also, on Hallowe'en he stuck a label on my back saying *don't give him sweets, he's not allowed any.* When I got home that night, that's when I found the label. No wonder no one gave me anything.

I have a plan how to stop him doing pranks. I'm going to tie him up in his house and put food around him every week until he learns his lesson. Will it work? I don't know, but hopefully it will.

*James Wagstaff (13)*
*The Prittlewell School, Essex*

## MY NEIGHBOUR FROM HELL

My neighbour is a real pain in the neck. One night we heard a *boom, boom, boom* and then a smash. That morning she came round. I opened the door. I saw her, she had two black eyes.

I told my mum and she told her to get off our grass and slammed the door on her. My mum said to me, 'Next time that druggie knocks on the door, don't open it.' The woman looked as if she had been pulled through a hedge backwards. She had bruises all over her body and a tattoo of a butterfly on her arm.

That night I had a nightmare about her. She was beating me up because I would not try her grubby drugs. Then I woke up with a thud and smashed my head on the shelf above my bed. I yelled with pain, then went back to bed with a headache.

In the morning, I told my mum of the nightmare and she said, 'That woman, I know she's a horrible person, but you have to live with it.' Then my dad wheeled in and told me to ignore her and try to sleep. That day at school I got told off for doing nothing. Well, not nothing. I had not done my homework because that woman would not let me think over the *boom, boom* of that loud radio.

Then, when we got a letter from next door, it was a letter of leaving. I yelled, 'She's finally gone!'

*Joe Freeman  (14)*
*The Prittlewell School, Essex*

## MY BROKEN LEG

It was a lovely day and my friends and I were walking home from school along the brook at the back of Prittlewell School. We were chatting and having fun and then my ankle gave way and I fell down the brook. At first my mates thought I was mucking about, because I am always falling over, but when I took my shoe off, my ankle had doubled in size. I was shouting in pain and my mates were rowing because they were scared. I wanted my mum and dad so I used my mate's mobile. My dad knew I was hurt by the sound of my voice. It felt like it took forever for my mum and dad to arrive.

When my mum and dad arrived, my dad took one look at my ankle, asked for a phone and called an ambulance. When the ambulance arrived, they couldn't find a place to lift me, so they called for the fire brigade and they lifted me up onto the bank.

When I arrived at hospital Pete, the nurse, said I had broken my leg and I needed crutches. My face dropped because I was sad.

The first night back was bad because I couldn't do anything for myself.

When I walk home from school, I realise what I went through and a tear comes to my eye.

*Sarah Jones (12)*
*The Prittlewell School, Essex*

## MY NEIGHBOUR FROM HELL

*Bang!* The walls of the house shook!
'Bob must be doing some more DIY,' Mum said.
Bob was our next-door neighbour. He was always doing DIY jobs, but if you ask me, his home is a tip! How do I know this? Well, it's because we got invited to dinner last week!

It all started on a Sunday morning. Dad was talking to Bob outside - even Bob's garden was a tip! Dad walked into the house. He didn't look happy and then he said to us, 'Bob has invited us next door for dinner. Do you want to go?' Mum just nodded, but I could tell that she didn't want to go.

I was doing my homework when Dad came into my room. 'Come on, it's time to go.' He walked off, so I went.
We knocked on the door. Bob's wife, Jackie, answered. Bob and Jackie didn't have children, but I'd always wondered what they would be like if they did. I imagined a boy with a scruffy haircut, quite tubby, and if they had a girl I would think that she would be friendly.

They showed us into the dining room. We sat down at the table and Jackie brought in the food. There was ham, tuna and cheese sandwiches. There were bowls of crisps. It was like one of those parties you have when you are little. When we went home I thought even though they are bad at DIY, they made a very nice dinner party.

*Larni Munns (14)*
*The Prittlewell School, Essex*

## A DAY IN THE LIFE OF MY RABBIT

It's Wednesday morning. Oh, here comes that girl again. Every morning at 7am she comes down here, feeds me and then she brushes me. I'm starving. *Feed me!* Yum, rabbit food! I haven't even touched my dinner and she's already going to brush me.

At last, away from that girl. She brushes and brushes until I have no knots in my hair. Now that the coast is clear, I'm going for a nose in the garden. Yum, look at all this grass! Oh look, what's that? Wow, that blooming ball nearly hit me. I'd better keep an eye out for other footballs that might fly over. *Oi!* That time it hit me. I'm going in.

Today, I'm actually looking forward to my owner coming and brushing me. She should be here any time now as it's 3.25pm. Ah, here she is. She's put me in my run. Wow, this is fun, I can run around.

It's 7.30pm now. I'm coming in the house. I can hear them putting the mat down. Ahh! This is warm in here. I don't want to go out on my own ever again.

*Amber Fletcher  (13)*
*The Prittlewell School, Essex*

# A DAY IN THE LIFE OF MY CAT

8.30am
Just waking up. What's that noise? Ah, my owner must be up. I can go and see if she's got any food.
'Here you go, breakfast.'
'Thanks, that'll do nicely.'
'Now, time to go out and explore the garden.' The door opens. Is she a mind reader or something? Sniff, sniff, sniff. What cat would dare to come into my home and use my garden? Despicable. I've had enough of this, I'm going in.
Come on, come on. I know what'll do the trick. I can just jump up on the window ledge until somebody notices me! Here it goes. Ah, here you are. (Door opens.) Thanks again. This is the life.
Right, I'm tired now. Let's find a comfy spot. Found one, this ironing should do nicely.
Zzzzzzzzzzzzzzzzzzzzzzz.
(Stretching) That sleep did me the world of good. There goes the door, it must be my other owner. I think I'll meet her today. (Door opens.)
'Miaow.'
'Hello puss.'
'Miaow.'
'Do you want to go out? Here you go.' (Door opens.)

Better see what's going on this evening. All clear I think. Better go in now, it's starting to get dark. (Door opens.) Cheers. Time for bed, after all it's another day tomorrow.

*Jenny Searle (13)*
*The Prittlewell School, Essex*

# NEIGHBOURS FROM HELL

My neighbours next door wake us up in the night. They wake us up with loud music and it happens every other day. Once, my husband and I were sunbathing and they soaked us with a hose. They set our fence alight and we had to put it out with our hose, as they just stood there smirking. When we called the police, they did nothing, so we were forced to move.

Before we moved, we had a cunning plan. We had been videoing the husband in their jacuzzi having an affair whilst the wife was at work. We eventually put it in the post addressed to the husband first, and then sent another one to the wife. She packed her bags and went as soon as they got the video. She didn't even stop to ask him why.

The next morning we saw her coming back for the rest of her stuff, but he was not there so she left him a letter saying *I hate you* and it was smudged with tears. That was it, she never even told him where she was going.

That night he came home fuming with rage. He kept us awake all night ranting and raving. He even bricked our house windows and let his dog mess up our beautiful garden. Well, we deserved it, but he shouldn't have been *the neighbour from Hell.*

*Scott Eagling (13)*
*The Prittlewell School, Essex*

## MY NEIGHBOUR FROM HELL

I would like to tell you about my neighbours. They are the ultimate neighbours from Hell. At first it started with little things, like loud music and tiny rows. That continued for about three months.

Everything was fine for a while - maybe one month or so, but then they decided to put a new fence up. The problem was they put it up 3ft on our side. We phoned the council and they went round our side and measured the width. It was well under what it should have been and this is a short beginning of the long list.

Another time, Mum was in the garden sunbathing and suddenly, it started raining weeds! Loads of weeds were being thrown over in our garden. Well, that was the last thing my mum was going to take. She went indoors and picked up the broom. She swept up all of the weeds, every last one, and threw them all back. I'm not lying - every last one!

My mum had had enough and got take-aways for nearly two weeks. She sat in the conservatory with a camcorder, waiting for our neighbours to strike again. They did, at 11.30pm. They climbed over the fence because the gate was locked. After this we had evidence, and very good evidence.

It's been two years from then and we have managed to sue them for £3,000. I think that will buy a lovely holiday.

*Jenny Harrold (13)*
*The Prittlewell School, Essex*

## My Neighbour From Hell

It was 2am. I felt my bed jump up from the floor. Then suddenly, I heard a *bang!*

I could hear banging all morning, so I got up and went to the kitchen to get a cold drink. I heard another thump. I put my hand on the kitchen wall, it was shaking so much I decided to go round there and see what on earth this man was doing in the middle of the morning. I knocked the door open and suddenly saw an old lady standing there with a hammer in her hand.

'I came over to say that I was woken up by the loud sound and thought it was you.'

'Yes, you're right. It was coming from here.'

'*What?* I mean, could you please keep it down, thanks?' I walked back home.

From that day on it was a total nightmare. All day and all night she was banging and crashing things. So one day I decided to phone the 'Neighbours From Hell' programme.

I was on TV and so was the old lady. It showed that I was ready for war. That night I was about to walk up the stairs when I suddenly felt the stairs move so much that I was about to fall. It was that old woman again trying to make me mad. So I did something about it and got her kicked out. That was the last of her.

*Hannah Parkin (13)*
*The Prittlewell School, Essex*

## A Day In The Life Of Brooklyn Beckham

Today I woke up and my mum got me out of my king-sized cot. She carried me down the stairs where she sat me down in front of the big box. She picked up this long thing with lots of buttons and, just like magic, the big box turned itself on. Mummy then picked up a colourful box and opened it up. On the front of the box was a picture of my favourite Teletubby, Laa-Laa. She got out the thing inside and put it in the hole of the thing under the box. Mummy was making breakfast in the kitchen and I watched the Teletubbies inside the box.

Daddy was away trying to win a cup. My daddy is a football player. He plays for a man with a chest united and eggland. When I grow up, I want to be like my daddy. He is rich.

Mummy came in with my breakfast. It was Coco Pops and they are my favourite. I ate my Coco Pops and Mummy got me dressed. Mummy told me she wanted to shopping in London and that I had to stay at home with the family nanny. Mum went out and I watched the big box all day. Mum came home with a bag full of shopping and she gave me a big kiss. I really love my mum.

*Carl Harrold  (13)*
*The Prittlewell School, Essex*

## MY ANT'S ODYSSEY

It's a hard life being an ant but sometimes it can be fun.

Things may look different like when we look up and see moving skyscrapers which block out the sun or a man who is probably sixteen stones eating a hot dog with all the tomato sauce dripping down onto passing people's shoes and small creatures like us, making us jump five feet into the air. I'm going to tell you my odyssey to school . . .

It was Tuesday 2nd of June 1981 and I had to go to school, my name is Lizzie and I am 13 years old. I go to a school within a school for humans. I wake up at 7.45am as I need to be at school for 9.00am. For lunch I would have leaves in barbecue sauce and chocolate flies. I would say goodbye to my mum and set off on a journey that all ants feared . . . the walk to school.

Firstly, on my journey to school I would pass a huge dog barking at the cat sitting on the wall of 5 Holy Bush Lane. I get scared but I would walk on. Further down the road the postman walks past me. *Thud, thud* his feet would go, sending me up into the air.

Secondly, I would sometimes catch a ride on someone who can't do there laces up. But often I would fall over in chewing gum which wasn't nice.

Thirdly, I would meet my best friend Mel. She is 13, the same age as me. When I would meet her I would be lucky to meet her at 8.45am because there was a little market on Mondays and Wednesdays, where people would always tread on small things like us. She lives down Ant Hill Farm Road. Me and Mel would arrive at school at 8.55am. The first lesson was on Safety When Around Humans and our last lesson was History In The Ant Times.

Finally, at the end of the day Mel and I would walk home together, Mel was coming round for tea. We would wait until the humans had left because we would get stamped on. On our way back to mine we would walk past a fish and chip shop, with temptation we were led to a death trap. We saw some chips which must have dropped onto the floor. We had a few nibbles and then decided it was time to go.

Later we arrived at my letterbox of a house and we climb up the long pole which is hard if it's frosty because we slide back down. Just think, we'll have to make this journey again tomorrow, will we survive or not? We will have to wait and see.

*Amy Louise Heathcote (13)*
*The Prittlewell School, Essex*

## A DAY IN THE LIFE OF DAVID BECKHAM

On the 21st of June 2002 we had a World Cup tournament. We played Brazil and we were 1-0 up until just before half-time.

David Seaman let in a goal and it was really upsetting for him and all of the team, but we are really proud that we had got this far as I think we all played very well.

When I arrived back home on a plane I was welcomed home with a kiss from my wife and kid, Brooklyn.

I was kind of pleased that I was back at home with my wife and kid but also I would love to be playing Germany.

*Jade Easterford  (12)*
*The Prittlewell School, Essex*

# A Day In The Life Of . . .

It was the 12th of October and the family was all sitting near the fire in the living room. Marie (the mum) had been told a few days ago that she was going to die in about two weeks. Everybody was very sad and very unhappy. The days went by and Marie was getting very weak. Eventually Marie died and they buried her in the nearby church.

A few months had gone and their dad Pete had just got a letter through the door saying that he has to fight a country with other men. The letter had told him what uniform he had to wear and what equipment he needed and that he had to get them by January. It was quite a shock but Peter decided that he would go and fight.

The days went on and Peter found two lovely homes for his two daughters, Lucy and Sophie. The two children were very sad and they didn't want to leave. Peter then decided to leave.

The war went on and on, after a few months of fighting Peter died. The two girls stayed in their homes until they were older.

Twelve years later and the long-lost sisters found each other at a family reunion shop and bought big houses next to each other. They were very happy.

*Charlotte Humphrey (11)*
*William Edwards School, Essex*

# A Victim's Nightmare

Hi, my name is Reece Jones and I'm 14 years old. My nickname is *Victim,* because I've been in so many accidents it's unbelievable. My dream is to be normal, not to be bullied, not to have my head flushed down the toilet every break time, not to be beaten regularly, not to be threatened by e-mail, letters and not to be called nasty names all the time. Is that too much to ask?

Let me tell you how the nightmare began . . .

It all started when the whole family, including me, went on a day trip to a theme park. We all had a fantastic time - nothing could possibly go wrong.

We were driving home late that night. It was pitch-black, about 10.30pm. Then all of a sudden this roaring car came speeding round the bend. Of course the car hit us - I was in it! There was a man and a teenage boy, a bit older than me in the other car. When the car hit us, we skidded a bit but that was all. However the other car wasn't so lucky, it somersaulted in the air.

We were OK, but the others weren't so lucky. The man died three hours later. The boy is the coolest kid in school, that's why I'm being bullied. The boy went to live somewhere else, but still came to the same school.

Six months later I'm still being bullied but I'm finally moving. Hey, nobody could stop it.

*Luke Stanton (12)*
*William Edwards School, Essex*

## DEAR DIARY

I couldn't believe it. When it first started we were told that it would only last until Christmas, but Christmas came and went and then Easter came and went and then Hallowe'en came and went.

I didn't want to go, I would have rather got a white feather and I did, but after I saw the adverts in the cinema and in the newspapers showing a German nurse pouring water onto the ground when a poor English soldier was dying of thirst I couldn't stand back and do nothing.

I came to protect and serve my country to show that I am loyal and worthy of the space I take up in my community, but to be honest I wish that I had stayed at home!

Now I'm here the sights and sounds, the smells and colours were overwhelming. There were puddles of red and red stained clothes everywhere. Heads and arms, limbs and torsos were scattered all over the place. We've been here for so long and I can't stand staying in the same clothes day in, day out. Sleeping in the same bed with no heating. Not being able to see my family but the worst thing of all would have to be seeing all of the dead bodies, all of my friends. Just imagine, that could be somebody's dad or uncle, grandparent or husband. Just imagine the heartache. Just imagine that could be me!

*Elizabeth Dale  (14)*
*William Edwards School, Essex*

## TEDDY ON THE TRAIN

One fine day, Sabrina and her bear got on a train to Manchester with Mum. They were going to her auntie and uncle's for a weekend.

On the train Teddy was having so much fun. He had a sleep, did some colouring in and played Bingo, looked out of the window until . . . a lady knocked Teddy onto the floor (just as they were about to get off). So excited Sabrina hadn't realised, until they had got off and the train pulled away.

All weekend she was upset, until she got back on the train and saw her favourite teddy on the floor with lots of gifts.

Teddy had been to lots of different places, Newcastle, Colchester, Southampton and many more.

Now Teddy was happy and so was Sabrina.

*Jenna Yeomans (12)*
*William Edwards School, Essex*

## I'M COMING, YOU CAN'T RUN

Becky looked down the staircase and saw a Jack like figure. 'Dad I'm so glad I've found you.'
Jack turned round and said, 'My sweet daughter, I'm glad I've found you,' in a relieved way. They ran to each other and hugged one another.

Jack slipped and pulled Becky down the staircase. Becky used a piercing scream as she fell down the staircase.

Meanwhile . . .

Andrew lived opposite Becky's flat and saw her every day. They worked in the same building and had the same job. Andrew drove into the car park and almost knocked over the laundry man, missed and skidded into the cart. Luke's body rolled into the car park as Andrew drove over the body with a bump. Andrew thought it was a speed bump so slowed down to a complete stop.

Andrew walked into the quiet and disturbing coloured back hall and headed for the staircase. A scream echoed from by the staircase. 'Who's there?' Andrew said nervously as he walked down the corridor. 'You can't hide.' Andrew walked closer to the stairs. 'Becky.' Andrew ran over to her. 'What happened?'
'My dad pulled me down the stairs.'
'What, Jack, he couldn't hurt a . . .'
*Bing, bing, bing!*
'Andrew, Becky, I know where you are.'
'Who is this?'
'I am going to get you.'
'If you're that little brat at number 52 I am going to tell your mum.'
'I am next to you.'
'Argh!'
'Run, run.'
'No, it's Laura.'
'Oh no it's not . . . she's dead!'

*Andrew Baker (12)*
*William Edwards School, Essex*

## THE HORSE FAMILY

There are two horses called Stardust and Thunder who are fully grown. They are wild horses and love running around fields. One day a man and a lady tried to take them, the horses ran away and got hurt by some barbed wire.

Another lady called Jenny came along and sees the poor horses are hurt. She goes back to her house and brings her horse carrier to put the two horses in. She tries her best to put them in but it was difficult. She took them back to her house and put them in her stables.

She made them better and put bandages on their legs. After a few weeks they were back to normal. She kept them because she always wanted some horses. After a year Stardust had a foal. Jenny called it Sparkle.

Jenny took Thunder to do a race every month and won. He was a fast runner and Jenny was proud of him. A few days after Thunder had completed a race the man and the lady came to Jenny's house and found out that Stardust had had a foal called Sparkle. They tried to steal the baby horse but Thunder woke up and chased them away.

Jenny woke up and went to see what was wrong. Sparkle was OK and so was Thunder. None of them were hurt.

A few months later Jenny went into the barn to get some hay for the horses and Sparkle followed. The man and lady wanted to take Sparkle and didn't know that she went in the barn with Jenny so they set the barn on fire.

Sparkle started neighing and Stardust and Thunder came over to the barn and started neighing too. Jenny then realised the barn was on fire, but didn't know what to do. Sparkle thought of something. She went and picked up a bucket of water in her mouth and splashed it at the barn door, she then bashed through the door and was out. Jenny quickly followed after.

The man and lady were caught and went to prison for a while. Sparkle was a hero for saving Jenny and Jenny loved her forever. She never gave Sparkle, Stardust or Thunder away.

Everyone was happy as they were and Jenny kept the horses forever. They were a heroic horse family.

*Katherine Furner  (12)*
*William Edwards School, Essex*

## TRAPPED

He ran as fast as he could through the thick lush grass covering him, trying to escape from the horrible sounds of gunshots behind him. He was being chased, but he didn't know why. He'd heard stories about 'The People' before, his grandmother told them to him all the time, but he had never actually encountered them before.

He dashed under a low branch and was about to leap over a tree when a tall thin figure came out of nowhere. A mischievous smile spread across the person's face as he slowly approached the fox. The fox backed away cautiously, scared. He heard a faint sound coming from the person, but he couldn't understand a word of it. He decided to run but the person was too quick for him. The person ran at him and threw a net over the fox's head.

The fox was extremely confused. He thrashed around violently trying to get out of the net and gnashed his teeth wildly, trying to scare the mean, thin man who'd caught him. The man just chuckled to himself, enjoying watching the scene. Suddenly the fox had an idea. He started chewing the net, hoping he would make a hole large enough for him to crawl through, hiding his work as he did it from the hunter.

An hour later it was ready and he silently crept through the hole. The man spotted him and ran but the fox was too quick and easily escaped. *He was free.*

*Luke Walsh  (12)*
*William Edwards School, Essex*

## DEAR DIARY

I was so excited this morning I couldn't think straight. All I could think of was what if I lose or what if I win. I got a lot of support from the make-up artists, camera crew and wardrobe, they were all so friendly. I met up with Will, he was just as nervous. I had butterflies as I walked on to the stage; I was hoping to win. There were cheers but they weren't for me. I was really starting to shake at that point. When the winner was finally announced I closed my eyes and prayed, then it was announced, the words I will never forget. 'The winner is Will Young.' I smiled and congratulated Will but inside I couldn't help feeling disappointed and slightly jealous. I had come so far but I had come second.

People came and said, 'Well done anyway,' and, 'better luck next time,' but there wasn't going to be a next time, this was my chance. I can't stand people feeling sorry for me so I got the courage to meet with the press. I just said I was happy for Will and hope he is very successful. When I saw Will being whisked away in a limo with screaming fans surrounding him I was jealous but it lifted my spirits when I got my own limo and screaming fans. When I got over my disappointment I realised I was going to be famous even if I didn't win.

Gareth Gates.

*Sarah Henderson (12)*
*William Edwards School, Essex*

# A DAY IN THE LIFE OF ANNE FRANK

As I get out of my uncomfortable bed, and see sunshine peering through the crack in the material that me and Daddy put up as curtains, my head has to function where I am once again. I realise I am in my new home. The cold home, the only home that can keep me and my family safe, from the Germans.

It came to the stage, where we were all petrified of the lorries driving past our house every five minutes. The thought that one of the lorries would stop outside our house and take us far away was frightening. We decided to call our special hideout the 'Secret Annexe'. But how much longer would the 'Secret Annexe' be able to protect us? One day, two weeks, three months, another year? I am scared, cold and hungry.

Burglaries, murder and theft went on daily on the streets of Amsterdam, life outside the 'Secret Annexe' was far from pleasant. And as we all sit on one of the beds listening to the radio, it starts to hollow, 'This is the day, the invasion has begun!' We thought, is it really the invasion? Thousands of planes flew over the 'Secret Annexe' non-stop. For me, the best part of the invasion was that I had the feeling that friends were approaching; and one day I could go out into the world once more and walk freely among its people without wearing a yellow, identifying star.

*Katie West (12)*
*William Edwards School, Essex*

## THE GHOST HORSE

She stood tall, proud and grand . . . Her name was Silver, that was her colour. She looked exactly like a ghost in the night, that's what most people thought she was, a ghost. There was one man though, he was called Bones not Jones, he always killed the animals, crushed their bones and smeared them all over himself, thinking that it would protect him from evil, but to be honest he was evil himself.

The thing about Bones was he loved stuffed animals and his ambition was to add the ghost horse to his collection. He had made a magnificent trap, all leavers and pulleys big enough to trap her.

There was one problem though, she was fast, as fast as the wind and no one had ever been able to catch her. Most people who had tried to were found unconscious in bushes and hedges with a tattoo of a horse's head on their arm.

One cold October night Bones decided to set up his trap in the wood, but he also had a shotgun, a super sword shot to be precise and it was dead accurate too. He stood and waited till she came running past after having a race with the rest of the herd and then . . . *bang!*

She laid there shedding blood everywhere, then he laughed, 'Ha, ha, ha, ha, ha!'

*Elizabeth Cooledge  (11)*
*William Edwards School, Essex*

## FAIRGROUND

Precious ran to answer the phone, her long blonde hair swishing behind her. She picked up the receiver, 'Hello, who is it?'
'Hi Precious, it's me, Brad.'
'Hello Brad,' said Precious happily.
'Would . . . would you like to go on a date to the fairground?' asked Brad cautiously.
'Of course, I would love to!' replied Precious, 'pick me up in ten minutes, OK?'
'OK.'
'Bye.'

Precious ran upstairs and pulled on a pale pink flowing dress, slipped on some sandals, plaited her hair, grabbed her handbag and went outside to wait for Brad. Brad pulled up in his car, flashed her a smile and opened the door for her to get in. Twenty minutes later, they arrived at the fairground.

They paid their entrance tickets and Brad asked what Precious would like to go on. 'You choose,' she said, smiling at Brad.
'How . . . how about the Tunnel of Love?' asked Brad shyly.
'OK, come on them.'
Brad paid for the ride and the two of them boarded, holding hands.

The ride started up and both of them were plunged into darkness. Precious felt Brad's arm slide round her shoulder, which Precious was glad of, because she didn't like this part of the ride. They stayed in the dark for a while. 'I'm so glad you're here, Brad,' said Precious.
Brad grunted a reply.
'Are you OK, Brad?'
Nothing. Silence. Precious turned to face Brad, instead of Brad, she came face-to-face with another man. 'Arghhh!' screamed Precious. The man smiled at her and laughed.

*Rebecca Gray (12)*
*William Edwards School, Essex*

# ELECTRO

Who am I? Are you sure you want to know? If somebody said I lived a normal teenage life, they lied. Here's my story. As the school bell rang, Gordon Thompson went in to face his doom, the local bullies expected $1 a day from every kid in Year 11 and Gordon is skint. The bullies give Gordon another chance at the end of the day.

He goes to his friend Norman but he is also skint. The final bell goes and the bullies close in, they torture him and he is pushed into the electric room. An electric surge rushes through his body as the cable shoots through his veins. Gordon goes cold and faints. The next day he finds himself in hospital.
'How do you feel?' a voice said in the background.
'Fine,' answered Gordon, even though he didn't know who he was talking to. 'Actually I feel better than ever,' he added. Gordon turned his head and found his mum, dad and doctor. Gordon felt he had the power of the world, he felt stronger physically and mentally. Two weeks later he was released from hospital.

One night Gordon couldn't sleep. He went to the top of the roof and looked at the stars. As Gordon was making the constellations with his finger a surge of electricity shot out. He went downstairs and designed his new suit. The next night he was on the roof again and shouted, 'New Yorkers prepare to enter Electro!'

*Ben Kelly (12)*
*William Edwards School, Essex*

## A DAY IN THE LIFE OF AN AUSTRIAN CIVILIAN DURING WORLD WAR II

My day begins when I wake up at 6am. Breakfast is imitation bread, which tastes like sawdust, and cornflakes with ersatz coffee.

At 7am I leave for work at the local hospital which is an hours walk through the town. Sometimes if Spitfires are on the prowl I dive for the nearest cover. If I meet someone in the street I have to greet them with, 'Heil Hitler'. I arrive at work and go to my desk in the accounts department dealing with the hospital workers' wages. There is no computer, everything is written by hand or on an old typewriter.

Lunch is at 1pm. I eat in the hospital as the food for the patients is better than I get at home. I either have a jacket potato or Wiener schnitzel with vegetables from the hospital garden.

I have to be careful when I talk to people as the Gestapo (secret police) might be eavesdropping and I could get into trouble for saying the wrong things.

I finish work at 6pm, hurry home, not stopping in case there is an air raid. Dinner is stew with bread. Afterwards if I'm not too tired I listen to the radio but not the foreign stations as they are forbidden. I often hear Adolf Hitler and his Nazi friends making propaganda speeches. In bed I listen to the enemy bombers flying over and bombing the local railways and bridges, the bangs and flashes seem like a giant firework display. I eventually fall asleep.

*Daniel Gray (12)*
*William Edwards School, Essex*

## The Guitar

I shuffle forwards, trying desperately to make out the figures of my friends. Strangers are bustling, pushing me away from my unknown destination. I feel like I'm suffocating in a strange jungle.

Suddenly the crowd surges as one, drawing me along with the wave of adrenaline. Feedback blasts into the sea of people. My senses heighten, eyes focus on stage. I anticipate the next burst of energy to break forward and lift me to greater heights. Everyone in the audience comes to life with the first great guitar riff that pounds from the speakers. Without realising it I have been sucked into the wild atmosphere, and all I can do is listen to the music which these masters are creating. My head spins with amazement, my body is ecstatic.

I've forgotten completely that I am separated from my friends, I feel at one with the other members of the crowd. I feel out of control, with no desire to lose this feeling.

As the set comes to an end I stare in awe at these artists. I think back to my dusty guitar in its lonely corner. I long to be able to produce the honeyed chords churned by the guitarist. Hang on! Why dream about being able to produce genius? I stroll purposely home, ready and eager to learn the guitar myself. Ready to make my own dreams come to life.

*Julia Alderson (15)*
*Wymondham High School, Norfolk*

# THE TALE OF THE HARD-WORKING PUPIL

Once upon a time there was a hard-working pupil named Johnny. Every day when he got home from school, he wouldn't watch television, play on his computer or go out with his friends, he would sit down and do his homework.

He was always well-behaved, smartly dressed and handed his homework in early. His room was well kept and clean, and he brushed his teeth twice a day.

His fellow classmates would have detentions, get girlfriends, go to parties, but Johnny just sat and did his homework.

One day, after doing a particularly hard piece of homework, he got a huge pain behind his eyes, like someone was trying to *burst* out of his eye sockets.

He went to the doctors for the first time in his life. The doctor suggested Johnny should just stay off school for a few days and should just relax.

But . . . he couldn't *not* go to school.

The next day, after a few hours at school, Johnny felt worse than ever - that throbbing pain behind his eyes . . .

He just *had* to go.

Every day the pain got worse during school, and while at home doing his homework.

Then one day, he woke up, and his head had exploded. He realised he had been doing too much. He got up for school, knowing he wouldn't be fanatical about work - he'd learnt his lesson.

But when he reached for his shirt, hanging on that coat hanger, his hand passed straight through it.

*Thomas Phillips  (14)*
*Wymondham High School, Norfolk*

## NARIDIAN WARS

The pain was unbearable; I could feel a sharp twinge going right through my body. I wiped my forehead and discovered my own yellow blood escaping from a dagger wound from just above my right eye. My long pointed ears sharpened. I turned quickly on my heels and quickly jumped behind a large metal crate.

'You will not survive this time T'Baage,' said a low and eerie voice that belonged to the man I hated the most right now. That man, D'Maegre, started this war 150 years ago against the Naridian people, my people. This time he would die. I would not fail the Senate.
'You underestimate me D'Maegre, I still have a few tricks left!' This time it would be his blood that fell. He had killed so many. He would pay!

I stretched out using my mind and my native powers kicked in. I heard a large thud and looked around the side of the crate. Another large metal crate had just slammed into him and knocked him against the wall. His weapon was about ten metres from him now. I could now make my move. I could sense his fear as I approached him. I raised my disrupter, aimed and prepared to fire.
'Would you really kill someone in cold-blood?' he asked slowly.
'You did!' I said gently, 'For the Republic.' I fired and an orange bolt of energy hit him and his body fell lifeless to the floor. It was over!

*Daniel Lee  (15)*
*Wymondham High School, Norfolk*

## YOUNG LOVE CAN BE HEARTBREAKING

The storm raged. Lightning hit low amongst the trees.

Jamie had always had a crush on Lottie, but he never knew that he would be trapped in the school canteen at 6pm (their dawdling after yoga class caused the caretaker to lock them in).

A slash of lightning thundered down.
'The sky's well angry,' said Jamie happily, as Lottie buried her head into his shoulders. 'I remember last time we had a storm this bad.'

Chazza, Greg and Marsh had just finished their regular Friday night gig. Swarms of Year Sixies herded towards them as they slid into their 60s van. The storm raged so much it was hard to believe the trees were still rooted to the ground. Rain was falling so hard that Marsh, who was renowned for his *super vision,* found it hard to see. 'The crowd were great weren't they?' remarked Chazza.
'Yeah, the best!'

A stroke of lightning thundered down in front of them. Simultaneously, a figure flashed before them. Marsh swerved the van trying to avoid it, coming to a smashing halt as they ploughed into a great oak.

'Died instantly . . . necks broke during the collision . . . no sign of the figure,' said Jamie. 'They say their music can be heard in this canteen at night.'

They stared at each other wide-eyed with fear as they began to hear bass music thumping to the rhythm of their heartbeats.

The pairs drowning screams could be heard miles away as their necks were broken in two.

*Kayleigh Miles  (15)*
*Wymondham High School, Norfolk*

## A Day In The Life Of A Doll

I used to be loved . . . no more. I was thrown away just as if I was a piece of rubbish that nobody wanted or needed any more. It was as if I was useless and that I served no purpose.

I used to be adored . . . no more. No more being adored. But instead crushed by the rest of the tightly packed toys that they did not want to adore.

I used to be worshipped . . . no more. No more being worshipped. But instead being trapped in a small space with the rest of them.

Thrown away into a small brown cardboard box at the back of a cluttered cupboard with the rest of the unwanted, dusty, old toys.

As my weepy eyes look up through the tiny hole I can distinguish a beam of light shining through on my porcelain cracked face. Gradually all the old unwanted toys are thrown out of the dull box until there is only me left in there. Just me all alone, waiting to be left once again, waiting for the beam of light to eventually fade away until it is not there any longer.

As I wait to be left again, I see a large hand coming towards me. As the hand slowly comes towards me and picks me up I realise that I will no longer have to stay in this dark place, but I will be loved once again.

*Carly Buckenham  (15)*
*Wymondham High School, Norfolk*

## SEEING IS BELIEVING

'In a small village, in the heart of England lived a ferocious dragon,' said my grandad, telling stories as per usual. Every Sunday I would go and visit him and he would always come out with a different story, every one more peculiar than the last.

'I'm not stupid, Grandad,' I used to say, 'I know these stories are absurd, they must be made-up.'

'Ah, my child, that's where you are wrong,' he would say in his husky voice, 'all my stories are very true.'

He would try and convince me that they were real, even though it didn't work. Until one day Grandad and I were just going for a brisk walk, it was wet, humid and groggy, typical English weather. I had to listen to Grandad rambling on again. Suddenly a strange noise and smell lingered around me. There was a slight trembling of the ground and a loud flapping noise. I pulled Grandad's sleeve, 'Can you hear that noise?' I cried.

'Of course I can, it's just a dragon,' he said.

At first I looked at him with disbelief, and then to my amazement, floating just feet above me in the sky was the most outstanding beast you had ever seen. It was a dragon! A thick muscular tail shaped like a spear, a body like Mount Everest, scaly and rough and a head with huge marbles as eyes. My grandad told some stories, but this one was true!

*Hannah Burroughs (15)*
*Wymondham High School, Norfolk*

## A Lonely Candle

On the window sill sits a lonely candle. The candle is burning, the more it burns the more droplets of hot wax fall and begin to form a thick puddle at its base. Gradually the candle diminishes, what was once tall, proud and powerful has become nothing but small, stumpy and ashamed. However, the wick keeps alight and the candle carries on burning, like a person just forgotten, ignored as if the person were nothing but a speck of dust, being pushed aside.

Often the door to the room will slam, a strong gust of wind would break out and circulate the room, the candle might quiver or maybe even flicker like a moth in distress but the candle will always regain its strength and always keep on melting.

For most of the candle's life it will bring warmth, glow and light to the cold, blue room but still it will remain unnoticed, no one will ever appreciate the candle for what it does.

Although the candle can survive through thick and thin, through gusts of wind, eventually the candle's wick will end, the flame will dim, the light, warmth and glow will disappear, and yet no one will have noticed and no one will be there to revive what was once the life of a human being.

*Stephanie Garnett (14)*
*Wymondham High School, Norfolk*

# MURPHY

Hazel had said his owners were strange, about how you have to be careful about how much you tell them. Things like, 'We turn him out every day weather permitting, he's really happy.' No that's not right according to their rules, 'He has to be stabled every day so he doesn't get laminitis.' Yeah more like, 'We keep him in a stable so he can't enjoy fresh air, so he doesn't put any weight on, so he doesn't get to play and thrive like other horses do.'

When he came to me my riding life picked up. He taught me, and I taught him. Wherever we went people said we had such a partnership, and I knew it was true. Between us we had style and aggression. Show-jumping a 3'6 course gave me the most amazing feeling of achievement, of euphoria.

My mum broke the news to me.
'They are taking him away?' I managed to stammer as my throat began to sob. She couldn't even give me a reason. Mum's tone was a mixture of anguish, resentfulness and anger. I continued to cry into a tissue that was already saturated. What did I do wrong? ran across my mind. Two weeks previously they'd come and gone after seeing Murphy, and left us with the impression that all was well. What must have been going through their minds? We don't know. But all I can think about is that they're taking him away, they're taking away my Murphy.

*Molly Harrison (15)*
*Wymondham High School, Norfolk*

## UNTITLED

The small tavern is pervaded by shouts of raucous laughter, intermittently punctuated by the clatter of tankard on stone. The air is thick with the scent of sweat and beer.

Staring into my drink I become aware that the laughter has died to a mere murmur as the room listens in anticipation to the crunch of footsteps outside, which draw closer and then stop. The room holds its breath. In the silence I can hear each wing beat of a moth drawn to the light emanating from a candle in the corner. As I gaze at the fragile, flickering flame, the great oak door is thrown back onto its hinges with an almighty crash. A large, cloaked figure is silhouetted against the heavens. As the figure enters, the mob remains hypnotised. The figure pulls back his cloak to expose a handsome face and bright blue eyes. The throng awakens and excited shouts and good-natured jeering break the silence.

The eyes scan the crowd until they eventually alight on me. Here, the face breaks into a rakish grin revealing two rows of white, even teeth flashing in the candlelight. He starts towards me through a sea of admiring faces, hands reaching out to pat him on the back and ruffle his shining gold hair, until he reaches the chair next to me - considerably more flushed than when he entered. Without meeting his eyes I stare into the cold, amber-coloured liquid. 'Nice entrance,' I remark shortly.

*Kate Cooper  (15)*
*Wymondham High School, Norfolk*

## MY DESTINY

There I lie, motionless, stiff, pale and hurt surrounded by my family who adore me, all crying into wet tissues clutching and sobbing over my fragile hands waiting for me to leap out shouting I was OK, but that would be a miracle. There I lie in a germ-filled public hospital, just one day after my eighteenth birthday, I lie dead.

Of course, I could see all this, I was not dead spiritually, I was actually very alive just somewhere else beyond human imagination where no one could hear, see or feel me, some place I would watch over everyone until it was their time to meet me and though my family thought my destiny was the hospital bed, it should not have been there for me physically.

The window above my bed in hospital let the bright, shining sun pour through its thick glass, onto my lifeless body at midday. My body was full of tubes and needles which were taken out. They could not help me, I did not want them to. I should have died at the scene of the crime that I committed, that I was guilty of, therefore I should pay. That was my real destiny.

*Laura Gedge  (14)*
*Wymondham High School, Norfolk*

## A Day In The Life Of An Egg

One day, whilst floating in his bubble, Egbert felt peculiar. The squishy liquid surrounding him started to shake and Egbert felt as if he was on a water slide.

'Wheeee,' he screamed.

*Boom!* he landed.

It was bright outside. Above him loomed a sky of reddish-brown feathers and the sound of clucking filled the air. I don't like this, he thought, I preferred it inside.

No matter how hard Egbert tried, he just couldn't move. Suddenly, he thought he had made it. He was flying high in the air. He was dropped into a wicker walled garden of straw. It itched and Egbert didn't like it. He wobbled his way across the farmyard as the farmer's wife went into the house.

Again, he was flying. This time he was in a kitchen. It was warm and Egbert liked it. The smell of fresh bread made the kitchen feel friendly. He was placed in a rack with lots of other eggs. I like it here, he thought, I can see everything.

As days went by the other eggs in the rack disappeared one by one. This confused Egbert. I wonder where they go? he pondered.

The next day, it was Egbert's turn. He was picked up in a plastic contraption and carried towards the shiny box in the corner. He could hardly contain his excitement.

'Ooooooh,' he screamed.

Below him he could see a jacuzzi. It was bubbling and warm. He wanted to stay here all day. He splashed about and was really enjoying himself.

After a few minutes, he felt dizzy. Slowly, he fell asleep and forgot everything. Egbert had been boiled . . .

*Hayley Goodrum (15)*
*Wymondham High School, Norfolk*

## SHORT STORY

I stumbled out into the rain, through the glass doors and landed on my knees. Rain shattered onto my back and drenched my jacket. Raindrops collected in my mass of black hair like glistening jewels. I heaved myself up and ran, I had no idea where to but just away. Away from him, away from his constant cheeriness and his continuous presence. I gulped for air. Rain was dripping down my face and my clothes clung to my body. I ran desperately through the mass of trees, trying to grasp the diminutive light ahead of me. I lost my footing and I thudded to the ground, my head sinking into the wet leaves. All I could focus on was reaching the calm, beautiful waves we had passed on the tedious drive up here, as I staggered to my feet and stumbled on through the unknown silence and inky black trees.

Suddenly I saw it. A glimmer of hope amongst a blanket of darkness. The moon's luminous light scattered onto the gentle, almost motionless water. I let the ice-cold water swallow up my fear. I slowly spread myself out onto the surface of the water. As I swayed back and forth I looked up at the star-studded sky and something inside me changed at that moment. I started to think for the first time about the last couple of years, probably the hardest of my life. I thought about what my mum and I had endured, faced and run away from. So what was I doing? Running away because I couldn't bear to see my mum laugh, chat and most of all be happy again. But most of all I couldn't bear to see who had made her all of these things. It wasn't me, but her new partner. He had nestled in and suffocated me so that he could get closer to my mum. And then I realised he wasn't horrible, but just a middle-aged man trying to make an unhappy, middle-aged woman pick herself up and carry on and smile. After all the things my mother had faced, for the first time I was happy, really happy for her. She deserved it and so did I, so why hadn't I just let it happen instead of putting up wary guards against him and me? There was no need.

I let the sea drift me towards the sand and then pulled myself out of the water. I felt lighter, much lighter and I retraced my steps and I knew, from that moment, that things would change. I had grown up and so had my attitude. Everything was going to be fine because Mum had me and Richard as her family, I thought, as I reached the forest and plunged back into it.

*Madeleine Piggot  (14)*
*Wymondham High School, Norfolk*

# A Day In The Life Of A Supply Teacher

How humiliating. Today was not running smoothly. As a supply teacher, I know I'm subject to teenage jokes but I'd made it worse for myself, stalling my car in front of a rowdy bunch, branded now, as a *typical woman driver!* Great start in a new school.

Dressed smartly, I moved in a 'I'm a teacher, don't mess-with-me' type of swagger. I asked some girls directions to the staffroom, and fifteen minutes later discovered they had sent me round in circles. I was breathing fire.

I had cute, innocent-looking Year Sevens all day, it had been a breeze. At lunchtime it started deteriorating; I slumped down into a comfy armchair. I shut my eyes only to have the life frightened out of me when a stack of papers was dropped on a table. I was told to *mark it* in a tone I daren't argue with. Teachers!

I received a warning about my final class; dreaded Year Tens . . .

I arrived to find the classroom had been ransacked; kids eating, swearing and near-enough hanging from the lights. I shouted for quiet, but they refused to listen. Smoke was pouring out of my ears in exasperation.

Once acknowledged, they talked and chucked stuff whilst I talked. They were driving me up the wall. I stared at the clock, time dragged as kids banged desks endlessly.

Finally the lesson ended and kids shot through the door like bullets. What a day. Never again. I quit.

*Kirsty Bell (15)*
*Wymondham High School, Norfolk*